NO BLOOD RELATIVE

by Terry Carroll

June 3, 1995

To: Wayne
Congrats on the new job!
Hope you enjoy the book

A *Midnight Original* MURDER MYSTERY

THE MERCURY PRESS

Terry Carroll

The publisher gratefully acknowledges the financial assistance of the Canada Council and the Ontario Arts Council, as well as that of the Government of Ontario through the Ontario Publishing Centre.

AUTHOR'S ACKNOWLEDGEMENTS
Many people had good suggestions about different versions of this book and I would like to thank them. They include: Nancy Kelly Carroll, James E. Smith, Clifford Maynes, Rhys Knott and Flora McPherson. Special thanks to Welwyn Wilton Katz and Beverley Daurio— your help and encouragement made publication of this book possible.

Edited by Beverley Daurio
Cover design by Gordon Robertson
Cover photograph by Doug Forster
Proofreading by Dan Bortolotti
Composition and page design by TASK

Printed and bound in Canada by Metropole Litho
Printed on acid-free paper
First Edition
1 2 3 4 5 99 98 97 96 95

Canadian Cataloguing in Publication Data

Carroll, Terry
    No blood relative
ISBN 1-55128-021-3
I. Title.
PS8555.A77N6 1995   C813'.54   C95-930475-4
PR9199.3.C37N6 1995

Represented in Canada by the Literary Press Group
Distributed in Canada by General Distribution Services

The Mercury Press
137 Birmingham Street
Stratford, Ontario
Canada   N5A 2T1

FOR NANCY
with love

PROLOGUE

Stephanie Basiuk was about to die. If she'd been told this, she wouldn't have believed it. For one thing, she was young, and the young believe they are immortal. For another, she'd been drinking. She knew about drinking. There was a lot of drinking in her family.

She was in a car with a guy who liked to get drunk and go cruising. Her kind of guy. Stephanie's fingers were rubbing the inseam of the guy's jeans, where guys like it, between his knee and wherever.

Her fingers crept toward wherever. The guy grinned a thank you at her and, with his free arm, mashed her shoulder against his chest.

He revved the engine, vroom-vroom, one cowboy boot on the brake, the other tapping the gas. He had a name, but what was it? She couldn't remember.

Stephanie was a little drunk, but so what? So was he. Everybody was drunk. If everybody hadn't been drunk, there wouldn't have been the problem with Joe. Everybody wouldn't have gotten so mad.

That was more or less how she had ended up in this car, after the guy got mad and started a fight. He was kind of cute, she thought, and he smelled nice.

"You like me?" she asked, her hand now on wherever, fingers roaming around down there.

"You're a fox," he said, saying it like one of those stand-up comics, his mouth coming slant-wise down in the corner, exaggerating the "fox."

Then he said, "I like you, baby. I like you a lot." This time it was the

7

"lot" which he drew out and extended and rolled around in his mouth before he let it go. "You and me..."

He revved the engine some more. Maybe he was afraid; his cowboy boot seemed nervous on the gas pedal.

"What?" she asked, nestling her head against him.

"Gonna do it up right," he said. "Mr. Wiggly wants to say hello. Yeah, what have we here?"

He took his foot off the brake, hit the gas pedal, and the car snapped her head back, it was that fast. Stephanie liked cars, the faster the better. She liked her cars and her boys the same, now that she thought about it, a little smile on her face.

Gravel plunked the underside of the car and the view through the windshield swayed.

The headlights were far away, coming at them. She laughed at the speed: it made her giggle, almost pee her pants.

Stephanie stopped laughing. Feeling the car slip out of control, she mouthed a single word, "No," silently. The word "No" was intended to bring the situation back under control. As if it ever could.

Those weren't headlights in the distance. It was one headlight, single, too close. She remembered now— somebody had punched out the pick-up truck's other light during the fight. But which side of the truck had the good light?

"No-o-o," she screamed.

Stephanie grabbed the steering wheel. He straight-elbowed her in the face. She let the wheel go and brought her hands up to protect herself.

The car lurched left, and then she saw, in the semi-darkness of the late June night, which side the headlight was on. It was on the left, she thought of it that way, on the left, on the driver's side.

She seemed to have a lot of time to think about the headlight and the front grill coming at her in slow motion, aware that she had no seat belt. Where was it? Too late. The digital clock said 11:03.

The vehicles hit solidly and the headlight went out.

Stephanie was a long time coming around.

Pulling herself out of the depths of unconsciousness, she felt cold, very cold for this time of year. Her head hurt and she went back under for a while, where it was warm and moist and dark.

She wanted to stay under, but she couldn't, so she surfaced again. It seemed dark everywhere. She couldn't tell where she was, which end was earth and which stars.

Her mother had a reliable test for accidents: if you can move it, it's not broken. This test was reassuring for little girls who fall off their bikes or run into fences. But she wasn't a little girl and thinking about her mother didn't help now. They had never gotten along, so why bother?

Stephanie tried her head. It moved a little on her neck when she asked it to. But it seemed heavy on one side. One leg moved slightly, she thought, and one arm.

Movements were almost too much for her, and they didn't add up to much— not enough to get her out of the car.

She seemed to be alone, and that frightened her, although nothing in particular told her she was alone. It was the absences that made her come to this conclusion: no breathing, no movement, no warmth. A small moaning.

Which meant that...

She wasn't sure what that might mean.

Down below there was a sensation of warmth and wetness. She was afraid her bladder had failed her. That would be so embarrassing, if anybody saw her.

It seemed odd to be hurt, so badly hurt she could barely move and could still feel no pain below her head, at least no pain in any one area. No specific pain. There was that moaning again. Stephanie realized she was the moaner. She felt detached from the moaning and the pain.

She was weak.

There was light.

She moved her head a fraction in response. The cracked Trans Am windshield glowed with light.

A car door slammed, then another. Male voices murmured. "Jesus

Christ," a man swore. Then again, "Je-e-e-esus," drawing it out, "Christ. Shit. Piss." Metal clanked. A man's kick, maybe.

She shivered and tried to turn toward these male voices, wanting very much to talk to them. But all she could do was change her moans. Now they came out louder, as "A-a-a-a-gh."

Fingers came through the open passenger window.

"She's still breathing," a man's voice said. "Christ, it stinks in here." She was embarrassed then, would have done anything to end the stink. But everything she tried to say came out as a moan.

The fingers withdrew and the man's voice said, "Get the sweater."

"The sweater?" asked another male voice, unsure of itself.

The pain, the general pain with no specific location, was beginning to settle down, locate itself.

The man sounded irritated. "The sweater. The Christly sweater from the back seat."

"I'm getting it," said the second man, sounding frustrated about something himself.

Boots crunched gravel. A car door opened and closed.

Stephanie smelled cigarette smoke. She moved, or tried to, wanting in her pain to assist her rescuers.

Something blocked the glow from the headlights. She tried to raise her head, desperately wanting to help him put the sweater on. It fell suddenly, with force, and blocked her face. She couldn't breathe. The crucial passages, her nostrils and her mouth, were plugged.

Stephanie tried to raise an arm, but it wouldn't move. Must be broken, she decided.

Her body heaved, her lungs gasping for air. The twin sister she loved came to her as a thought. But no help came for her. No air.

For the second time that night, the lights went out.

CHAPTER 1

Waiting in his Volkswagen Beetle for the car ahead of him to park, Marc LePage had one of those insights that might never have occurred to him if he were sober. The emergency vehicles, he thought, weren't assembled solely to safeguard the public good. The young people scattered around the periphery weren't whooping and hollering just to amuse themselves in the almost-dark of another Alberta June night. Coloured lights weren't pulsing simply to make people keep their distance.

No, the way he was going, this scene was a harbinger of what was in store for him. The blackness he'd been carrying with him for so long would end under a blanket, emergency lights flashing above.

Not that he cared one way or the other.

Marc took a pull from his vodka bottle. As he set it on a ripped floor mat on the passenger side, the liquor sloshed inside.

With a useless degree in philosophy, questionable drinking habits, and a checkered newspaper career, Marc was headed for Nowhere, Alberta, fast. Newspaper publishers who were going somewhere didn't end up on weekend photo shoots in the middle of the night. Not if they could get anybody else to cover for them. Well, he'd tried, he thought drunkenly. Reporters hid behind answering machines these days.

It wasn't like the old days, when you worked day and night for peanuts and didn't complain. "Hah," he laughed at the night.

A cop approached to wave his car to the side of the road. Marc took a quick drag on his hand-rolled cigarette, exhaling to smudge over the smell of alcohol in the car. He glanced up and it was weird: Lars Ericksen was looking through the window. What was a Mountie doing here? Oh, yeah. Right. They were in the county, not that far from the village of Rose Hill. Somebody had decided to put up a grain elevator in 1921 and the next thing anybody knew, there was a village. RCMP jurisdiction.

He rolled down the window and Lars leaned toward him, smiling. "Wanna get this hunka junk off the road, Marc?" Lars said Marc's name the French way to tease him, rolling the "r" just a little, barely pronouncing the "c."

Marc snorted a laugh out the window. This was no hunka junk. This was Das Kapital, Volume 2. That's what it said in gold plastic letters above the licence plate of his robin-egg blue Beetle with robin-egg sized flecks of rust on the hood. Volume 1, the 1964 version of the same car, had died on him the previous December, the winter of his first newspaper job in Alberta. The original Das Kapital had taken him west when Marc's ex-wife, Cindy, had gone east to Toronto with Sky, the only daughter they had left after that other accident— the one that still troubled his dreams. Marc had taken a job at *The Crooked Elbow Sun*, with the Brownrigg Corporation, the same group he'd worked for in Ontario before the breakup of his marriage.

But why was he thinking about that now? Because it was Friday night. That's what he did on Friday nights when Lise was working. Got drunk and thought about the past he was drinking to forget.

Marc forced his attention back at the police officer. "No safety check laws in Alberta, Lars. You know that. At least, big guy like you should know that. Don't look at me that way. You know what I mean. Big guy." Calling Lars "big guy" snapped him out of his funk. The phrase struck Marc as funny for no reason at all and he started to laugh.

Lars said, "Big guys like me also know some guys shouldn't be driving under certain conditions."

Marc asked an obvious question to change the subject. "What happened here?"

"It's a Stones concert, Marc. Fans got out of hand. You know something? You look like shit. Aren't you sleeping?" Despite his sarcasm, Lars sounded concerned.

Marc didn't like that question. He shivered and pulled his head away, didn't say anything.

"Okay, don't listen to your friends. You mind parking this excuse for a car off to the side? And stay away from my *confreres* in uniform. These boys pack Breathalyzers."

A pick-up with a poor muffler ran up behind the Beetle, its headlights jumping in Marc's rear view mirror. Bright lights bothered him when he was drinking. In Alberta in June, there was too much light as it was.

He parked and yanked his Pentax K1000 out of the camera bag in the back seat. His sleeping patterns were nobody's business. When had he discussed them with Lars anyway? Memory lapses— they were a major down side to the booze.

Film in the camera: check. 400 ASA: check. Shutter speed at 60: check. Flash on: yes. Batteries: no. Where were they? Marc rummaged around in the bag, found four double A batteries and snapped them in place— wishing he'd stopped at the office for the big flash.

Hunched over like a soldier trotting into combat, he slipped past a police car and started to shoot.

A Trans Am faced the road, long nose crumpled, windshield cracked but still in place. Its rear wheels squatted in a shallow ditch among tall grass and wild rose bushes. Dense canola grew in a field beyond the ditch. Rape, they used to call it, because of the way it robbed the soil of nutrients. Growing in small tangled bushes, it smothered all other vegetation in a field. A suffocating plant that yielded a sweet, suffocating smell.

Across from the Trans Am, water seeped from the hood of a Chevy half-ton, almost new and badly damaged. It had been hit, hard. Its hood and grill were collapsed on the right side. A body lay beside the road, a blanket over it. Not much blood.

A stereo boomed "We will... We will... rock you!" from a Corvette parked on the west side, beyond the accident. Three young people danced on the gravel in the uneven light washing over them from the police cars and the fire engine and the single ambulance.

Kids shouted to each other. Horns honked. "Need a hand, fat boy?" somebody called. An RCMP officer, waddling over to help a volunteer fireman attend to the body beside the half-ton, ignored the offer.

As soon as Marc's flash went off, another Mountie hustled over, shouting, "Excuse me. You're not allowed on the site."

"'Scuse *me*. What the hell do you mean?"

"They asked us to keep reporters away."

"Who's 'they,' Tony? Whose butt we kissing this week, the Queen of England's or somebody's closer to home?"

"Fuck you, too, okay, Marc?"

"Hey, it's a public road. Last I heard, the Charter..." There was something about his legal right to be here, but Marc had had either one too many or one too few drinks. He couldn't remember what the Canadian Charter said about freedom of the press.

"Just stay out of my hair, okay? We got a request from Crooked Elbow city cops to try and control the media feeding frenzy. This isn't Crooked Elbow jurisdiction so I don't know what it's all about. But we said we'd co-operate, so stay behind the barricades."

"Don't that strike you as weird, Tony?"

"Yeah, well, several things about them small-town cops strike me as weird."

Marc knelt on the road, talking to his camera so his boozy breath wouldn't drift up toward the cop. "Give me a clue. What do you think happened here, Tony?"

"Nothing official, but if I was you, I'd be checking the road for wings and feathers."

"Yeah?" Marc was concentrating on his lens— should he keep the 50 mm lens or switch to the wide angle? The wide angle solved most of the focus problems at night, but it took a lot of flash. He decided to stick with the 50. Go with high realism, see if any readers noticed or cared. Besides, the 50 was already on the camera.

Tony kept talking. When it came to cop talk, he couldn't keep his mouth shut. "A game of chicken. These kids, they never learn. You look at her car and it's smashed mostly on the passenger side and you look at his car and it's smashed on the right, so somebody was on the wrong side of the road. I took a boo at the skid marks in the gravel, what's left of them, and they crossed the road, both of them. And surprise, surprise, there's alcohol involved. Guy smells like a brewery. Took the edge off that oil rigger smell. Been having a Friday night snort or two yourself?"

Marc ignored that. None of Tony's business. He wasn't driving at the moment. "Any idea who the victims might be?"

"Yes."

"Going to share that with me? Hey!" Crouching on one knee hadn't worked for Marc. When he'd stopped paying attention, he'd tumbled over.

"How much money you got?"

Marc rolled back up. "On a weekly newspaper salary? You must be kidding. Unlike some policemen we know."

"Allah be praised! Well, look who decided to show up. Time to play crossing guard."

Sirens rose and fell. Coloured lights danced like the aurora borealis before Marc's eyes. A late county ambulance roared in, upping the flashing light complement. It skidded on the gravel, narrowly missing a teenager who had darted in front of it at the last minute. Generously bellied men in white uniforms jumped out and rushed to the Chevy. They pushed back the blanket, feeling around the young man's neck. His head looked battered. Somebody tried CPR, gave up, and covered the young man with more blankets. They hoisted this bundle onto a stretcher and rolled it into the ambulance.

Slow ambulance response time. Now there was an editorial angle...

"How many people in the Crooked Elbow area are suffering, dying, because some ambulance— paid for by the taxpayers of this city and county— is unable to get to the site quickly enough to save lives? Maybe it's time that somebody besides a bevy of dead cats and penguins was elected to city council..."

"I'm back." Tony the cop interrupted Marc's mental editorial writing. He might have been unfair anyway. The ambulance hadn't arrived much later than Marc. Volunteers, they had to get to the station and then to the scene. Whereas cops and newspaper types took the call and came from wherever they were.

"What's the status of the victims?" Marc asked.

"That guy by the truck, that's the last firewater he's going to chug-a-lug. We're not sure about her, the girl in the Trans Am. Good thing she's coming out the driver's door. They'd need the Jaws to get her out the passenger side."

Marc yawned. He reloaded his camera and swayed, in slightly sideways fashion not helped by vodka, toward the bystanders. The small bar at The Wild Rose Cafe hadn't been overly fastidious in checking I.D. tonight. Or he was getting old. All these kids looked about 14.

He told them who he was, what he was doing, and one of them couldn't resist the oldest joke in the area: "*The Crooked Elbow Fun*, eh?"

Marc forced himself to smile, feeling better now that he'd been in action for 15 or 20 minutes. A reporter, not some desk-bound editor or publisher. He asked whether anybody knew any details. Who was in the Trans Am and the truck?

A tall boy with long hair said, "Might be Steph. Everybody says she was with some drunk guy at the bar. Then she starts acting all pissed off... Like it's the Miss High-and-Mighty Teen Competition and she's winning. You look again and she's hanging with another guy. That's crazy shit." Insanity sounded like something the long-haired boy could admire, and he looked the part. He wore a nose ring and an open blue jean vest. Tattooed snakes and dragons crawled across his chest.

"Yeah, it was Stephanie. You been partying, dude? We have," pouted a girl beside him. Black jeans clung to her calves and thighs like tights. Her left ear was rimmed with delicate steel studs. She gave Marc a stoned, stupid look and swung herself into the protective arms of the snake-and-dragon man.

"Um, I may not be totally familiar with this person. Does she have a last name?"

"That's your problem, eh?"

A boy in a cowboy hat laughed as if what the girl had just said were hilarious. He lost his breath, gagged, and stumbled into the tangled wild rose bushes beside the canola field. "Jamey's yawning in Technicolor. Again," somebody yelled after him.

Marc was losing patience with these young people, giving the impression that they were too cool to care about anything. One of the girls looked so much like Sky that a wave of despair gripped his heart. Could his daughter avoid a similar fate? Probably not, especially with no dad around. He was a newspaper man. He knew the statistics on children of divorce, raised in single-parent families. Though what kind of a role model had he been, the hours he'd kept, his moods, his drinking?

How old was Sky now, 12? 13? He shook his head and hair whipped past his ears. "Seriously. Who's in the car?" he asked a girl in a Cowboy Junkies T-shirt. "What's your name, you don't mind me asking?"

She answered him softly, a hint of primness in her voice. "Joan. And it was Stephanie Basiuk in the car. At least, we're pretty sure. She was with different people so I don't see how anybody knows exactly what happened?"

The name got his attention. "How's that spelled?"

She attempted the spelling for him— telling him not to quote her on it, she could be wrong— and Marc printed it in his spiral notepad. The accident scene closed in on him. For a moment, he had trouble breathing. "Teresa's sister, right?" he asked.

Red and blue strobes of light splashed over the girl's face. "You know her?"

"At work. The inserting crew. Part time. They put flyers and sections together. Sharp looking girl." More than sharp looking. He'd talked to her a couple of times, kidding around, and she had seemed to like him. He found himself thinking about her at odd moments, how she was only a few years older than Sky, but the same age as he had been when he started going out with Cindy. Everybody was dedicated to causes back then. His genera-tion had never figured out how to communicate the good stuff: the commitment to peace and love and changing society. These kids had to deal with AIDS and ethnic cleansing and manipulated images of Woodstock.

"So's her sister. Was. They're twins."

"What?" Marc said, startled. He'd drifted away again.

"Her sister's sharp looking, too. They're twins." She sounded frus-trated. Women hated it when you didn't listen the first time. He'd learned that much from Cindy, the bitch banker, mother of his daughters and most of his troubles. She made twice the money he did, but she'd be after child support if she ever found him. Every day when he went through the mail at the office, he expected a garnishee.

"Who's in the other car?" he asked.

"We're not sure. Somebody said his name was Joseph. Some oil rigger guy. New to town. He came to the bar by himself and he seemed all right, dancing and everything. I saw him on the floor with her, seemed to be having an okay time. And now this."

"So Stephanie Basiuk, she come with anybody?"

"Yeah, well, I guess so."

"A boyfriend, maybe?"

She hesitated, and when she answered she sounded indignant, as if he didn't know anything. "God, she's not going out with anybody."

Marc gave up on his notetaking in the poor light. "What's that supposed to mean?"

"Well, you know, it's Stephanie."

A siren's wail distracted them. An ambulance pulled away with the victim from the Chevy truck. Hot radiator odours mingled with the sweet, stifling smell of canola.

Two men in white eased the girl out of the Trans Am. She flopped on a stretcher, face up. One cheek and her nose were a mess. The men quickly covered her with a blanket.

"O-o-o-o-h," said one of the girls, covering her mouth.

"Gag me with a spoon," said one of the boys. Nobody laughed.

Marc was 50 feet away, too far for his little flash at night, and he was sure the pictures would violate community standards of publication. But he pressed the shutter button anyway. Moved closer. Shot again. Waited for his flash to recharge. Shot until he felt the awful tightening at the end of a roll of film.

"You have to do that?" a volunteer firefighter growled, sounding angry enough to hit him.

"My job," Marc muttered, and then felt awkward about the way the paper intruded into people's lives.

Spectators drifted away, leaving Marc to contemplate his trembling hands, the shortness and brutality of life, and the stars in a deep, deep blue night fringed with dying light. What was it, one in the morning? It never seemed to get completely dark in Alberta in June.

He needed a drink and he needed to avoid Lars and Tony. Now was not the time for a lecture about his best friend, Al Cool. As things turned out, dodging the Mounties was easy. When Marc left, they were helping each other measure skid marks, one of them at each end of a long tape.

Lars raised the middle finger of his left hand in a salute to the Volkswagen or the sky or life in general, and grinned at Marc's departure.

Turning at the green and white sign for the village, Marc passed dark houses and a machine shop and swung up the main street. Rose Hill sloped more than most Alberta towns. Its hills ascended from Rose Creek, a small river meandering through glacial rock, sparse pasture and cactus until it joined the Crooked Elbow River some 15 miles north of the village.

Vehicles crowded the streets in front of the only hotel in Rose Hill, The Wild Rose Cafe. More vehicles spilled down the street and around the corner— Cadillacs and Mercedes among medium-priced cars and polished half-tons. The occasional BMW. The bar was open until three.

"Vegas Style Dancers Thursday Through Saturday. Four Different Shows Nightly," boasted four-foot neon letters on the false front of the building. The sign was a tribute to the business acumen of Nicky Kuchik, one of the fattest of the Crooked Elbow fat cats.

Nicky had picked up the rambling hotel cheap when it closed five years before. People said he was soft in the head, buying a hotel in a village on the skids. But Nicky fooled them all. He renovated the men's lounge into a sports bar on one side and built "Alberta's longest bar" on the other. He added honeymoon suites with red jacuzzis. When he built a stage and brought in revue-style entertainment, word spread to Edmonton, the gateway to the north, the city of champions. Enough champions made the two-hour drive south to make Nicky rich.

"Show girls," he liked to tell people, "aren't strippers. It's like comparing satin to polyester."

Marc let the curb stop his Volkswagen in front of the hotel. He locked the door on his camera equipment. Patting his jean jacket, he found some crumpled last-call money. Just to be safe, he unlocked the car, treated himself to a long pull of free vodka, and had trouble locking the door again. Drinking was funny, he thought. You'd be floating along on one plane and, bingo, everything would change. Tonight, the liquor, the weariness, the accident, they all hit him at once, nearly knocking him over. He was disgusted with himself— he never knew when to stop.

Two men had already claimed the cement step leading to the small bar off the side, not exactly blocking his way and not exactly sliding over so he could get by. They quit talking as he approached.

"If it isn't Acting Mayor Klaus Axel. Evening, sir," Marc said, miming the doffing of a hat to a superior. "And Robbie McLean, *n'est-ce pas?* May your supermarket never run out of pre-baked pizza or I may run out of nourishment."

The mayor of Crooked Elbow was in Europe taking a cure following a nervous breakdown. Klaus Axel, rumoured to be even richer than Nicky Kuchik, had taken over the mayor's job in his absence. "Marc LePage," he said. "What brings the press to this part of the world?"

"An accident up the road. Nice level spot for a game of chicken— gravel road, top of the hill. Know what I mean?" Marc's feet shifted on him without warning.

"Looks like you're tying on a good one, my friend. Some kid said it was the Basiuk girl. And some white trash living like an Indian." Robbie McLean spat on the street as if he were cleansing his mouth of the word, "Indian."

"Thought you boys might be there. I saw some volunteer firefighters hanging around in case somebody farted and lit a match at the same time." A knee gave out on him; Marc righted himself to keep from falling over.

"Hey, Deadeye Dick, you take a camera with you?" Klaus Axel smiled and stood up, as if inviting Marc to join them. Klaus wasn't a tall man, but he was a lot taller than Robbie. People called him BM1 behind his back. A scatological reference, but also a reference to his status as the Biggest Man in Crooked Elbow. Robbie McLean they sometimes called BM2.

Marc spread his hands wide, and spreading them nearly keeled him over. "No camera," he said. "None." He couldn't remember where the camera was.

"Good." Klaus bumped him with his shoulder. "Stephanie Basiuk was a local girl and negative shit in the press is bad for business. By the way, you ever need falling insurance, you come and see me."

That remark prompted a question from Marc. "You're in the insurance business. What happens in a game of chicken?"

"Nothing special. We pay them. They pay us. Everybody's happy."

"But what if her car's worth more than his? Never mind. I can't think straight. You know something else? I was thinking on my way from the accident, what's a girl her age doing in a Trans Am? Everybody treats her like she hasn't got two wooden nickels to rub together. And she's driving a new car."

"I don't know," Klaus said. "Maybe it was a gift. Maybe she blew somebody until they came like a radiator on a hot day."

Robbie thought that was pretty funny. Laughing a high, unpleasant chuckle, he looked at Klaus and said, "Yeah, maybe she did." And laughed some more.

Robbie was wearing a white cowboy hat and boots with heels that made him a couple of inches taller. He stretched, still laughing, and stood up, the brim of his hat threatening Marc's nose. "We was thinking about one for the road, and I guess we wouldn't die and go straight to everlasting perdition if we stood the press to a drink."

"Thanks gentlemen, but it's late and I need to get... If I don't watch my waist line, who will?"

"A very good question, guy," Robbie McLean drawled, in an accent that was a credit to his admiration for all things American. "See you around. If you happen to get stopped, somebody wants to check your point-zero-eight, let me know. I'm a personal friend of the police commissioner." He laughed at Klaus and slapped his back. The two of them went inside.

"Good people to have on your side," Marc said to the street. "I mean my side. Too bad they're such bourgeois assholes." He had trouble saying "bourgeois," but he knew what he meant.

It was a long ride home, not as long as the ride Stephanie and Joe had taken that night, but long enough. He hit the shoulder twice and gravel woke him both times before he could hit the ditch.

He still had last-call money with him when he dislodged himself from his car in downtown Crooked Elbow.

"Need a nightcap. Maybe a coffee. You jerk," he said.

Laughing with inebriated self-loathing, he missed a step on his way up to The Victoria. "Like Alberta bars. Open till three. Let the dead bury their dead." Whatever that meant.

He thought Lise might still be at the bar. Lise and he had some kind of a thing going. Maybe if he saw her again, he could keep it going. But she wasn't there.

He joined a white-haired rancher who was pretty far along. They had a drunken discussion about why Immanuel Kant never left Koenigsberg all his life. The rancher's opinion was that Kant's horse probably wandered into the German forest and never came back.

That was the problem, the rancher said.

Marc argued that such behaviour was more up Hegel's alley, but the rancher didn't seem impressed.

CHAPTER 2

Sunlight oozed brownish yellow through a bath towel covering a window high on the wall of Marc's basement kitchen. It was two days later, Sunday, nearly noon. A day too bright for his eyes. He closed them and saw swatches of colour and remembered the lights at The Victoria the night before. Some locals called this hotel the centre of the universe. A densely populated universe, if he remembered the previous night correctly.

Lise had been there, but did she start off with him or did she come later? Later was fuzzy. With a big yawn, he shoved himself away from the kitchen counter that served as his breakfast table and went out to a world that was entirely too bright for the retinas of any drinker. In it, squatting like a dull blue toad in the brilliant sunshine, was Das Kapital, Volume 2, without a new scratch or dent on it that he could see. He didn't want to know how the car had gotten home.

And Marc didn't want to talk to his aunt and landlady, who lived a few short steps away from the side door against which he was now leaning. She didn't mind leaving her waxed floors and picture-perfect curtains to discuss her black sheep nephew from Ontario and his errant ways. He felt like a kid around her.

He hurried downstairs again, although his head didn't appreciate his haste. He made more coffee and scrambled some eggs with cheese and green pepper in an electric frying pan. When he took a bite, his teeth ached and the right side of his jaw hurt. A little of the night before came back to him. Somebody above him at a table. A contest. Two forks clenched between Marc's teeth. A beer mug balanced on the forks, somebody pouring beer into the mug. People chanting, Lise leading them, "Mark-ee! Mark-ee! Mark-ee!"

Later, he'd asked somebody for details about the car that had been smashed in the accident. What had he asked and why had it made somebody mad? Marc couldn't remember, so he let it go, and something else surged into his mind. Another reason his jaw felt like mush. On his way to the washroom, somebody'd hit him. That part was clear now. A couple of bull riders, celebrating their loss at the Saturday afternoon rodeo in town, had gathered above him. They wouldn't have minded a brawl. Klaus Axel had come over and turned down the temperature.

Sunday afternoon. Nothing to do, once he'd rinsed off his plate and put it away.

He took the *Critique of Pure Reason* down from its place of honour between the basic works of Plato and Aristotle. But the question of how synthetic a priori judgements were possible paled in comparison with the lure of somnolence.

Marc drifted off and when he woke again, he went to the McLean Gym and Public Pool and did some curls, leg extensions, and bench presses. Fifteen minutes in the pool, a shower, and he was home for a late afternoon snack— grilled cheese with dill pickles on the side— eating them with aching teeth. A quick coffee. The headache didn't go away, so he took two more pills and threw his gym stuff into a laundry basket in the corner. Trying to read some more Kant, he fell asleep on the couch in his bedsitting room.

He dreamed Teresa Basiuk was in the press room, naked. His estranged wife, Cindy, pulled him away from her toward the press units, where Anne-Marie, their oldest daughter, was standing. He was overjoyed to see her alive again. The units were tall as the building and getting taller, thundering at him. Marc resisted his wife, but it wasn't working. She was stronger than he. Besides, he had to follow her. Anne-Marie was being sucked toward one of the press units. The bells warning of a press start-up rang and rang. He knew it was the phone and woke up, feeling empty and depressed, as he did every time he dreamed about Anne-Marie.

Addle-headed, he banged his way to the kitchen. His forehead was slick with sweat, his tongue thick, his throat pasty.

"Hullo," he croaked.

"Marc LePage?" It was a southern TV evangelist's voice, so it had to be Robbie McLean. Some days Robbie sounded like a good ole boy from Tennessee, just in from trout fishing. He always said Lee-Page, pronouncing the second part of Marc's name like the page of a newspaper.

Marc grunted and didn't answer. Robbie kept talking. He was part salesman and didn't like silence. "I know you and me don't always see eyeball to eyeball. That's okay. But I respect the job you're doing at the paper."

"That's cool. Thank you." Marc rotated his head and let his neck crack. The headache was weaker but still hanging in there. He gave up on a dry day and tossed back a snort from a bottle sitting on the kitchen counter between a bag of chocolate chip cookies and the electric frying pan. Yellow margarine had congealed in the pan. Marc came alive when the alcohol hit.

"Yeah, well, it's a hell of a lot better paper since that Brownrigg company bought it. But there's one little bitty matter we need to discuss. I hear you lied to us. What say we get together? Tomorrow."

"Lied to you? I never lie," Marc yawned. "Tomorrow's not a great day. We finish the paper— most of it— Monday, so we can dazzle the citizenry with literary gems Tuesday afternoon."

"I know when the paper comes out. That's why I got to see you."

They settled on 3:00 p.m. Monday at the newspaper office.

Marc had asked Carmen, the receptionist, to make Robbie wait until 3:10. But at 2:57, according to the clock in the cluttered newsroom outside his office, the man strolled in as if he'd just assumed the deed to the place. Two short men in white shirts, red ties and dark polyester pants stepped in after Robbie. Brass name badges were clipped to their shirt pockets. Carmen poked her head around the door, raised her eyebrows, and mouthed, "What could I do?"

"Kept them out," Marc mouthed back, angry. His office was a disaster area, and Robbie McLean was already running this meeting. There'd be no Hegelian dialectical debate— thesis and antithesis evolving into a new synthesis. Instead, everything would be rolled into a ball and dumped in Marc's court, whether he wanted it or not. His cheeks felt hot; beads of sweat loosened in each armpit.

Robbie winked at him. "My meat manager and my produce manager, Jake Halliday and Ollie Johnson. Say hello to Marc, the Marquis de Sade. I brought them along so there wouldn't be any misunderstandings about what goes on at our meeting. By the way, I hope there's no hard feelings from Saturday night."

"Of course not. I understand," Marc said, but he didn't.

They shook hands and Marc found them all chairs. Jake and Ollie pinched the creases in their trousers and sat without saying a word. Marc settled behind his desk.

Robbie patrolled the office, his tiny fingers linked behind him, Napoleon inspecting the barracks. He stopped in front of a row of community newspaper awards flanking a large print of the Canadian Charter of Rights and Freedoms. "That thing's ruining the country," he said to Jake and Ollie.

They nodded and squirmed on their vinyl chairs.

When Robbie came back to the desk, his mood changed. He scowled at the mess and tried a grin to cover his disapproval.

"Bad day for paper," Marc said. A stiff vodka and grapefruit juice would go down nicely right about now, he thought. Lots of crushed ice.

The mess didn't end with his desk. Paper of all colours— white, chartreuse, magenta, canary— covered a chair, a small filing cabinet, part of the carpet. Robbie stacked some of it neatly to one side, wiped his hands, and leaned forward, his knuckles white against the imitation wood top.

"The accident out by Rose Hill. You got there late, after some of us volunteers was already gone. We didn't see you till the hotel, later. A little birdie tells me you lied to us. You had a camera with you."

Robbie slid an American cigarette from a shirt pocket embroidered with flowers. The cigarette in mid-air for effect, he stopped, as if waiting for Marc to acknowledge his efforts as a volunteer firefighter. Marc nodded and said "Uh-huh," an old reporter's habit to keep an interviewee talking.

Robbie scraped a flame from a gold lighter and puffed. "Well, as you no doubt know, there was young people involved. I just wanted to confirm that the names of these youngsters aren't going to show up in the paper."

"What makes you guys care one way or the other?"

"This is me talking, eh? Not some guys. And you listen to me. The girl was 18, but he wasn't, eh? We're dealing with juveniles here. Hell, leaving the names out is probably so routine, it don't need mentioning."

Marc leaned back in his chair and studied the flecked white ceiling tiles, his legs stretched under the desk. "You know the rules, Robbie," he said. "We can't tell you how we're handling a story before the paper comes out. Otherwise, the bourgeoisie'd be running this paper. Running it into the ground."

"Yeah, yeah, we been through this before. But once the genie's out of the bottle, he don't go back in."

It occurred to Marc that negotiating was Robbie's life, what he did best, which meant that his life was 90 per cent hot air. It had made Robbie rich at a tough game, running an independent grocery store against the food giants in the province. But Robbie McLean wasn't a man you could trust, unless you only trusted him to look after his own interests.

"Her father," Robbie said. "He's not only a close personal friend, he's done a lot for this community. Johnny Basiuk's had his troubles, but you don't know what he once meant to this town. You're too new. He was the best in his day. It'll kill him if his girl's name trickles out in a news story.

Confidentially," he said, his eyes dead serious, not even blinking, "the doctors think suicide's not out of the question."

Between the mesmerizing hand motions and the you-all voice, Marc was of two minds about Robbie's sales pitch. But when he threw in suicide, a bubble of relief burst in Marc's chest. He bit the soft balled part inside his cheek and counted the strands of gold nestled in Robbie's greying chest hairs to keep himself from laughing. There were five strands. A hickey the size of a quarter discoloured the tan above the gold chains.

Robbie turned away. Clumping around the office in grey snakeskin boots, he waved one hand as if he were appeasing a delegation at a city council meeting. "It's not like we'd even be asking, if these was adults. That's not right, to try and control the press in a democracy. But there's kids involved. And who knows? You help us, maybe we can help you some time. A little mutual back-scratching never hurt the bears."

"You still haven't told me why you care so much about the names in the paper," Marc said, although he knew the drill. People with vested interests often tried to keep names out of community papers. The trick was figuring out what their interests were. "Look, there's no future for me in a fight with one of the biggest men in Crooked Elbow. So if you just go away, I'll pretend this never happened."

Robbie's shoulders bunched inside his jacket, like a bantam rooster swelling its feathers to attack. As he leaned over the desk again, the air was suffused with aromas: tobacco, cologne, peppermint lozenges. "Now you listen to me, you Kwee-beck bastard. I don't know what rock Brownrigg finds socialist creeps like you under. But I put a two-page grocery spread a week in that rag you call a newspaper— colour— and Klaus Axel uses a page and a half for the real estate and insurance, sometimes colour. None of that has to happen."

"You know I'd like to help you. I really would."

"Fine, so help us."

"I can't."

"Can't? Or won't? Not even this once? We're not trying to influence the story. We're just talking names."

"I thought you had more sense than to come in here, using advertising as a threat. One newspaper in town, it's not like you're blessed with options."

Robbie eased his cowboy hat back on his head, tilted it slightly to the right and checked his reflection in the office window. A wide peacock feather spread across the front of the hat. His voice was quieter. "What good's it going to do, washin' linen in public like that? It's bad for the town's image. Ah, what the Jesus H. Christ... Sometimes I don't know why I bother. C'mon, guys, let's go. We'd be further ahead having a chat with the brick wall across the street."

His associates smiled into their laps, stood, brushed the wrinkles out of their pants and smoothed their ties straight along the buttons of their shirts.

"It was an experience meeting you," said the meat manager.

"Have a truly nice day," said the produce manager. Raising a warm, moist palm, he shook Marc's hand vigorously.

When Robbie was at the door, he spun around on the toes of his cowboy boots. "I've got news for you, boy. Everybody's got skeletons in their closets. I'd advise you to keep yours very well hid."

That made Marc mad. Anger wasn't as good as liquor, but it sometimes focused him, made him feel wonderfully alive. Forget the mess on his desk, the reporters scurrying outside his office window, the paper he had to put out. Robbie McLean had just earned himself a shot.

"Before you go," Marc said, his voice steady, his fingers trembling, "how'd you like to fill me in on the Agriplex?"

Robbie's grocery associates stared down at their boots as if to demonstrate how little attention they were paying.

Marc slid a spiral-topped notepad from under some papers. A twisted apple core toppled over and joined an overturned ashtray and cigarette remains on the carpet. Flipping pages cluttered with his scrawl, he came to a blank one, and scribbled the date with his left hand. "You and Klaus did the gasohol plant with government help and now the agricultural society wants this Agriplex. Correct me if I'm wrong, but I haven't seen any public meetings or anything. Is this going to be a repeat of the gasohol fiasco, you and the good ole boys pushing it through? By the time we hear about it, it's a done deal?" Marc looked up into brown eyes staring full and unblinking at him, as if shocked by the question.

"That Agriplex's been on the back burner for years. Between the city, the county, and the province, we've just about negotiated the life out of this sucker. All's it is, is things finally coming together."

"Groovy," Marc said. "But we're talking land and buildings in the five million dollar range. And there's been no public meeting since I've been around."

Robbie flipped his hat to one of his associates. White blotches rose high in Robbie's cheeks, mottling his summer tan. "That just shows what some people don't know, eh, boy? Negotiations in these matters are very delicate. But all you care about is running kids' names in the paper— the community can go cornhole itself."

"Okay, but everybody's broke— the city, the province. Where's the money coming from? Or maybe I should cut the bullshit and ask the obvious, why you're so interested in the accident."

Something popped into Marc's head, about the fight Saturday night. Some girl— was it Teresa?— had started talking about the car. Marc, half snapped, had picked up on it, and Robbie had taken a swing at him. Why? Marc still couldn't remember many details.

Robbie rotated slowly on his heels, his mouth open, an index finger wagging a threat— the little boy angry that mommy was threatening to take his toys away after she had said he could have them. A facial muscle twitched high in his cheek, under his right eye. His lower lip trembled. "No comment, okay? You think you got that? Everything here was off the record. You print Word One and you'll be talking to my lawyer, you goddamn French hippy. You think that's funny? Well, I'd be surprised if the story's any closer to right than usual. That dead guy'll be an Indian before you're through with the story, *mon* fucking *ami*."

His face scarlet, a vein bulging near his temple, Robbie snatched the notepad from Marc and tried to tear it in half. When that didn't work, he pulled at pages, two and three at a time, twisting them, balling some up, ripping at others.

Grabbing a slim paste-up knife from the desk, Robbie slid open the blade and slashed at the pages. They wouldn't cut fast enough for him and that made him furious. He held his breath, expelled it in a yell, and moved behind the desk, slashing the knife at Marc's face. Marc put up his right hand to protect himself, needing his left hand for editing. The knife sliced a precise cut in his palm. It didn't hurt at first, although it felt numb and he could see blood.

"You can't go around assaulting people. I'm calling the cops."

"You do and it's the end of you in this town," Robbie snarled, his eyes red, the colour leaving his cheeks as if his heart had started sucking instead of pumping. He clicked the little knife shut and tossed it back on Marc's desk. He was breathing heavily through his mouth. A thin line of spittle hung from his lower lip, threatening to fall.

The spittle fell and Robbie laughed. "Call the cops, asshole. Go ahead." Shoving his embarrassed associates through the door, Robbie slammed it hard enough to rattle the long, frosted pane of glass running up the side.

Marc inhaled slowly through his nostrils and exhaled through his mouth, his eyes closed. He sucked at the cut on his hand and pressed it tightly with a piece of gauze, the kind normally used by the composing room to wipe wax off layout flats. The cut wasn't deep, but the gauze quickly reddened.

"Workers' Comp, for sure," he said to nobody. "That neo-Luddite bastard."

Rolling his head in a slow semi-circle, he controlled his breathing— slowly in to the count of four, slowly out through his nostrils to the count of four. In. Out. Counting. Then he punched two numbers on the telephone and asked Carmen for the date and time of the Basiuk funeral.

"You're beautiful," he said when she told him.

Palm roughly bandaged, black tape dispenser in his good hand, he resigned himself to the task of taping together what he could find of his notes.

He needed a few quotes if he was going to put out a paper the next week.

CHAPTER 3

By 11:30 Tuesday morning, Marc had finished dummying the front page of the paper— sketching in the placement of pictures and copy. He left the composing-room staff to do the rest— paste it up, get it ready for the press— while he went for lunch.

He decided to stretch his legs. The newspaper office was two blocks off 50th, the main street and also the most direct route to his favourite hotel. It was only five or six blocks to The Victoria, but he was sweating as he walked. After three blocks, he took off his jacket and waved to a member of the local middle class in a store window, the merchant obsessing over his clean-cut image. Polishing. Dusting. Rearranging.

A block later, Marc watched a round, dry weed tumble down a side street toward him. The sight of it was so typically western, it gave his eastern heart a lift. The wind brought many questionable things to town— dust, weeds, old newspapers, irritation. But it was a constant in people's lives and it usually cleansed the air. Day after day, it blew in hot and dry from the west or southwest, losing its moisture in British Columbia before sweeping across the plains to the parkland surrounding Crooked Elbow.

"Restaurant side's pretty full," a harried waitress puffed at him when he reached The Victoria.

"Okay, any room on the lounge side?"

"Only about a hundred seats." She popped her gum, looked worried and left him on his own to find a table in the lounge, a dim, air-conditioned room with the faint burnt tobacco smell exuded by poorly washed ashtrays.

A table of men with sweat-stained caps and two-day beards stared at him and went back to their beer. Near the far wall, a woman with white frizzy hair told a story— animated by hand gestures— to the remains of her cigarettes and six beer glasses, mostly empty.

Marc ordered a beer and a salad and they arrived together, both cold as ice. "First of the day," he said, tilting his glass to the old lady. She didn't return his toast. Crazy old ladies know better than to mix with editors who start work at six in the morning so they'll have time to grab a little courage before a funeral.

In his shirt pocket, Marc found tobacco and folded photocopy sheets from the morning— early drafts of the lead story and an editorial, with names. Take that, Robbie McLean. Suggested banner headline for the lead story, all in capital letters, TRAGIC CRASH KILLS 2. Later revised for more length. That just about killed George, the composing-room supervisor. George hated last-minute changes. The usual Tuesday morning scenario.

"Two people are dead," the story began, "following a two-car pile-up on a gravel road just south of Rose Hill last Friday night.

"Dead are 18-year-old Stephanie Jo-Anne Basiuk of Crooked Elbow and 17-year-old Ronald Joseph Woscicyk of Edmonton, temporarily living in the city of Crooked Elbow.

"Royal Canadian Mounted Police Staff Sergeant Ben Muttsi said the blood-alcohol level of both victims was high, a game of chicken was suspected, and the investigation was continuing."

Prize-winning material, here. Too bad Mr. Pulitzer didn't provide for Canadian publications when he set up his prizes.

Marc's other photocopied sheet contained an early version of his editorial, which took pains to mourn the loss of the young people before demanding an investigation into ambulance response time. "In the interest of saving the lives of our youth, particularly in rural areas, something drastic must be done. Something as drastic as getting our local politicians out of the coffee shops and into the council chambers where the business of governing this community is supposed to be addressed."

Not bad, he thought. Good enough to earn him more than foam in his beer glass, especially since he'd accomplished a minor miracle, getting Barb Zelnak off her butt the night before to finish the gasohol story she'd been assigned three weeks before. Her page three feature said the plant, under construction for the past year, would soon start production. Although the project was late and over budget, Klaus Axel was quoted as saying, "I'm delighted to be doing something to benefit the environment as well as Alberta farmers."

Not to mention your own pockets when the government grants come through, Marc thought.

By the time his last beer came, he and the waitress had the place to themselves— just them and four wild horses stampeding in a painting above the seat vacated by the old lady. Marc munched popcorn as cheap and salty as the conversation in The Victoria at night, finished his beer and left.

The funeral home on the highway had been converted from a grocery store after Robbie McLean sold it and built his new supermarket downtown, closer to the Safeway. Marc was late, but there were lots of parking spaces. He pulled in beside a tan Cadillac flecked with gold, and bumped its passenger door when he opened his.

"Oops," he grinned at the door. "Shouldn't park where the proletariat can get at you."

The wind seemed hotter and more irritating than it had downtown, but the lobby of the funeral home was cool and soothing. An usher greeted him with a nod, managing to wrinkle the edges of his eyes and stretch his lips across his teeth without quite smiling. "We're a little behind schedule," he murmured. His fingers smoothed the hairs of a black moustache trimmed too short to need smoothing. His eyes darted to Marc's grey leather tie, his blue jeans.

Marc signed the guest book, "H.L. Mencken, Chicago," and followed his dark-suited escort down the centre aisle. The carpet exuded the lingering pine smell of a cheap motel. A large portable cross dominated the room.

"Do you prefer a side, sir?" the usher whispered.

"Sure. The winning one. Up near the front."

Marc hated funerals and he didn't want to sit alone. He stopped about four rows behind the reserved section and the usher stopped with him. A family of five, all in dark blue, bumped over apologetically to make space for Marc. Across the aisle, high school girls exchanged secrets and the occasional giggle, shushing each other.

Ahead of him in the reserved section, Klaus Axel sat beside a tall woman with bottled blond hair piled high. Two boys were on the other side of her.

One seemed to be about 16, the other much younger. Kneeling on the carpet, Marc made the sign of the cross and thought, "Yeah, there aren't that many tan Cadillacs in town. But what's he doing here?"

Flourishing loosely fleshed arms, the organist launched into "The Lord Is My Shepherd." People joined her, singing half-heartedly. One of the girls across the aisle began to cry.

A priest in white robes walked to the lectern and opened a Bible— Father Larry, the only person who'd been any help to Marc in dealing with the losses in his life. They'd started talking after a council meeting before Christmas, on a night when Marc was half in the bag, wondering whether he'd make it through the holidays. Larry asked him to stop by the rectory the next day. It was the weirdest thing: the priest had hardly said anything, but they talked for three hours.

Seeing him again, Marc felt guilty that he hadn't been to church since. Or cracked the book Larry'd given him, *The Cloud of Unknowing*, allegedly written in the Middle Ages by a priest who requested anonymity.

"Stephanie Basiuk was not a regular churchgoer," Father Larry was saying. "But the family came back to the Church in its time of need, as many of us do. Death brings the family together and the wider family, the Christian community of friends.

"This afternoon, we've asked friends and relatives to help with the service. Teresa— the twin sister of the one whom God has called to be His own— will do the first reading. Teresa?"

In a pink dress, looking more like an awkward woman than a girl from the inserting crew, Teresa shuffled impatiently past her family in their reserved chairs and walked loosely to the front on white heels. Her brown hair, streaked with blond, was layered and puffed up in front. Her lipstick was pink. As she lowered the microphone, a ruffled sleeve slid back, showing hints of black undergarments. She read well, keeping her eyes on the paper in front of her.

"A reading from the book of the prophet Isaiah:
    On this mountain,
    The Lord Sabaoth will prepare for all peoples
    A banquet of rich food

On this mountain, he will remove
the mourning veil covering all people
and the shroud enwrapping all nations
he will... he will... destroy death forever."

Teresa looked up— maybe to prove how tough she was, that she could do it— but looking up was her undoing. Her last words came out hesitantly, as whispers, the eyes of the congregation rooting her to her spot. A shiver coursed through her, loosening a stubborn portion of sorrow. She wept openly. Outbursts of grief, answering her from the congregation, circled like small, hot dust-eddies over summer fallow until they settled on one girl who hugged herself, rocking, her voice keening against her sobs. A woman led the weeping girl to the back, where grocery carts had once been lined up for patrons and check-out tills had once whirred.

"Sorry for all this, like, bawling," Teresa snuffled, clearing her throat, straining to talk. "Stephanie was a good person. No matter what you think. No matter what anybody thinks."

The priest stepped toward her and wrapped an arm around her shoulder for comfort.

"Don't touch me," Teresa yelled. Squirming away from him, she wiped at her nose with the back of her hand. "Just don't touch me."

Father Larry patiently squeezed her into the curve of his arm, like a coach escorting an injured player off the field. She let her head go limp against him. Tears dripping from her cheeks, she allowed herself to be led a few steps from the lectern toward her seat.

Klaus Axel half rose in his pew, then sank back down. As if this were his cue, Teresa's father lumbered to his feet. To Marc, he looked more like a hockey goon gone to seed than a local sports hero or a potential suicide. The man patted the pockets of his dark jacket, as if checking to see whether his wallet were still in place. He seemed confused. "Your Worship," he said unsteadily to the priest. "I'd thank you for taking your hands off my daughter."

"Daddy, it's okay," Teresa managed. "Hang on. I'm coming."

The priest let her go. He ran his fingers through his hair and made washing motions with his hands. His lower lip trembled. He bit the lip with uneven front teeth and took a moment at the microphone to compose himself.

"The second reading this afternoon..." He shoved back a loose sleeve, checking his watch "...is from a letter of Paul to the Romans. It's by Stephanie Basiuk's homeroom teacher, a woman I know was a godly influence, Anna Kradnick."

Marc used the family beside him as a refresher course on when to stand and when to kneel. He nodded off and woke, startled, to see girls lining up for communion. Sleepily, he admired their youth and their roundness, sometimes in surprising places— a cheek, under the chin— watching for a fawn-like glance that would lock on his. But nothing drew him like the streaked head of hair in the front row, leaning toward Stephanie's mother's shoulder, not moving.

Marc couldn't bring himself to go to the gravesite for the final words and the lowering of Stephanie's casket. The thought of watching a replay of Anne-Marie's final moments above ground was more than he could bear. Far too much to do at the office, he told himself.

"So how was the party?" Carmen asked as he wandered by her desk, checking the pigeon hole for messages. Her almond eyes smiled at him.

He laughed out loud, with post-funeral relief, glad to be back among chemical smells and newspaper people hustling about. "It was okay. Cathartic, as these rituals should be."

"If you say so, Mr. Walking Dictionary. I'm surprised you stayed away from the wake."

"I had lunch before the funeral."

"Could be a mistake. It's the Basiuks. Can you see Johnny doing a wake sober?"

"Don't know the man, Carmen. Teresa read at the funeral. She did well. I don't think I could have gotten through it, but she did okay. Only broke down at the end."

"Brave girl. I'd be careful, if I was you. We used to be neighbours. Don't dip your dink in the company ink."

He laughed. "What's that supposed to mean?"

"The stories I could tell. About that family."

"Such as?"

"You don't want to know." She coloured slightly when she said it and he believed her.

"So that explains your transformation into the party animal we all know and love."

"Something like that."

Classified order forms, invoices for ads, and two pink message pads cluttered her desk. One message was for Marc, rewritten Carmen-style: "His Royal Highness, the exalted company prez Jeremy Brown, requests the company of your presents in your office tomorrow morning, nine a.m. Rehearse your bowing and scraping."

Another note requested a photo reprint from a paper two years before. "Tell them we lost the negs, will you?" He crumpled the note and lobbed it at Carmen. She made a face.

More paper had been piled on his desk— handwritten columns from correspondents in Rose Hill and West Berwick and New Scandia; glossy recipes from food companies; a promise that he was one of the very few people who would win a car if he returned this form NOW. News releases, news releases. Everybody and his cousin wanted something in the local paper, free if they could get it.

One envelope had his name typed on the outside, all upper case, with PRIVATE, CONFIDENTIAL typed underneath it. Carmen was under instruction to open all his mail except for items with "confidential" on the outside, most of which turned out to be gripes about stories or staff.

He slit open the envelope with a letter opener given him by the Optimist Club after he delivered a luncheon speech called "The Newspaper— Roadster of the 21st Century, or Road Kill on the Information Highway?"

A single sheet of paper was folded inside— foolscap, three-hole punched. The letters were typed, all in capitals:

PLEASE LEAVE THE CHICKEN ALONE.

I THINK YOU KNOW WHAT I MEAN.
I'M TELLING U 4 YOUR OWN GOOD.

He read it three times, looked at the envelope, checked the type style—from an IBM Selectric, a kind of typewriter kicking around most offices.

Being threatened was nothing new to him. Nothing came of the threats, usually. Or so he told himself, though the next piece of paper, from a community correspondent, trembled when he picked it up.

Marc edited several local columns to take his mind off the note. "Visitors this week with the Mouse family motored from Daffyton and Ducksville..." He'd love to print that, see if anybody would notice. Some weeks, he was sure the *Sun*'s readers must be as bored with the social notes as he was.

Carmen's voice paged him. "Marc, line one. Marc, line one."

"Would you take a picture (deep breath) of the Lions Club president (second deep breath) presenting a cheque for $2,000 (major wheeze) to Beaver Park for picnic tables? You (second major wheeze followed by chest-rattling cough) better do better than last time. Monday night at the Lions Club meeting (final cough)."

Cheque presentations bored Marc almost as much as Catholic funeral services and community correspondents. He had to get away. He recorded the cheque presentation in the daybook and went back to the front desk.

"Be out for a while, Carmen. Maybe all afternoon."

"Going to the wake, are we?"

"On assignment."

"Have one for me." She winked, either at him or his weakness, he wasn't sure which.

Grabbing his camera bag, Marc took Das Kapital on a trawl for feature photos. Retired farmers nodded on benches in the shade of trees and bushes planted by the downtown business association to beautify 50th Street. Trees and interlocking brick were the downtown's answer to the lure of big-city malls. If it took precious water to keep the little trees green during dry spells, that was the price that had to be paid for progress.

"It's all so quaint," Marc said to Das Kapital's steering wheel. "Quaintly boring and boringly quaint."

He turned left by the Safeway store and meandered out to the suburbs, West-El Park, near the gym where he'd been exercising on Sunday. New people had filled up the park when the petrochemical plants were built north and east of Crooked Elbow. It was a typical Canadian suburb. Parents rushed their kids to soccer and ballet and gymnastics on Saturdays when they weren't too beaten up by the rigours of shift work or the aftermath of Friday nights on their neighbours' decks. Their stucco houses had aluminum or vinyl fronts, as if unconsciously aping the western tradition of building stores with false fronts. Families mortgaged their homes to the hilt, leaving the *nouveau pauvre* to choke on the smell and haze the plants generated near downtown when the wind blew wrong.

Two girls with ribbons in their hair sold lemonade from a stand on the sidewalk in front of a stucco and aluminum bi-level. They held up their pitcher and he clicked the shutter. Cute kid pics: the salvation of weekly newspaper editors during the slow summer months.

Down the block, a girl in purple shorts and halter top darted in front of his car. He slammed on the brakes and Das Kapital obediently shuddered to a stop.

"You idiot," he shouted, his heart pounding. "Cars kill people." Beeping the horn, he leaned out the window and yelled, "Watch where you're going."

He pulled a U-turn in front of Our Lady of the Blessed Harvest School and drove fast to the Moose Hall. He could use a drink.

Voices hummed like grasshoppers. Bowls clattered in the kitchen like binders in wheat. Chairs scraped the cement floor of the hall like stones caught in a moving blade. He saw a few people who had not been at the funeral. Robbie McLean, standing by Klaus Axel, ignored Marc and kept on talking to a tall man, shirt tail spewing from the top of his pants. Nicky Kuchik sipped coffee, watching impassively.

"Excessive wealth is the true obscenity," Marc muttered, wishing he had the nerve to walk up and insult them openly, see what they'd do about it.

Instead, he piled potato salad, cold brown beans, green salad, celery, radishes, pickles, and two buns on a floppy paper plate. A large woman slid thick slices of roast beef on top of this pile.

Marc took his food and a waxed paper cup of orange drink to a wooden fold-up chair standing against the wall near the Basiuk family. Empty plates were stacked at one end of their table. Teresa's mother, her mouth slashed with red lipstick, sat with her back to the family, staring at the room, her shoulders unnaturally squared.

A thin man with blotchy skin approached. She flinched when she saw him. He slapped Teresa's father on the back. "How're you doing, Johnny? Sorry about the kid." His slim fingers picked at dandruff on the shoulders of Johnny's jacket.

"Clem!" Johnny swung a damp gaze in Clem's direction. Johnny's black hair was combed Elvis Presley style, partly to hide his patchy baldness. "That you? Sit down. We're heartbroke. It's awful, just awful. Have a little smash to ease the pain. Suz, quit your fooling around." Johnny swept the small girl away from the table to make elbow room for his friend. Pulling a bottle from under the table, he twisted the cap and splashed whiskey into a foam cup.

The two food lines soon splintered into a third— a ragged line, mostly men— sidling along so Johnny could pour "just a little, just a touch... whoa, that's good" into their coffee before they picked up their dessert. Marc resisted the temptation to join the line. Father Larry would have been proud.

Another bag appeared on the table. It was imprinted with black letters: "Don't drink and drive," a message from the Alberta Liquor Control Board. Johnny swung an arm over his wife, forcing her to slide around and face the family. "C'mon, honey. How about a little drink?" Leaning into her mother, Teresa shook her head, no, at him.

Clem poured for Teresa's mother with bug-eyed concentration, as if the liquid were as precious as transubstantiated wine, topping the cup with diet cola from a can. The woman downed it and held the cup out, empty, looking around the room, as if embarrassed by her need. Johnny did the honours on the next one.

"C'mere, sweetie pie," Clem said, with a sly wink at Johnny as he pulled the pale girl Johnny had earlier swept away from the table onto his knee. She wore a light blue dress with tiny white flowers. A scarlet ribbon bobbed in her pony tail. She smiled and a gap showed between two yellow front teeth.

"You want a drink of uncle Clem's special Coke? The kind little girls like? Am I right, or what, boys?" Clem shouted the last words, swinging his innocent-looking eyes to people around him who roared their approval and immediately went back to discussing the weather and crops and what a shame Stephanie's death was. He separated some of Mrs. Basiuk's second drink into a waxed paper cup. The little girl tipped the cup, sucked greedily, and made an exaggerated sour face. Clem buried a red-veined cheek in her hair and rocked her, laughing, "You love it, don't you baby?"

His hand moved up and under her dress. The girl strained her arms and locked them tightly around his neck. Basement noise roared in Marc's ears like surf. He longed to escape this suffocating room, to go out where the prairie sky spread wide and the breeze swept in fierce and hot from the southwest.

His heart pounded, his blood a river roaring and boiling through his wrists and temples. He carried his plate and plastic cutlery to a table where two stout women cheerfully attended to such matters. Coughing into a shaking fist to clear the tightness in his chest, he borrowed a cigarette and a light from an old farmer with a purple birthmark on his forehead. When the cigarette was going, Marc made his way to the Basiuk table, squeezing between tables and chairs. Coming at Clem from behind, Marc dug his fingers, as hard as he could, into the cords running from Clem's neck to his shoulders.

"Sorry about your daughter," he said to Johnny. Clem wiggled away, let the girl go.

"Eh?" Johnny said, swinging around to see who had interrupted his drinking. Tobacco and cologne and stale sweat odours were awakened by his turning.

Marc's upper lip curled; salty phlegm rose in the back of his throat. "I'm sorry," he managed, his voice so controlled it bordered on sarcasm. "Forgive my bad manners. I'm Marc LePage. At the paper. *The Crooked Elbow Sun*."

Teresa answered him over her mother's shoulder. "Yeah, they know. We saw you at the service. I told them I knew you from the paper. This is my mom and dad, Shirley and Johnny Basiuk." Brown eyes. Arms tanned a light coffee colour against her pink sleeves.

"Do you... Does anybody need a ride or anything?" he asked.

Teresa looked at him again and seemed to take charge. "No, like, the family'd better stay together for now. We'll drive my dad home or get my uncle or somebody to help. If *he's* in shape." She stared boldly at Marc and then away, shutting him out. The little girl, Suz, crawled up on the table and curled her legs. Using her mother's black purse as a pillow, she pretended to sleep. Marc felt sweaty and useless, so he decided to leave.

Halfway up the basement steps, Marc turned around for a last look at the room. Her eyes glazed, little Suz played with the ribbon in her hair with one hand. Her chapped lips busily sucked a thumb. Klaus Axel stood beside Teresa along the wall across from Johnny Basiuk. Klaus slipped an arm around her waist and gave her a quick sideways squeeze. Teresa moved away. He sidled over beside her again. The hand moved lower and fondled her left buttock. Without looking at him, going right on listening to her dad, Teresa reached behind her and lifted the hand off. The hand moved down and she seemed to give up. She didn't move it away.

Marc waved a feeble good-bye to nobody in particular, feeling sad and excited and a little jealous for reasons that weren't clear to him. Angry at what he'd seen, though nobody else seemed to care, so why should he?

Nobody waved back at him.

Outside, the wind was stronger than ever, and its direction had switched to west and north. Marc stopped for two vodkas on the way home, tall with a lot of ice. They disappeared. He didn't feel like going back to the office. One more drink might do the trick.

The wind was wild by the time he left the lounge at The Victoria, but he wouldn't have wanted to guess at which direction it was blowing. He was at least three sheets to it, and he let the hot rushing air carry him to the parking lot. Das Kapital knew the way home, and took him there without a hitch.

CHAPTER 4

The wind finished its swing around northern Alberta by switching to the northeast. In its changing, it brought rain— great dollops of water— before it died down overnight. Rain as extreme as the dryness had been.

Water rushed down sidewalks, spilled from spouts, hammered on roofs. As Marc was leaving for work at 7:30 in the morning, the clay cracks in his aunt's lawn were filling in. Her lawn of bluegrass and fescue was once again slick and dark green.

A chemical smell, trapped by the clouds, pervaded the city. A similar phenomenon had happened during a January snowfall. The wind's change to the northeast had been followed by stillness, low clouds and heavy snowfall. He'd written a column using the factories and the sewer gas smell as metaphors for Alberta society— pulling oil from the clean earth, extruding clean plastic from it and, in the process, leaving a disturbing haze in the once-pristine air. The citizens of Crooked Elbow were middle-class scum if they did nothing about it, he had argued.

The column had gotten a lot of response, much of it suggesting he leave town.

Water gushed from the downspouts of the newspaper building, a square stucco affair converted from a car dealership in 1957. Marc hurried around the outside of the *Sun*, making sure the spout extensions were in place. Running for the front door, he caught a glimpse of a Mercedes convertible sweeping into the parking lot. He waved quickly and was through the door, his jean jacket and cowboy boots soaked.

He made a quick trip to the bathroom to dry his face and comb the water from his dark hair, sleek with rain. In the mirror, the tie he'd worn to impress the president was rain-splatted and wilted. The face that stared back at him looked young for 35, hardly experienced enough to be running a small city newspaper.

"Oh, well," he said, "you've got good cheekbones," and grinned ruefully at the pitiful imitation of corporate success he saw there.

Jeremy Brown waited for him by the front counter, chatting with Carmen as if this were the sunniest Alberta June day on record. Marc shivered and said, "Morning, Noah. Nice day if it don't rain."

"Great weather for ducks."

Marc smiled broadly at this witty repartee from his boss and offered his hand. He hoped the sarcasm had left his smile.

Jeremy shifted the handle of his umbrella to his wrist, took Marc's hand and smiled back, "Enough of these weathered clichés. Let's go to your office. What happened to your hand?"

"Nothing."

Carmen smiled. It was a morning for smiles.

The smiles ended with the closing of the office door. Jeremy was a tall man with a black fringe of hair and trimmed black beard. He looked more like a medieval monk than a businessman. But he was no holy man and this was no mission of mercy.

Slapping a leather briefcase on a relatively uncluttered patch of Marc's desk, he adjusted two gold dials and winced as he snapped open the case.

Inside, a white number 10 plain envelope nestled on top of several neatly stacked manilla file folders. The envelope had a name on it— Marc LePage— and Marc recognized the loopy handwriting: Natasha in payroll at the Edmonton office. Jeremy smoothed its edges with his fingertips. He glanced up quickly, and then back down, as if the envelope, not he, were the true messenger.

"I'm afraid we have some bad news," he said. "We've decided to re-examine your appointment as editor and publisher at *The Sun*."

The first thing Marc thought was "We? As in you and who else, *mon ami?*" Then he played with the sound in French, "*Oui,*" and thought about agreement or acceptance.

Finally he said, "What the Christ do you mean?" though he knew in an instant that the question was as useful as asking a man like Jeremy Brown what Karl Marx had meant by alienation. Jeremy would have done his homework. The company had had a wrongful dismissal suit at one of the dailies. Whispers of discontent were out on the grapevine, only a little louder than the suggestions that the newspaper guild was talking to people. Jeremy would have met with his lawyers in a hushed boardroom before deciding to terminate a publisher.

Maybe to ease the shock, maybe because he felt guilty, Jeremy kept his tone neutral, like a banker turning down a loan application. "We've decided we need some changes at this division. Frankly, it hasn't been performing as well as expected.

"As we pointed out in our April 15 memo, the, ah, first quarter performance was somewhat disappointing. The second isn't much more promising. As you know, we felt we would need to review the situation with you after your first six months. Remember? When we rehired you at this division just before Christmas? We knew you had mostly editorial background with us in Ontario and it might work out, it might not, like many things we tried when we bought this paper. After a lot of soul searching— and I mean a lot— we've decided we need to, ah, find somebody with a little more background in public relations. Somebody who..." His long fingers finished the sentence, lamely, in mid-air.

The wording for a classified ad filtered through Marc's brain: "Publisher required for growing weekly newspaper in N. Central Alberta. Solid sales background essential. Must be good at dealing with management asshole types who fire people out of the blue..."

Marc felt like a man tossing in an airplane in turbulent weather. His guts churned and spilled adrenaline that had no place to go. His ears plugged up, rang with a high-pitched sound. He swallowed and noticed other sounds again: the rumble of presses deep in the building, the dull thud and squeal of a typesetter, a cough in the hall outside his door.

Life goes on, said the sounds. With or without you.

Marc took a deep breath and said, "Excuse me, but what's the bottom line? Is there one? Or are *we* just dumping *me* on the scrap heap of life?"

"Um, yes, well, we have a couple of options." Still this "we" business, oblivious to Marc's sarcasm. "We're willing to consider a transfer to another division on the editorial side— nobody's quarrelling with your editorial skills— or we have a generous lay-off package, if that appeals to you. In any case, we'd like you to continue on here until we bring in the new publisher. We have no doubt about your dedication to this paper. And a smooth transition looks better in the community."

"Ah, the community. How generous are we being with this lay-off package?"

"Well, we have somebody in mind for the position, but we want to do some training on the sales side. So we'd like you to fly the helicopter till then. After that, 15 weeks' severance pay, unless you decide to transfer to one of our other weeklies in an editorial capacity. We could use your talent near your old stomping ground at a couple of papers. So what do you say?" Jeremy said this enthusiastically, as if it just might be opportunity knocking and Marc should answer.

"Well," Marc said. "I could sit around for a couple of days and think about it, but I can't see myself moving back to Ontario. Christ, after everything I tried to do here? You know how long I've been in the business... I'm talking too much. I should have been talking to the guild when they called."

"I'll ignore that. We also know some of the personal problems you've run into."

Marc ran his fingers several times through the damp hair combed straight back from his forehead. "Yeah, we all know that. So I guess there's nothing to think about." He pulled at the knot under his neck, slipped the tie over his head, and flipped it on the desk among the welter.

"What exactly are you telling me?"

"Let's make it easy on you. I stay for a couple of weeks and take the severance package. Funny, you can work your ass off, that still doesn't mean you're cut out for the corporate bullshit. I was starting to like this boring, redneck town. Anyway, is that a big cheque in your hand or are you just happy to see me?"

"As a matter of fact, it is a cheque. And, not that we don't trust you, but there are a couple of other angles we need to cover. Business is business. I've got half the severance package here, with the balance due when you finish your couple of weeks on the paper. To our mutual satisfaction. Or whatever."

"This week's paper's in the bag, obviously. So I'll do one more for you and be out of here a week from Friday. Okay?"

"Perfect. Thanks. Oh, yes, one more thing. We have a copy of our standard two-year non-competition agreement for your signature. I hope that's no problem."

Marc took the envelope. It didn't weigh any more than a regular cheque. He slit it open. Over $4,000 after deductions. He glanced at the non-competition agreement. "Thanks, I think. Thanks but no thanks, maybe. Ah, what the hell, you guys are right... I don't golf. And this'll buy me a holiday or something. Now, a little quid pro quo. You mind telling me something? This have anything to do with a call from one of Crooked Elbow's leading citizens? Maybe a complaint about this week's paper?"

Jeremy looked up fast and his eyes were opaque, fish eyes. They shifted down, to his hands, and then back up and they had cleared, that fast. "Nothing. Of course not. I have no idea, ah, what you're talking about."

"That's good." Marc offered his hand. "Sorry things worked out this way."

"Yeah, so are we. You're a man with a lot of talent. I know you'll do well. A word of advice for the job search. You might, ah, want to spruce up the wardrobe, and invest in a hair cut. Just a suggestion... We also offer counselling."

"Thanks, but I'll skip the couch sessions. Sorry, did that come out wrong? Not the usual Brownrigg cheerleading?"

"Don't sign the non-competition thing until you've had a look at it. There's also a form releasing us from any liability after you take the money. Look at them both. Send them in tomorrow's dispatch, once you're comfortable. Or the day after."

"I'll sign the release right now, but I'm not sure about the non-competition thing. What are you worried about? That I'll write for *The Edmonton Journal*? And if I do, so what? I have to make a living."

Jeremy smiled. "Now where was that spunk when we wanted you to sign up advertisers? You're right. We're not worried about you working for *The Journal*. If you sign the release and finish the two weeks to our satisfaction, we'll be happy. Second half of the money comes your way a week from Friday."

Marc signed the release, took the cheque, and let Jeremy find his umbrella and his own way out. Jeremy said good-bye but Marc didn't answer him or bother to look up. When the man was finally gone, he sat down and stared at his desk.

For ten minutes, he sat there, not doing anything, not thinking, angry and staring without registering what he was seeing. Then, he slammed his left fist against the desk, and grinned fiercely at the papers unmoved by the blow.

In his bottom left hand drawer, at the very back behind several hanging file folders, nestled the oldest cliché in the newspaper business. Marc pulled it out, looked at it for a while, twisted off the cap with his good hand and poured a generous slug into his coffee mug. Not the cleanest cup in the world, but vodka should sanitize it. He swallowed it fast and it burned his insides, so he poured himself another. Picking up the letter opener the Optimist Club had given him for his speech about the media in our time, he twirled it with his fingers and settled it briefly in his palm like a knife. He flung it across the room. Knife throwing was obviously not a career option. The opener banged against the drywall and thumped to the carpet. Marc felt a little better, but not much. He went to see Carmen.

"You've heard of the golden handshake?"

She said she had.

"Well I've just been given the bronze one. No, erase, not even close. The rhinestone kiss-off. Anyway, I'm out of here."

"No," she said. "That can't be. You're the best thing that ever happened to Crooked Elbow. How long you staying? We'll have to get a party together."

"We'll do that," he said. "More than once. I've got a couple of weeks. My last day's a week from Friday."

"What're you going to do? What are we going to do without you?"

He ignored the second question. "Unpack the guitar. Write an earth-shattering paper on Catastrophic Categorical Imperatives in Kant's Writing. Finally get down to some serious drinking. I don't know, Carmen. He offered me a job at one of the weeklies in Ontario. But can you see me going back to edit the *East Bunghole Chronicle*? It wasn't so hot the first time around. And what's he going to pay me? Eighteen hundred a month? I've got my ex-wife's future to worry about."

Carmen came around her desk. When she hugged him, she was lithe and very warm. Her head rested briefly against his shoulder. Her hair was vaguely scented and clean. A strand tickled his chin. He thought about the possibilities. Was her husband good to her? "I'll miss you. You've been great," he said.

"That's nice." She let him go and went back to her desk, swaying in her plaid pleated skirt, smoothing it under her as she sat down. "Who's taking your place?"

"Sounds like some ad guy they're training."

"Oh, yuk," she said, and wrinkled her nose. Marc didn't think it was from the chemical smell in town.

CHAPTER 5

By Thursday, Marc's palm was red and only partly healed. He went to a walk-in Medical Centre. A nurse directed him to a doctor's small office. While he was waiting for a doctor, he thought about getting cut one day and fired the next. He'd never been fired before, at least not from a newspaper job. He could feel his blood pressure rising as he was mulling over the unfairness of it all.

After a 15-minute wait, a ponderous, flat-footed doctor in a Hawaiian shirt walked in to clean and bandage his hand for him.

"How'd it happen?" the doctor asked. His voice was so steady that Marc wondered if he really wanted to know, or was just making conversation.

"Knife slipped. At work."

"Oh? You'd better start looking after yourself."

On the way back to the office, Marc decided to follow the doctor's advice. He called the RCMP from the *Sun* and asked for Lars.

"Hey," Marc said when he had Lars on the line. "How ya doing?"

"Not bad. Enough paper work, it's showing up in my stool. Other than that, I'll survive. What can I do you for?"

"You can do me for some advice."

"Ann Landers at your service."

"This is a little out of your jurisdiction."

"Oh, great."

"We're talking city cops."

"Some of my best friends are city cops."

"Yeah, right," Marc said. "How about this for a headline in the paper? 'Prominent local businessman attacks publisher with knife.'"

"That could be assault."

"That's what I thought. Then prominent local businessman tells publisher he'll never work in this town again if he goes to the cops over it."

"This businessman have a name?"

"His initials are BM2."

"I was wondering."

50

"Why's that?" Marc asked.

"We got this request to run your name through the computer from a cop in your fair city. According to our files, you were one active son of a bitch in your youth in the civil disobedience area."

"What else is new? So can I charge him with assault?"

"Technically, yes, but you've got a couple of problems. The local constabulary isn't going to be enthused about the idea of charging a member of the police commission with anything. Which leads me to the main question. What happened?"

"He got mad at me, Lars. Came to me after the Basiuk accident, trying to keep names out of the paper. When I failed at Sucking Up 101, he grabbed a little paste-up knife and cut me."

"Any witnesses?"

"Two."

"They testify?"

"They both work for BM2."

"Great. So you've got a cut on your hand from a little knife, no witnesses, and the charges could be against a member of the police commission."

"I guess so."

"I have two words for you."

"I hope they're not swear words."

"They are 'good' and 'luck.'"

"I didn't want to hear that. I was hoping the Mounties would come to my rescue."

"Maybe. But we hate to investigate our brethren in the enforcement game, even if we don't like them. A cut hand with no witnesses won't get you very far."

"Thanks for nothing."

"Before we get too bitchy, let me remind you that any citizen can ask us to lay charges. You asked for my opinion, not what the book says."

"Bye, Lars."

"Bye."

Word had gotten out that Marc was leaving, and some of the staff had gone drinking with him the night before. Today, he couldn't stand the idea of hanging around the office, wondering if people were going to treat him with pity or contempt. He had to get away.

To make it look good, Marc took his camera equipment with him. But if a photo assignment was his excuse, he decided he might as well capitalize on it, do what he could to raise class consciousness among his readers.

The paper was forever running pics of cute kids and pets from West-El Park. "To hell with that," he thought. "In my last paper, we'll prove that cuteness knows no socio-economic boundaries."

Das Kapital bumped over railway tracks and passed grain elevators towering over wartime housing— small bungalows built in the 1940s.

He stopped for a picture of three girls playing hopscotch on an outline sketched in chalk on the sidewalk. When he got out of the car, he thought that today's breeze— westerly and fresh— made petrochemical emissions seem non-existent. Unlike yesterday in the rain, when the fumes would have seared the throat of a smoker in this part of town.

A girl skipping over chalked lines was beautifully framed in the lens of the camera when something bumped Marc's shoulder.

"A little young for you, doncha think?" It was a young woman's voice, registering low, followed by a quick laugh. "Just kidding."

Marc swung around on his heels and squinted up into the sun. The sky was cyan brushed with wisps of white after the storm. His daily hangover was at the vestigial stage. The light didn't bother him much, especially once he'd shielded his eyes with his hand. "Oh, hi," he said. "What're you doing here?"

"Trying to stay out of trouble." Teresa's eyes locked full on him, then swung up the street. A jacked-up restored '53 Ford with wide tires squealed away from a stop sign. "How are you?" she asked.

"I'm cool," he lied, and then came closer to the truth. "Erase... let's go for 'not bad.' I was, um, let go yesterday. And we went to the bar, if you know what I mean."

"No. I don't know what you mean. Let go? You mean they fired you?

So what're you going to do about it?" Her questions ran together, more like one question hyphenated with quick breaths.

"I don't know," he said. "I mean, I've got a couple of weeks. I'm finishing this paper and doing one more. That's part of the deal."

"I wouldn't."

"What?"

"Work for somebody if they fired me. No way. They could suck slough water through a dirty straw."

Marc wondered for a minute if that's what he should have told Jeremy, but then he said, "You're so young. Inside, I'm really pissed off. But I said I'd help do one more paper and I usually meet my commitments. Besides, I need my final cheque."

"I'm not that young. So you doing anything important? You want to go for a drive or something, talk to me about it?"

He raised himself from his hunkered down position. One knee cracked. "Sure."

Jamming the Pentax into his camera bag, he swung the bag over his shoulder like an awkward purse and walked to the car with her. They bounced over the tracks and down 50th Street together. Crumpled pop cans glinted like clunky imitation jewellery in garbage receptacles lining the street. Horns honked. Cars swished by. All poor attempts to distract him from Teresa.

"So what's the problem?" she said. "I mean, the paper's going good and everything. It's what everybody says, even my parents."

"I don't know. The prez says they need a PR type. Which I personally think is prime Grade A Alberta bullshit."

"Yeah? So tell me about the bullshit."

"I can't. I don't know enough."

"But you've got ideas, right? C'mon, you can tell me. Man, that must have been some drunk, the way your eyes look."

"I'm coming around. Look, I think this thing started before I got the boot. There are a few things that bother me, starting with the night your sister died. First the cops put on this low-key show, trying to make it difficult to get pictures. Then, on Monday, Robbie McLean comes to see me, nuts about keeping the names out of the paper. You know him? The guy with the southern drawl at the hall after the funeral? I told him I can't pull names just because some asshole asks."

Teresa turned pale, wouldn't look at Marc. He felt awful for mentioning her sister.

"Sorry," he said, just to keep talking. "Erase. I didn't say they were assholes to his face, but he got the message. So, my opinion, he goes to Jeremy Brown, the president of our little company, and convinces him I'm bad for business. And they can me. I've got no proof for any of it. It's just a theory, and I've got a hundred of them. God, I'm thirsty. Staff parties are murder on old guys. Want to grab lunch?"

"I don't care. Sure. And I don't think you're old."

Carl's Ice Cream Emporium was chilled by three air conditioners, whirring at the back like prop airplanes waiting to take off. Teresa said hi to some skinheads with black leather jackets, work boots, and earrings in their left ears. "Yo, T," said one. The others grunted into drink cartons all bearing the same soft drink logo on the side.

"Friends of yours?" Marc held a chair for her, feeling both gallant and a little hurt that she knew boys who looked like that.

"God no, they're just guys. What's it to you?"

"Nothing. So, are you okay?"

She looked away.

He ordered. Large colas, burgers— no onions— and french fries, from a greasy-haired teenager with a bad complexion and a uniform the colour of aging plaster.

"Thanks. God, I'm starved."

They munched steadily in silence. Being with Teresa made Marc conscious of how he ate: not the tidiest, chewing fast, wiping his lips constantly with a napkin. She pushed her tray at him after eating half her burger and a few fries. "You want to finish this? I'm stuffed. Got any smokes?"

"Yeah, in a way." He rolled one using stringy Drum tobacco and she laughed when he lit it for her.

"It's like hash. Man, these are strong. I'm getting a buzz."

He ate three more fries and quit. "Okay, something else. Klaus Axel, do you know him?"

"Can we talk about something else?"

"We could... But I wonder if Klaus put Robbie up to that visit to my office. Klaus is the real mover in this town."

"On council or something."

"Yeah," Marc prompted. "That much some of us already know."

"Don't be like that. He's not my favourite guy, but he's a relative. Doesn't mean he's not geek of the week, which he is."

"He's your relative?"

"He's my uncle. I babysit and they pay good. Which I appreciate. But I've got no respect for the man. He's BM1, with his friends and his megabucks, but it don't mean shit to me. His wife's nice, Aunt Anne, she's my mom's sister, and if she's a relative, she must be okay. One of the best." She slapped Marc's arm quickly and said, "Just kidding."

Marc whorled the last of his cola out of the bottom of the cup, considering before he said, "Tell me about your uncle and his friends."

"You know, they're guys. Men's night out, crap like that. They hang out— Uncle Klaus and Mr. McLean. Nicky Numbnuts or whatever. Even my dad, the big loser of all time."

"Poker night with the boys?"

"It's like I don't want to talk about it and I don't have to." But she couldn't quite stop. "It's something from before I was born, started with sports or something. Dinosaur chauv stuff. So what're we going to do?"

Teresa's hand found Marc's arm. Her palm was warm. It unleashed a spasm in his gut. He didn't trust his motives, but he didn't move his arm away. His fingers trembled. "I almost hate to ask, but you want to give me a hand looking into this? You could be a big help in checking out a few people in this town," he said.

"Yeah, sure I do. You want it done right, ask a woman."

"Let's see if I got this. You're Klaus Axel's niece and he and your dad are members of this club. Don't get offended, but that still surprises me. I saw Klaus and your father at the hall and the families don't look like they move in the same circles."

"What did you see?"

"Nothing."

"At the hall. You saw something."

"Nothing." He looked away until she said "Forget it," and he looked back.

She was running her fingers through the front of her hair, over and over, flipping the hair back with her left hand and letting it tumble forward. "Look, my dad's got his problems, okay? Man, does he ever. And the funeral hit him hard." Her hand left Marc's arm. She looked across the street at the menswear store, where a dummy in a navy sports jacket stared stonily at cars drifting back to work after lunch. "You have to go way back to understand it. Mom says they were high school buddies, super sports freaks. There's a scrapbook at home. My dad..."

"If this is too tough, we can do it another time."

"Yeah, well, life's a bitch and then you marry one, right?" She forced a smile, the edges of her mouth turning down. "It started before we came on the scene, me and Steph.

"Okay, you want something, I'll give you something. I played with the truth a little back there, you know? I'm no blood relative to anybody. And they lied when they put it in the obit that Stephanie was John and Shirl's daughter. We're adopted, me and Steph. We were nine when they got us as foster kids. Adopted us a couple of years later, good ole Johnny and Shirl. But they never really gave Steph a chance. Nobody did."

Teresa's lower lip trembled. She ducked her head. Her hair obscured her face. He stared at that wind-blown hair— long and gleaming— wanting to comb it for her.

She shook her head and left quickly for the washroom. While she was gone, Marc watched the skinheads scratching swastikas in the formica table top, when they weren't shoving each other around. Things ran to extremes in Alberta— money and weather and politics.

"Sorry about that. You want to go?" Her eyes were streaked but her make-up was fresh. Grinning like freaks in a Saturday morning cartoon, the skinheads stopped emblazoning the table tops long enough to stare at her.

"On one condition— you promise to help me check things out?"

"Yeah? I don't know what good I'd be. But I'll try anything once. Except." Slightly cross-eyed, she sucked the last of her soft drink through a straw. Freckles sprinkled her cheeks, her nose, like cinnamon.

"What?"

"I get any good stuff, you promise to go out with me?"

"No boyfriend?"

"Not right now. I haven't thought about guys in a week. Really. That's some kind of record. For me. Since the funeral, I'm just not... So what are we doing? You spare a few minutes, take me to the park? Or you have to go back to work right away?"

"Not really. Not necessarily right away."

Foaming at the edges after the rain, the Crooked Elbow River ran full and dirty through Beaver Park a short distance from the factories. Teresa and Marc parked by a brown campground sign and walked down to the river.

Marc wanted to take her hand, but he wasn't sure how she might react, any more than he was sure what he was doing. Or where Lise fitted into any of this. Lise hadn't returned his calls since Saturday. It was possible she was sending him a message— he was on unfamiliar turf with Lise.

"You know why they called it the Crooked Elbow?" he asked.

"Because of all the elbow-bending in town, Charlie?"

"No. And why did you call me Charlie?"

"Just something I call guys sometimes. They call the river that because of the big bend it takes in the middle of Alberta. And they call this Beaver Park because of all the girls who lost it parking down here, right?"

Marc laughed. "No. Because of all the beaver they used to catch where Rose Creek meets the Crooked Elbow. Before we trapped almost all of them, with the help of the Cree and the Blackfoot. And said thank you by killing the natives with tuberculosis and the reserve system."

"I thought the Norwegians killed them all at the OK Corral. Then they moved right into pig farming and the petrochemical industry."

"Yeah, right. The Norwegians didn't come up from Minnesota and the

Dakotas until almost 1900. Farmers and coal miners in the '20s. But it was the spill-over from the Leduc oilfields and our proximity to water and rail that gave us the boom after the war."

She teased him before turning serious again. "O-o-o, 'proximity.' I like it when you use big words. History and grammar lessons all in one. How do you know stuff like that when you've only been here a few months?"

"My job. You have to know a little background."

"Teach me things," she said.

They were quiet, strolling together through trees a safe distance from the churning water. Sunlight filtered through poplar leaves above them. Dappled shadows moved across Teresa's face, darkening the freckles. In the hollows between poplar and cottonwood lay dirty fluff, pounded there by yesterday's storm. Marc found a long twisted stick and used it as a cane, hobbling through soggy leaves and fluff, an old bum, acting the fool for her. Teresa's clown.

She tried not to, but she had to laugh.

"See those leaves?" he said, waving the stick at a poplar.

"Yeah, Charlie."

"See how yellow they look, like fall leaves? I noticed that in the spring. We tried to get a story on it— pollution and its effects on the city."

"And..."

"Nothing. A great blanket of silence descended from the executive suites and City Hall. Their PR flunkies knew nothing, said nothing, never had a complaint. We didn't have the budget to pursue it."

They lugged a clumsy picnic table near Rose Creek where it eddied and swirled over a beaver dam, the creekwater hurrying to get to the river. She jostled him, told him to shut up, a beaver might show itself. He stretched out on the table. The gurgling stream worked on his hung-over brain like a tranquillizer. He drifted briefly to sleep.

"I guess we'll never see them," she said, waking him.

"As if I care."

"It seems so totally awesome, like they do all this work together and they can't even talk. Doing everything by instinct, but good instinct, you know?"

"I think you're a little nuts," Marc said, yawning. He was still half asleep, lying on the picnic table.

"Nuts?"

"Cuckoo."

A sleek head rose near the bank. Teresa tugged at Marc's arm, whispering loudly, telling him to shush.

He raised his head to look and it didn't hurt at all. "That's a muskrat," he said.

Clambering down to the seat of the picnic table, he leaned back to study a few clouds drifting through the light blue sky. "Your big shot uncle... sorry, but I don't like him very much..."

"That's okay. Liking him isn't the point. I never met anybody who did. At least anybody I'd go out with."

A hawk, gliding on invisible currents above the park, suddenly dove straight down to kill something. A horn blared, a truck downshifted on the highway, gears grinding. "Um, at the risk of sounding like a cheap talk show host, do you want to talk about it?"

"What? My uncle? I don't follow you. Sometimes you're all over the frigging place."

Marc smiled. "No, dummy. The accident."

The muskrat climbed the bank on the far side and wiggled itself into a comfortable sunning position in the drying mud. Teresa said, "I don't think I can. You don't want to hear about that family crap."

Marc sat up, walked away, tossing twigs toward the stream. The twigs whirled end over end and fell short in damp yellowed leaves. "I don't know," he said, inhaling quickly, a sneeze tickling the edges of his nostrils. "Maybe I do want to hear about it. People like me who never really had a family, sometimes we get curious about the details."

"You never had a family?"

"The one I had fell apart on me. And the one I had before that, the one with the mom and dad, was a little weird. My mom was ahead of her time. She left when I was five. I thought of her as an angel, telling me she loved me before she went away."

"Cool," Teresa said.

"But I guess that memory was a little inaccurate. A conclusion I came to in my teen years, since she never came back. My dad, he was mostly gone. He tried but there were a whole lot of things he was more interested in than me. Or maybe he never had the energy. He was always working construction. I walked out when I was 16 and I've never been back."

"I wish I'd done that. My mom tries, but I don't know, I hate her sometimes. We have our days. It doesn't help that Steph didn't make it. Maybe I'll get out of here. Steph was the main reason I was staying around— her and little Suz. Do you think it was an accident? I mean, I know it was an accident but was it, like, accidental?"

He sneezed violently and his jacket fell on soggy summer grass clippings. "I was there, taking pictures. It sure looked like an accident."

"Yeah, well, they can think what they want."

"You don't agree?"

"No. Yes. Look, there's nothing I can prove. Steph was, how do I put this nicely? Impulsive. I know that. I know all about impulsive. But I can't see her getting in a game of chicken with some guy she hardly knew. Or, erase, as you like to say. I can see it in a way, but in a way, it makes no sense. Is that just because she's my sister and my best bud and I still can't believe she's nowhere? You come down for breakfast and you expect her to be there. You know?"

"I know. I lost a daughter."

"Sorry. No, I am. How old was she?"

"Thirteen. She'd be 14 now."

"Tough, eh?"

"The worst. They think it was suicide, but with drugs, how do you tell?"

The muskrat had slid back down the bank into the water, and was swimming in circles, its slick black head visible. Like me, Marc thought, staying on the surface, keeping out of the deep. Barely.

"Man, that's the shits." Teresa paused. "Maybe it was destiny, with Steph, I mean, her turn to die, like a Romantic poet or something. Poetry's great. I even write a little. Try to, anyway." She sounded shy about that.

"Jesus, I don't go for any of that predestination stuff," he said.

"Don't say that."

"What?"

"*Jesus.* It violates one of the commandments."

"That bothers you?"

"Yeah. It's taking the name of the Lord thy God in vain. Though as you may have noticed, it's the only commandment that does bother me. It says something in the New Testament about that, too. Like if you curse God or Jesus, you go straight to hell." Teresa wrapped her arms around her chest and drew her legs under her heels on the picnic table bench, rocking. "I don't know why I'm telling you this stuff. I must be crazy."

"You're pretty amazing," Marc said. "Not to mention pretty. And a poetess, no less. Who would have guessed?"

"Very funny, your stupid little rhyme. I'm not," she said.

"What? You just said you write poetry."

"No, not that, dummy." She slapped his arm. He slapped his other arm. Mosquitoes had discovered humans near the shade. "Pretty," she said. "I don't think so."

"Think whatever you want, but you're very photogenic. You could model. I've done a little fashion photography." Marc moved closer to her, not sure he was liking himself very much.

"You think so? Maybe some day. I don't understand why you're down on metal. I don't like all the headbangers, but Alice Cooper's old videos are too cool for words. And he was no kid." Her shorts were pulled high, exposing a circle of flesh white as marble above the tan line. "It's the same thing... the music feeling and the poetry feeling."

She leaned over and prodded him with his walking stick.

"These skeeters are going to eat you alive," he said.

"I'll show you how to shed those suckers." She launched herself off the table, a gymnast in competition, and landed on the balls of her feet. Arms outstretched, hair whipping around her face, she whirled and whirled in her low-cut running shoes on the grass, eyes closed, chanting, "Who's your favourite? Who's your favourite? Who's your favourite?"

"Poet? In English?" he yelled at her. "You mean my favourite poet? Thomas I guess. And Yeats."

She came to a dead stop, showing no sign of dizziness. "Who's that?"

"They're both dead. But their works aren't."

"Well, maybe you can show me their works. I don't know anything. I'm just an ugly, dumb girl. You have to teach me things." She stuck out her tongue and whirled again on the grass.

"Yeah, maybe I do," he said, the blood pulsing hot through his body. He could feel his heart roiling in his chest. Teresa would give him angina before he had a chance to teach her anything.

They went back into town. Teresa said she felt like a drink. He took her to the centre of the universe, The Victoria, where he had one beer and then another, still not sure where this was going, wondering where he should let it go. Teresa started with beer and switched to gin and tonic. Madonna came on the jukebox, "Like a Virgin," and Teresa sang some of it to him, a little downward smile for his benefit.

"That's more like it," she said, and later, "Got to find the little girls' room," still humming Madonna. He lost track of her. Time passed. He caught a glimpse of Teresa sitting in the lap of a biker with the arms and belly and age that went with Harleys.

"Hey, Roach," Marc heard her say. "What's happening?" Whatever the biker said must have been funny. A man at the table with bib overalls and tattoo-infested arms hooted and stomped his spur-studded boots.

Teresa stole Roach's black leather cap, brought it with her to Marc's table.

"What?" she said, using her lips-turned-down smile, running her hands through her hair, donning the cap so the little peak tilted over one eye, a campy young Marlon Brando.

Marc didn't say anything. He sipped his beer and looked away. She pouted, he could hear it in her voice. "I hate it when guys get like that. I was just having fun. Pisses me off when you do that."

"What?"

"Get possessive."

Marc looked at her. She wasn't smiling and her drink was finished. "Besides, the guy's gruggly," she said.

"Gruggly?"

"Little Suz's word. Little bitty sister. From gross and ugly. You want to see something?"

"With you I'm never sure."

"I think we need a couple of drinks on the house and then we should go some place."

"I like your style, but you'll never get away with it."

"Watch me. Tom's on tables and he likes me."

A huge man, bare arms matted with black hair, T-shirt stretched across his belly, emptied their ashtray and dabbed at the table with a cloth. "How you folks doing?"

"We'd be a lot better with a couple of drinks." Teresa's voice wavered, somewhere between recently lost waif and newly found kitten.

"An Ex. And a gin and tonic?" Marc asked her.

"Double panty remover, please, for ladies, and I think you should buy us one?" Chin tilted, she kept her eyes wide on Tom. The lids blinked.

"Man, oh man, Teresa," the waiter said, looking anywhere but at her.

"Didn't you miss me? Admit it, okay? Nobody's nicer to you in the whole bar."

He rattled their empties on his tray, paying no attention to Marc. "You know, Teresa, you're something."

When he brought the drinks, Marc insisted on paying, but Tom wouldn't take any money.

"Thanks, Tommy, you're a sweetie." Teresa was all but purring.

Tommy smiled at her. "And when I'm on the bread line over this, you'll be thinking of poor dumb old me."

"Yeah," she said and laughed her quick laugh.

A toe caressed the inside of Marc's calf under the table. "That was too easy. He loved it, couldn't you tell? Now, we're going to negotiate our way to your so-called car with these. They should last us to Rose Hill. And believe me, I have connections in that bar. I spent enough time there this summer, I should get shares in the place." It was supposed to be a joke, but her face paled as she said it.

The Rose Hill bartender, running the small bar off to the side, looked about 19. He had straight blond hair, tied in a pony tail, Bette Davis eyes, and no lips.

"It's the divine Miss T. And who's the new guy? I don't believe I've had the pleasure. Introduce us, Terrible T."

Teresa kissed Marc on the lips quickly— she pulled him down to do it— and the bartender on the cheek. "Phil, meet Marc. Marc, Phil, as in Fill 'Er Up. Did you miss me?"

"Does the ocean miss the shore? I always miss you, dahlink."

"That's sweet. So this is my date and he's the editor or publisher or whatever of *The Sun*."

"Edmonton or Calgary?"

"No, dumbbells, Crooked Elbow."

"Aha, *The Fun*."

The standard joke. Phil the bartender laughed. Teresa smiled. A leather-faced cowboy at the bar grinned. Marc grinned until his cheeks hurt. Then he looked away.

"They're playing my song. C'mon babe." Teresa grabbed his hand.

Marc didn't consider himself much of a dancer and he didn't recognize the song. The bass line he would have called funky 15 years ago, but he didn't dare call it anything now. Teresa danced loosely— light, jumping, circling— absorbing and self-absorbed. She made him smile, just watching.

Another double gin and tonic for her. "We should get a room, baby." Her head lolled against his chest, her fingers roamed his ribcage. "I think they've got movies and everything. I like you. I mean I really like you."

"I like you, too..."

"So?" They were alone on the floor, tight, not dancing, just taking a step now and then.

"I think I should be getting us home. You're a little drunk." he said. Lise flashed through Marc's mind again briefly, either a case of inebriated loyalty or fear.

"You think this is drunk? Man, you don't know shit from drunk." Ripping herself away, she marched to their table, downed a gin and tonic and smiled at him, her eyes staring, not moving. "Now sweetheart, I'd like a drink. A real drink, if you don't mind. Paralyzer time."

Marc stuck to beer for a while. Switched to cola straight up, no ice, when she ordered her third paralyzer. The paralyzers didn't knock her over, but they narrowed the scope of her playing field. "Man, doesn't anybody in this barn know how to dance?"

"You've danced with half the guys in the place still standing. And the rest couldn't miss you on the floor."

"Are you pissed off? You are, aren't you? You're getting pissed off. I hate it. Hate it, hate it. You know I only want to be with you. You know that. Where's Steph? Where is she?"

"She's gone."

"I know that." She slapped his forearm. Tears sprang to her eyes. She brushed them away, wouldn't look at Marc.

"Drink up. We've got to go. Where'd you learn to drink like that?"

"Start young and practise. That's the ticket. Practise. Practise, practise. Okay, you want to be a party pooper, be a party pooper." She kissed Phil the bartender, hard, before they left, ground her body against Marc, harder, and danced her way out of the bar. She managed to sneak the last paralyzer out with her— how, he didn't know. Maybe she had an arrangement with Phil.

They two-stepped side-by-side to the car. Her tongue found his ear as he fumbled with the door locks for Das Kapital.

She rolled into her seat still talking, the drink balanced between her knees. "Yes, yes," she said. Then, "No, no." He looked over at her just before the Rose Creek bridge. The drink upright between her knees, she slept, her forehead gently bumping the window.

Marc stopped at a phone booth by the 7-Eleven in Crooked Elbow to look up Teresa's home address. She didn't wake up. He located the address and drove to the side of town he had found her in. Pulling up behind a ready-mix concrete truck that loomed like the back end of a pregnant hippopotamus in front of her house, he hissed, "Teresa," shaking her. "Teresa."

He couldn't wake her up, so he hoisted her out by her armpits, heaved her over his shoulder— awkward as a roll of carpet— and lugged her up the steps to her house.

Inside, lamps burned in a small living room. People were drinking beer around a table. Swinging Teresa down, an arm around her to prop her up, Marc fumbled for the doorbell.

Her father heaved himself out of his chair and lumbered to the door. "Yeah?" he said.

Teresa began to slither through Marc's drunk rubbery arms toward the concrete slab that served as a landing at the top of the steps. He wrestled her back up, leaning her awkwardly between himself and the wrought iron railing.

"What the Jesus you doing to my girl?"

"I think she passed out, sir."

"Eh?"

"She's a little under the weather."

"You got my little girl drunk?"

"Not exactly."

"You're lying. You're a miserable excuse for a human being and you're lying." Johnny Basiuk pushed Marc on the shoulder and bent to take his daughter.

Breathing heavily, he grunted and lifted, carrying Teresa inside as if he were a pot-bellied Dracula with a blood-drained victim in the night.

CHAPTER 6

"**Y**ou've got ad people waiting," Carmen told Marc when he showed up late at the office the morning after he'd been bar-hopping with Teresa. "I didn't know what to tell them."

"What?" Only half listening, Marc had been checking for messages. None.

"The ad people. Remember? Friday morning? The launch of the *Best of Summer* campaign. Something to perk up July. Or is that all over, now that we're losing you?"

"No," he caught himself saying before he'd really thought about it. "I'm on payroll for another week. We know how important it is to perform for Mr. Brown while we're on payroll. You got time to look at my resume this weekend, maybe rework it for me?"

"I'm looking forward to it."

"Where are they, this charming ad staff of mine?"

"My guess? They're hustling the coffee pot, hoping it'll pour them an ad."

Marc found two salespeople in the lunch room, another one in composing, and brought them together for a meeting.

"Like all good ideas, this one is stolen," Marc began once they were settled in his office around his silent telephone that was not yielding any more advertising than the coffee machine. "The *Best of Summer* is an idea I saw in *The Paris Star*. That's Ontario, not France. Reporters go after the 'The Best of...' in Crooked Elbow. The best view. The best rodeo grounds. The best garden. And you, good ad people, sell space to businesses eager to prove they're good at something. The best shoes, the best service. The best headache remedy for weekly publishers."

"Feeling the effects of last night, Marc? You poor thing. Let me see a copy of the one from Paris. I think it's a terrific idea," effused Fiona, the top advertising salesperson. "We can hit all those non-advertisers. The industrial park people. The offices. Government, even. I think this could be a big, big seller."

On the cusp of his departure from *The Sun*, Marc knew he had a winner. If Fiona thought it was a wonderful idea, she'd have the other reps so excited about it, they'd forget to sell the regular paper.

Letting Fiona take over, Marc faded out of the meeting. He wanted to go home, where it was warm and safe, curl up in the foetal position and stay there. When the meeting was over, he'd tell Carmen he was leaving, at least until the afternoon.

A comment from Fiona snapped him out of his reverie, "Barb said she was going to be here."

"What's that?" Marc said.

"Barb. She said she was going to be here this morning. To discuss how we're handling the editorial side. Then she got called away."

"How did she know about this meeting?"

"I must have told her," Fiona said. "Did I do something wrong?"

"No, I guess not," Marc said. "Editorial's going to have to get involved right away if we're going to pull it off in July. Sorry, if *you're* going to pull it off in July. So, everybody's clear on deadlines and the concept?"

All three sales reps nodded and Marc said, "Thanks for waiting for me this morning. Fiona, can you do a handout for the businesses and one for the staff so everybody knows the idea and the deadlines?"

"Sure, Marc. And just in case we have any questions, you're here till next Friday?"

"Yeah."

"Great."

There was markedly less enthusiasm when Marc checked in on the editorial side. According to the daybook, Barb was supposed to cover planning committee at 11:00. But nobody, not the receptionist, none of the reporters, could tell him why she wasn't in.

Carmen had one piece of information. "Barb called in about 8:30. You weren't here, so she told me to tell Fiona and I did. Is there a problem?"

"Yeah, there's a problem. She was supposed to cover a meeting. Why didn't you give me a note?"

Carmen's cheeks coloured. "I told Fiona, like Barb said. Sorry, I guess I figured it was time to start passing on messages to other people."

Marc walked away. "I wish somebody'd give me a funeral before they bury me."

He dialled Barb's home number and got a recording of a rock group redoing "Hello, I love you, won't you tell me your name?"

After leaving her a message she wouldn't soon forget, he tried to talk another reporter into covering for her. No soap. "Sorry, Marc, got an interview."

The reporters were as tired of covering for Barb Zelnak as he was. Marc took his notepad, his camera bag and his management inadequacies into the brilliant sunlight of a dry Alberta morning. And almost passed out when he encountered the brilliance.

Planning committee met at City Hall around a large wooden table in a downstairs room that was air conditioned and fluorescently lighted.

Marc expected the usual routine— polite discussion before the passing of predictable resolutions. Instead, a babble of voices sifted down the hallway as he approached.

About 15 people occupied wooden fold-out chairs along one wall. Marc recognized a lawyer, Jordan Hamm, in a dark blue three-piece. Beside him sat a man with a clerical collar. Maybe the collar was too tight. The preacher was sweating, his face red, despite the air conditioning.

Robbie McLean called the meeting to order.

The balding city planner smiled and stood. "Mr. Chairman. As I'm sure we're all aware, the Evangelical Assembly has made application for the rezoning of half an acre of Agricultural Land to Institutional..."

Marc took notes mechanically. He'd heard the arguments over low-income housing too many times over the years to think that anybody was going to offer anything new. He found it so exciting that he had trouble keeping his eyes open. To wake himself up, he left his chair and had a look at a large area map pinned to a wall. Keeping one ear tuned to the discussion, he used the numbers from the planning committee agenda to find the location of item number three, the proposed Agriplex, on the map.

A block of land, just east of Crooked Elbow, partly within city boundaries, partly in the county. Five acres on the highway. Across the road, Beaver Park, acting as a buffer between the rezoned land and the petro-chemical plants.

Returning to his seat, Marc picked up on his note taking. But he was right the first time— he could have tape-recorded the comments from ten similar discussions he'd heard over the years and boiled them down to one concern: "Not In My Back Yard."

Marc gave up and caught a short nap. Robbie McLean's call for the question on the Agriplex land rezoning woke Marc at 12:30. The motion passed unanimously. Robbie McLean declared the public part of the meeting over and thanked everyone for coming. "Planning committee will break for sandwiches and coffee before going in camera," he said.

Marc picked up a cheese and lettuce sandwich and stopped Jordan Hamm in the hallway. Pictures of every mayor since the city's founding in 1908 lined the wall. "So, Jordan? You weren't on the residents' side?"

"Not my arena, Marc. How are you?"

"I've been better. What were you doing here?"

"I was in abeyance in case there was any opposition to item number three."

"The rezoning of five acres of property?"

"That's correct. Perhaps we should find a place to sit ourselves askance for a moment. You look tentative, to say the least."

"Where did you learn to talk like that?" They walked back down the hall together.

Jordan treated the remark as a compliment. "One picks it up in the drama of the courtroom. It can be defibrillating if one's caught with one's words down, so to speak."

Marc's head felt enough clearer after his night with Teresa that he decided to ignore the "No Smoking" signs. Jordan disapproved. Marc could see it in his face. But Jordan said nothing, and once his cigarette was going, Marc tried a question. "So what's the owner going to do with those five acres now that he's got the zoning?"

"First, let me mollify you that it's a consort of individuals whom I represent, people of sustenance in the community, people with the pecuniary paddles to put together a deal of this sort."

"Like who?"

"The group's nomenclature is not public at this time. They're operating as the numbered company in question on the zoning application. I think it's up to the city to decide the utilization of the property. They're inveigled in the purchase along with the agricultural society, I believe."

"So the Agriplex is going ahead. That should be good for business."

Stopping outside the committee-room door, Jordan smiled at Marc. "Oops, did I just let the proverbial cat out of the bag? It's ebullient news for the area. The parties involved in this project include the city, the county, and the province as well as the private section." Jordan was a handsome, friendly man, so friendly that Marc sometimes forgave him for being an enthusiastic mangler of the English language.

"Tell me about the private section."

Jordan Hamm laughed and then stopped abruptly. "They're a group of forward-looking citizens who've assembled the land and now have a very articulate package for the agricultural society. They want to construct the kind of faculty this area has needed for a long time."

"Just facilitating the faculty."

"Yes, I like that."

"So why can't you tell me the names of the people wrapping up this package?"

"I'm sorry, but that is secretive client information." Jordan's hand found Marc's arm and squeezed it before he said, "Sorry to hear that we're misplacing you. I realize you're not popular in all quarters, but I've always been a fan of your paper. It's had subsistence. And I hear Barb Zelnak is presuming a larger role?"

"Excuse me?"

"I hear she's going to be the new publisher?"

Marc was so surprised that he paused before saying, "Where did you hear that? They were looking for an advertising type."

"I'm sure I don't know. Barb is rather well-liked in the business community, I understand. Well, all the most to you."

Jordan shook his hand and Marc said, "You do a lot of work for Klaus Axel."

"We do a lot of work for a lot of people. Have a satisfying day."

Stunned by the news about his replacement, Marc returned to the committee room. Klaus Axel was talking to two tanned women from a group objecting to a church's subsidized housing proposal. Marc joined them. The women tipped foam cups at each other and went looking for the coffee urn.

"Don't do that, guy, scaring the women away. I'd rather talk to them than you any day. And don't look so glum, that was a joke," Klaus said, winking.

When Marc didn't reply, Klaus said, "You feeling okay?"

"I had a hard night with a girl I barely know."

Klaus winked again and squeezed Marc's elbow. "I know where you're coming from, guy. You know the difference between sucking and swallowing?"

"No, Klaus, I don't think I do."

"Doing it and liking it."

Marc pretended to laugh. "So you're involved with the Agriplex?" he asked.

"We're involved. The city is. I have to give Jordan Hamm a lot of credit."

"For what?"

"For coming up with the concept. Otherwise, there'd be no Agriplex."

"But *you're* not involved."

"Personally? Course not."

"Don't you think this is coming together awfully fast? I mean, I've been around town a few months and I haven't heard any public discussion about it."

"Maybe you don't move in the right circles. Listen, congratulate Barb on her new position, will you? We're sorry to see you go but we'd rather have her running the paper than some stranger who doesn't understand the community."

"Word travels awfully fast in this town."

"I could use a bright young man like you to help me. I need somebody who's good with words to help me do promotion. We should have lunch some time."

"I hope you're buying."

"Course I'm buying, guy. We're working on new directions for the city and a journalist like yourself should get on board. I can't imagine you lining up with the other losers at the pogey window."

"I see you have a lot of sympathy for the unfortunate victims crushed by the inevitable downturn in the cycles of capitalism."

"What?"

"Never mind. Why would I work for you?"

"You know the old expression. If you can't beat 'em... Gotta run."

Klaus ran, stopping at the sandwich board before his in camera meeting. Marc called Teresa's house from a pay telephone in the city hall lobby.

"How are you?"

"I'm okay," she said, yawning. "Just got up. How're you?"

"Can you meet me?"

"I guess. Sure. Anything new?"

"We can talk about that. I just found out that Barb Zelnak is taking my job."

"The one with the short blond hair? You got a problem with her?"

Marc said, "I get to the office this morning and she's gone. Later, I find out, to Edmonton. Stupid me. That means head office. So I cover this meeting for her and I find out from Jordan Hamm and Klaus Axel that she's taking over."

"I guess that's kind of embarrassing."

"Kind of. So can I see you?"

"Sure, where are you?"

"City hall. Can I pick you up?"

"I'll walk, okay? It's only a mile or so. Give me a chance to clear my head."

CHAPTER 7

Twenty minutes after his telephone call, Marc stepped outside City Hall and saw Teresa loitering on a strip of grass near the trimmed caragana bushes which lined the civic lawn. Rocking on her heels, she was swinging a little black purse back and forth. Tiny rounded caragana leaves riffled in a steady breeze out of the west, whispering secrets to her. Rocking and swinging her purse, Teresa seemed as oblivious to their messages as she was to Marc's arrival.

She wore a black denim mini-dress, zippered up the front. Small, silver-coloured chains dangled from her breast pockets. Her hair was in a ponytail. Two slim chains dangled from her left earlobe. In her right, she had inserted a stud and a purple stone.

A red MG sports car darted past and Teresa turned to watch. The driver was going bald at the back. The rest of his hair was long, whipping around his eyes. When she turned back, she saw Marc and her eyes narrowed like a cat's. She pounced— one short, theatrical jump straight up, legs together, knees bent. When she landed, she jogged toward the City Hall steps— in exaggerated slow motion, going for the video effect— and hugged him.

"Hey," Marc said, embarrassed, looking around. The only person watching was an old gent with a walker making slow progress on the public sidewalk past the caragana bushes.

Hugging Marc's arms and his camera bag together in a huge embrace, Teresa squeezed him again and almost tipped him over. "Did you miss me?" she asked, looking away, eyes down, bottom lip showing. "I thought you might hate me or something, the way you sounded on the phone."

"It's not you I'm mad at. The whole morning pissed me off."

They walked the block around City Hall, as if they were both teenagers with nothing better to do. Strolling with her took the edge off Marc's frustration. Barb. Lazy Barb Zelnak, invading his office. He'd leave the mess for her, too.

A block away, the sidewalk was cracking, but around City Hall, public works had recently poured new concrete. When they reached the new stretch, Teresa let him go briefly and skipped over the clean lines, playing at hopscotch. Returning to him, smiling, she pressed her cheek against his shoulder.

"Your folks know where you are?" Marc asked.

"Step on a crack, break your mother's back. Step on a line, break your father's spine... School's out for the summer. I'm 18 years old. Where I am is the last thing on their minds."

"So, in a word, 'No?' Your folks don't know you came to see me?"

"How do you know I came to see you? Just kidding."

"How's daddy today?"

"He's okay. How're you?" She reached up, touched his face. Softness came to mind: kittens, baby tigers.

"I'm going to make it, I think, thanks to some over-the-counter pharmaceuticals."

She ran her fingers lightly over his jaw, pulled him down so she could kiss the tip of his nose. "A little slow this morning myself. But, c'mon, we've had worse days. Right? I mean with me here, how bad could it be?" She forced a laugh, stopped suddenly and said, "Just kidding."

"I've had worse days. Aren't you even a little hung over?"

The back of her hand brushed his cheek. "I never am usually. Sorry if anything happened last night. Daddy's got temper problems, big time. I keep telling him, but he won't listen. He just loses it. I guess it's not even his fault exactly. Did he hit you?"

"No. But tell me something— if his temper's not his fault, whose fault is it?"

Looking unsure of herself, her eyes everywhere but on Marc's, she covered her uncertainty with a laugh. "Lighten up, will you?" she said.

They were behind City Hall again, their second time around the block, strolling past a compound with a high chain link fence where the city stored stubby-wheeled garden tractors and mowers. A huge plywood cone containing winter salt hulked above the lawn equipment.

"So what ya want to do today, Charlie? You got any plans? Maybe I could help you figure some things out. You said I could." She said it like a baby, grabbed his arm and stretched up to kiss his cheek.

Her moves were so childlike, he couldn't help it: thoughts of his own daughter hit him from nowhere. He wondered where Sky was right now and what she might be doing. Or a better question, what was he doing, going out drinking with a woman barely out of high school and calling her the next day?

Well, he reminded himself, Teresa wasn't his daughter. Teresa was a young woman with her own free will. The idea that women were men's property was a degrading capitalist notion. Besides, if he was going to sleep with anybody, it would be Lise, and he certainly wasn't being unfaithful to Lise by talking to Teresa. Was he?

"A loonie for your thoughts?" Teresa squeezed his arm to her body.

Shaking his arm free, he said, "Now that's inflation. It was a penny when I was your age. Guess I should grab a bite of lunch. You want to join me?"

"I'm only about three-quarters starved. I could only eat about half a cow."

"Okay, let's do the lunch thing. And then in fairness, I really should check in at the orifice. My old friend Immanuel had a saying to cover moral dilemmas such as what to do when you are fired: always act in such a way that your actions can be brought into universal accord. Though my other friend, Karl, had different ideas about the working man and his obligations to his employer."

"Yeah, well, I don't see why you give a rat's ass about that place."

"Maybe it's stupid, but I'd like to see what Barb's up to. I'm cooling down, thanks to you and the walk. But I'm starting to wonder about the powers-that-be and the Agriplex. They pass a major zoning change and treat it like requisitioning a new sidewalk."

"So do a story on it."

"I don't have time before I go. Too bad, because I'm about the only guy in town capable of investigating something like the Agriplex— unless you count Barb. Fat chance of her doing anything if they've already co-opted her."

Teresa hurried Marc along, now that they were back in front of City Hall. It was one of the few completely brick buildings in a city that favoured stucco. Two flags, one a red maple leaf and one blue with a provincial crest, flapped in the breeze on either side of a green city flag. A blue swatch in the middle of the flag depicted a river with a large bend, the product of a design-the-flag contest sponsored by the recreation department. Marc despised flags, and he hated the design of this one, but he'd sent a reporter to take a picture in the spring when the contest winner was announced. Mayor, recreation-board chairman, flag, and pretty 13-year-old contest winner, you couldn't go wrong.

Teresa said, "I've got a surprise for you. You buy me lunch and I'll show you something to investigate."

After lunch, she insisted she wanted to surprise him, and she had to drive.

"Ever drive a standard?"

"What a stupid chauv thing to say." She grinned at Marc and slapped his arm and said, "Just kidding," but he wasn't sure she was. Her teeth, when she smiled, were endearingly small. But they were sharp, with tiny gaps, like the teeth of a small, predatory animal.

She lurched and stalled and clutch-popped the Volkswagen through crowded downtown streets and across the tracks where Alberta Wheat Pool and Pioneer elevators stood guard over graceful poplar trees that gave way to fixed-income duplexes and struggling commercial enterprises.

Well into the commercial area, Teresa turned right, a wide turn, the car jolting along in third gear. "Close your eyes. Go on, close them. And no peeking or you're dead meat."

He thought he'd be dead meat anyway; she'd swing the steering wheel while she was trying to shift and force the car into the path of the first cement truck she failed to see. He'd die a slow, crippling death. She'd pretend she was just kidding and find some new guy to take to the bars.

"Go on," she said. "Close your eyes. Close them. Or I'm pulling over— right here— and throwing away the keys."

How did Teresa know he had no spares?

Reluctantly, he closed his eyes and did not peek.

The car bumped over something; he heard gravel crunch and smelled paint and tar and a fainter metallic odour.

"Where are we?"

The car came to a sudden stop and stalled.

"You can open your pretty eyes now."

They were parked in a yard facing an olive green metal building with a large red and white sign: Larry's One-Stop Auto Wreckers and Body Shop. "Your Crunch Is Our Lunch," said a yellow portable sign by the street.

Teresa took Marc's hand and they went inside. Everything, including the air they breathed, seemed to be dusted with fine powder. A dusty metal door opened onto a dusty hallway. The cement-block walls of the hallway erupted occasionally with brilliant light from a welding rod. Rock music, 630 CHED, competed with the steady crackle of the rods.

"Larry, hey!" Teresa yelled through the door. Nobody answered. She looked annoyed. She couldn't compete with welding rods and rock music.

One wall had 5-by-7s of repainted vehicles taped around a tool-supply calendar. The woman on the calendar looked as smooth and shiny as plastic, her body as flexible as hose. On the opposite wall, a runner-up for Miss Nude World smiled for the camera. Her face was half turned. She looked back at the world she'd almost won with a smile and suspicious eyes. Her breasts were unnaturally pointed, her waist unbelievably slim. As attractive as he found her, Marc also wondered about women who were paid to strip for the camera and what eating disorders contributed to a body this slim.

The welding stopped. Teresa whistled, a shrill whistle, index finger and thumb spreading her lips. "Hey, dummy."

A skinny man in grimy coveralls duckwalked out of the shop. He wore huge boots splattered with paint. Blinking at them, he worked a cigarette to his lips. He'd apparently seen Miss Nude World runner-up a hundred times. She didn't earn as much as a glance.

"The divine Miss T. Who ya callin' a dummy?"

"We're here to see the car," Teresa said.

The ends of the man's fingers were webbed with cracks, the lines in them dark as metal. He used them to brush at metal filings imbedded in his greasy, paint-smeared pants. "That depends," he said.

"On what?" Her voice was feline, edging toward purr.

"On whether you promise to be a good girl."

"Larry, I'm always good. You know that." "Larry" came out "La-wwy," in her kitten voice.

"Yeah, but are you careful? Who's your friend?" Larry cranked a thumb the colour of gun metal at Marc.

"My main man." Throwing her arms around Marc's waist, she pressed her main man to her. "He wants to see the car with me."

"The Trans Am?" Mouth splitting wide, like a yawning wolf's, Larry grinned at her. "If I do, and the boys in blue object?"

"I'll buy you a beer. And be your friend forever."

"Please... my devoted wife... what would she say? This way to the royal boneyard."

Larry led them outside, past a rust-brown engine and a piece of road equipment leaking oil, to a row of vehicles in various stages of decomposition. A dog growled. Larry unlocked a gate to a compound guarded by chain link fence and a German shepherd. It charged around the corner of the building and took a running leap at the fence at about eye level. Marc knew there was a fence between them, but he couldn't help himself. He jumped back, adrenaline pumping.

"Down, Lassie," Larry yelled, as if the dog made him proud and angry at the same time. "Just a minute, folks."

Letting himself through the gate, Larry grabbed the dog by the collar. "These is friends, girl. Settle down." The dog glowered at them with damp, mistrusting eyes and let itself be dragged over to its leash.

"There she is," Larry said. "In the corner."

Teresa and Marc started for the car. "Hey, Teresa," Larry grunted, showing her a grimy palm. "You know why you can't masturbate with this hand?"

"Larry, I think I heard this one. Okay, why?"

"Cause it's mine." His grin grew to fiendish width and Marc expected the cigarette to drop. But it clung to Larry's lower lip, defying exhaled laughter and gravity.

Teresa grabbed Marc and giggled. "You're bad. Isn't he bad, Marc?" She pulled Marc around and murmured. "Never mind him."

A black Trans Am with a crumpled front end squatted between a pick-up with a crushed fender and an old green Bel Air that didn't seem to have much wrong with it.

"Okay, this is it."

"This is it?"

"Yeah, the surprise, why I brought you here."

"Yeah, well, I haven't been this surprised since last Christmas when I didn't get anything."

"It's a Trans Am, dummy. The latest. Used to be my favourite car, next to a Corvette." Her gaze drifted away to a field of barley, its stalks undulating in lime green and white waves beyond the old sheds and industrial buildings that crowded this part of town. Teresa's lips trembled.

"The car in the accident."

"The car Steph was in." Teresa bit her bottom lip with her small teeth and looked at the car instead of him. "Notice anything?"

"It's not going anywhere. Well, erase, maybe a demolition derby, if you spent six weeks on it first."

"Some people get the obvious right away. And then there's me, who's lucky enough to bring along Sherlock."

"Care to fill me in?"

Teresa sauntered to the Trans Am, to the side that was smashed the worst. As she leaned over the hood, the hem of her mini-dress rose. "The damage is mostly on the passenger side."

"They were playing chicken. The pick-up is mostly damaged on the same side. Somebody swerved at the last minute. Or, for all we know, somebody's steering went screwy. Busted ball joint or something."

"Yeah, or an alien landed on the highway and blasted them both. Look, it means the impact was on this side. I mean the most impact. On this side. The passenger side," she said.

"Right, Miss Marple, the passenger side."

"Don't be like that. This is serious. I'm very serious." She was pouting again and Marc was sorry. He said so.

"Okay, now look at this crack. Larry let me in before. He's an all right dude, some days. I had a good look at it. If you look right here..."

Stretching across the hood, she moved her finger from the shattered part of the windshield along a crack almost dividing it in two. Marc did his duty. He looked at the windshield crack, an award-winning performance, since her skirt was riding the edge of panties which were red and not very new. "Yeah," he said.

"The crack started on this side of the windshield, on the passenger side. That's where the impact was."

"So you think that's where Stephanie was? You think she hit her head on this side of the windshield?"

"Yeah, genius, that's what I think."

"So?"

"So, think about it." Teresa sounded angry but he couldn't be sure whether she wanted to bop him or cry.

"Half the windshields in Alberta are cracked. Stephanie could've been thrown across the seat. If there were no seatbelts. Or she wasn't wearing hers, I mean." He moved to get a closer look at the spider web fracture and the uneven line that ran from it. Inside the car, a blue garter fringed with lace dangled from the mirror.

"Maybe, but I don't think so. Grade 11 physics. Elementary, my dear Watson." She pointed. "For every action, there's an equal and opposite reaction. The car gets hit on the passenger side at the front. Does the driver go bouncing around, over to the passenger side? I don't think so. I think he goes bouncing against the steering wheel on his own side, or into the door. Or if he's lucky, maybe right out the door."

"Okay, erase, back up. For the sake of argument, let's say you're right. Where does that leave us? People who play chicken when they're full of booze are liable to do anything. Including driving from the passenger seat."

"No easy stunt with bucket seats and a console in the middle. I don't think you did such a great job on the story. Where'd you get your information?"

"From the police. Where else? That's what we do. We need police reports every week, so they tell us what they want us to know, and we pretend it's the truth and act grateful."

"It was my sister..."

"I hadn't been fired when I wrote the story, and I barely knew you then... Look, journalists play the game."

"Especially in Crooked Elbow." Teresa ran her fingers through her hair, fluffed up the front of it. "You like this dress, don't you? I can tell. I like your tacky belt and those jeans. And I like the cowboy bit with the boots. We're cool, but so what? I read your story. You missed the main question."

"Which is?"

"Why was there no autopsy? And, lots of black Trans Ams around, but who happens to be the registered owner of this baby?"

"Stephanie, I guess." Teresa's evasiveness was getting to Marc. She seemed to know the answers but wasn't giving him any. Still, he couldn't tell whether she actually knew more than she was revealing or whether her reticence was grounded in teenaged arrogance. "I'm sure I have no idea," he said. "You tell me."

"Always got ideas, baby." She pulled him to her and kissed him full on the mouth, quickly. Her breath was warm and young against his lips.

"So what happened here?"

"You're the reporter. You do the investigating. I'm just a dumb girl who hears things and wonders what's going on. But there's only so much she can say, 'cause she may be dumb but she's not an idiot."

He detached himself from her, though it was an effort, like ripping apart Velcro. He couldn't look at her.

Whining and slobbering at the end of a heavy chain by the building, the dog watched them for false moves. Somebody had spray-painted "Lassie! Beware of Dog!" on the dog house. Banging and clanging reverberated inside the building. Larry was in there, painting cars and smashing metal.

Reaching through the Trans Am's passenger window, Marc flipped down the sun visor. A mirror and nothing else. He walked around the car and flipped down the visor on the driver's side. The underside of the visor had a film of dust, a blank space the size of a business card, and nothing else. Leaning across, he opened the glove compartment, removing an owner's manual and a small plastic insurance folder. The insurance folder had an Axel Agencies business card tucked inside. Nothing else.

He slipped the manual out of its plastic envelope and ruffled through the pages. Nothing fell out. Inside the plastic cover of the manual were a business card from Johnny Baker's GM dealership in town, warranty information and a plastic card guaranteeing repair work anywhere in the United States or Canada.

"Nothing, right?" Teresa said.

He didn't answer her.

"I could have told you that. I already checked. You know what I think? I think the cops took the I.D., the pigs. Either that or the driver. Or maybe the owner, who could also have been the driver."

"It wasn't Stephanie's car?"

"You kidding? The way that girl went through cash? Maybe somebody gave her a car I never heard about. It's not exactly impossible. But I think I would have known. She didn't buy it, that much I know. She had trouble keeping cigarette money."

"You know other things about the car you're not telling?"

"A guy's car, from what I hear. Some guy who may have been in the bar. Who may have had a fight with some other guy. Maybe over him dancing with Steph. Sorry to say, but that makes sense. Not exactly the first time for something like that." Teresa's eyes clouded over. Their murkiness bothered Marc.

"What are you saying? That Stephanie was friends with Joe?"

"I heard that, but I also heard other things. So I think you should do your job, find out who owns this car. And print that in your paper before you're gone, if that company you work for has the guts— which they don't. Maybe you can slip it in. Because if I'm right, some people are not going to like it."

"But you won't tell me what you heard?"

"I heard nothing. I brought you all the way down here and shared what I knew with you. If I tell you any more and somebody wants to give me a hard time, which they will, I'll be in deep shit. You take it from here, Charlie. I'm just helping out, like somebody asked me to."

"Okay. Why don't we rewind this conversation? I thought we were on the same side. I don't see why you're pissed off at me all of a sudden."

"Let's blow this pop stand," she said.

He copied the serial number of the Trans Am in his reporter's notebook before they left. His hand was definitely better.

CHAPTER 8

"**F**riday nights, I have this other job." Teresa hesitated. "At the restaurant. You have to get me home right away."

After dropping her at her house, Marc watched her gyrate, an 18-year-old in a mini-dress, up the front walk to whatever awaited her inside the drooping bungalow. Its paint had started peeling by the aluminum front door and kept on going. The house looked as sorry as he felt.

Marc stopped by the office. The place wasn't being consumed by flames so he went home. His apartment was empty and stale and almost as cool as it had been that morning. Friday evening television was as exciting as Friday evening television ever gets in the summer. It depressed him so badly, he switched the TV off and went outside.

Bent double over a hoe in her garden, his aunt weeded yellow gladioli, her back to him. The hem of her flowered cotton dress bounced above her knees to the rhythm of the hoe. Brown nylon half-stockings ended abruptly above her calves. Purple and blue veins discoloured the flesh between the nylons and the hem of her dress. He couldn't help it— he thought about the difference it would make, slipping the same stockings on Miss Nude World runner-up. Or Teresa, for that matter.

"What's happening?" he said. Things were bad when talking to his aunt struck him as better than no conversation at all. She openly disliked Marc, said she only let him stay for the rent. One night when he was a long way from sober, he'd pestered that much out of her. As nearly as he could tell in the shape he'd been in, she thought Marc and his father were to blame for his mother leaving them.

His aunt straightened and turned, shielding her eyes. Soil had dried grey as potter's clay on her pale fingers. "Well, hello stranger. It's a fine kettle of fish when a person finds out from her neighbours that her nephew's out of a job."

"Sorry, been busy."

She flipped the hoe around and scraped her foot against the blade. Dark clay peeled off the toe rubbers protecting her wide-heeled shoes. "Basiuk busy. From what I hear," she said, studying the hoe, not him.

He ignored that. "How're the glads this year?"

"Never you mind the glads. A body can tell by looking how they are. How're you?"

"Okay. Tired."

"Why am I not surprised?"

"Meaning?"

"Meaning, blood will out. Meaning, you're more like your father than I care to think. You might know something about the news business, but I've got a good nose for the monkey business."

"Yeah?" Marc was hot. The woman and the conversation further depressed him. He wanted a long shower. Wasting hot water infuriated her.

She turned back to her gladioli, grumbling more to them than to him. "Some people don't know what's good for them. That Johnny Basiuk should've been shown the Greyhound bus depot years ago. The stories I could tell you about that family would curdle your milk."

He left her to her glads and her grumbling. Going inside, he had a shower, extraordinarily long and as hot as he could stand it.

When he finished, he noticed that the cheque from Jeremy Brown was still on his kitchen table. Marc took it downtown and deposited it, using the bank machine.

Looking at the new balance on his little bank machine slip didn't cheer him up. He'd just spend the money, and then where would he be? He took out $100 and bought vodka and beer and hamburger and buns and went home. His aunt pretended to ignore his purchases and he pretended he couldn't see her in the garden.

Just to prove that he wasn't the hopeless drunk she assumed he was, he made a hamburger with fried onions, and had a Coke with supper. He called Lise at the police station. A woman running the night answering service said she couldn't be reached. The woman said she'd take a message.

Marc said, "Please tell Lise Champlain she has to call me. It's Marc LePage and I'm at home. Underline the part about she has to call me."

Lise didn't call back. She had her ways when he'd been ignoring her.

Nothing to do. Sleep came nowhere near him.

He decided to board the fast train. Two glasses of vodka. The burning train, the train on fire. He slowed it down, let it coast into the station with a couple of beers. Only problem was, this train carried too much baggage. He poured another vodka so he wouldn't have to inspect that baggage too closely.

That didn't seem to work.

He opened more beer, paced, very sober. Got a cigarette going. Looked on the bright side. He didn't have to get involved with Teresa, a woman who was obviously too young for him. He had Lise. She understood a drinking man. She should, she worked with drinkers. Cops, they all worked hard and partied hard. Lise appreciated a good time, didn't ask too much of him. What else mattered?

More vodka. Christ, the bottle was half gone and what was it, 10:00, 10:30? It was going to be a long night. He poured a short one and was halfway through it, thinking about Sky, how he'd been fired and what if she found out? Some role model— bad and getting worse.

His little brown telephone directory, what was it doing on the kitchen counter? Phone numbers from Ontario and a few from Alberta. He must have pulled it out for a reason.

"Oh yeah, Father Larry's number," he said.

Fumbling with the book, he found the number and called the priest. A calm, fatherly voice had done the recording for the answering machine. "Hello, this is Father Larry. I'm not in the office right now. Office hours are 8:30 to 5:00. Mass times are Saturday at 5:00, Sunday mornings at 9:00

and 11:00." The voice offered the numbers for the head of the parish council and the Crisis Line, in case of emergencies.

Marc had dialled most of the number for the Crisis Line when he realized how stupid that idea was. He'd never pull it off, talking to some well-intentioned obsessive/compulsive volunteer about problems he could solve on his own if he pulled himself together. It wasn't as if he didn't know what his problems were— he'd been over them a million times in his mind.

Technically, Marc was way over the limit, but he still wasn't feeling it. He figured he could drive drunk as well as 90 per cent of the people who were sober out there. Better than 90 per cent.

The east side of the rectory was dusky, except for light glowing through a many-paned window on the second floor. Marc banged on the door, threw gravel at the window, shouted, "Hey, Father, quit reading that stuff in bed," and sat down on the lawn. Maybe he was finally a little drunk. That was a comforting thought, so he sat and drank some more.

The front door opened. Father Larry peeked out. He was wearing jogging clothes.

"Going for a run, Father?" Marc asked. He didn't know what he'd expected. White starched cotton, perhaps? A long nightshirt with a frilled gathering around the neck?

"Who is it?"

"The newspaper boy from hell."

"Marc?"

Marc didn't answer.

"Would you like to come in?"

Marc still didn't answer. He got up off the grass, mounted the steps, followed Larry down a hall to a little room. The priest yawned, showing uneven teeth. He lit a candle and set it on a small table between two chairs.

"Sit down," he said.

Marc sat.

"I think we should rest quietly for a moment, aware of God's presence in our lives."

They sat quietly, their eyes closed. Marc couldn't think of anything to pray about, certainly nothing as profound as God's presence in his life. A battery-powered wall clock chugged away the minutes. The priest said, "In the name of the Father and of the Son and of the Holy Spirit. Amen."

Marc kept his eyes closed. A while later, he heard the priest say, gently, "You've been drinking."

Marc waved the vodka bottle at him, unscrewed the top and took a drink. "You want one?"

"No, thanks. I'm trying to quit. It's been three years now. You want the number for AA?"

Marc shook his head. "It's in the paper every week."

"So how you been?"

Marc shook his head again and looked at the carpet. It was clean, but needed replacing.

"What's happening in your life? I thought maybe I'd see you in church, but I haven't. Not since before Christmas, except at the funeral."

"Yes, the funeral. I've been to lots of funerals. Too many funerals."

"Want to talk about it?"

"No." Then Marc couldn't help himself. Tears seemed to come all the way from his gut. His chest ached and his throat ripped with the vain effort of trying to hold them in.

"Ah," Marc said, rocking. "A-h-h-h. Man."

Father Larry gave Marc a Kleenex and he wiped at his nose, his eyes. "I can't," Marc said.

"Can't what?"

"Go on."

"Probably not."

Marc had a little trouble breathing, but he got it out. "You're not supposed to agree with me."

"I think I meant you probably can't go on the way you're going."

"I lost my job. Only a few days left."

"That's very hard."

Marc let out another throat-wrenching sob and poked at his nose with the Kleenex. "Yeah, well, I thought I was getting it together."

"Maybe you were."

"Now I'm hanging around with Teresa Basiuk."

"The sister. A lovely young woman."

"It's not that I don't know."

"Know what?"

"That it's all very Freudian." Marc tried to smile, but his lips were heavy. He felt like a punch-drunk boxer must feel when he tries to smile. "Like she's got a father problem and I'm trying to make up for A—. For A—."

He couldn't get her name out. The tears flowed. His chest heaved. His nose ran.

"For Anne-Marie," the priest finally prompted.

"Yeah," he managed.

"They are God's children first. Then they are our children."

"But now I'm not there for Sky."

"You and her mother didn't get along."

"We don't. But I'm still not there for Sky. And now, people in town are after me. They hear things about me before I do and I've been threatened. I've got no job. I've got nothing."

"Except Teresa."

"Teresa and Lise."

"Teresa and Lise? You have two women in your life?" The priest's voice was unrelenting in its calmness but Marc thought he detected a touch of interest or surprise. They had to wonder, these priests, about some of the things their parishioners were up to.

"I'm only dating one," Marc said.

"And that one is..."

"Lise."

"And we mean by dating?"

"I've only been to bed with one of them. I only..."

"Teresa is a friend, then, one who needs you?"

"I suppose. Maybe. That scares me. In what sense we might mean that."

"You haven't slept with her?"

"No."

"You want to?"

"Maybe."

"You are not going to want to hear this. You may not even remember it tomorrow. But for many of us who drink, or used to, the question is this: will we hit rock bottom and start to rise, or will we die first?"

"You want to give me that AA number, don't you, Father?"

"That's up to you. But at the risk of sounding like a bumper sticker, I think you've got to forgive yourself."

"For what?"

"You know better than I. But maybe you should also tell God. How long has it been since your last confession?"

"You want to hear the confession of a drunk?"

The priest smiled. "Drunks and sinners and whores."

The feeling of relief lasted into the next morning. Marc slept until 9:00 and woke refreshed. He pulled down a Good News Bible the priest had given him months ago and it fell open at the story of Jonah. He read some of it, didn't think much of the translation or the stick-man pictures, but when Lise called at 10:00, he was still reading it.

"Got your message," Lise said. It wasn't the friendliest opening Marc had ever heard from a woman, but at least she was still talking to him.

"Yeah," he said. "That's good. Why didn't you call last night?"

"I was working. So did you want something?"

"You, of course," he said.

"You left a message that I had to call. And you did that so you could flirt with me? Am I supposed to be flattered or insulted?"

"I don't know," he said. "Be what you want to be. I was a little upset and I thought I'd call."

"And when I called back, there was no answer."

"You must have called late."

"I was off at 11:00. What were you doing?"

"Had to see a man about a confession."

"Sins of the flesh?"

"You wouldn't understand. I feel a lot better today."

"I can't understand what you won't tell me. I'm off today. Meet me for a drink."

"No drinks."

"Okay, babe, coffee."

Lise was already at the Tim Hortons on the highway when Marc got there. She was sitting at a corner table with her back to the wall. A table of Blackfoot natives with rich black hair, wearing rodeo garb, occupied tables on either side of her.

Marc ordered a coffee and a muffin at the counter and regretted the nixing of drinks as soon as he sat down. If he had gotten Lise alone, poured a few drinks into her, he could have kidded her along, improved the mood. But cold sober at 11:00 a.m. was a different story.

"Good morning," he said.

Lise didn't reply.

Staring at her coffee cup, she ran her short, strong fingers through her thick hair. Naturally as reddish brown as ripe durham wheat in the field, her hair had been highlighted with blond. She wore it in a style they'd called a bob when Marc was a teenager. It was probably now called androgynous or hermaphroditic; who could keep up with such trends? Shaved at the neck. Thick on top. Straight all around. Her olive T-shirt was two sizes too big and it managed to simultaneously cover and emphasize her chest.

Head bent over her cup. Not a tall woman, but muscular— big in the shoulders and the chest and the hips. More the look of a Ukrainian peasant than a French name like Lise Champlain suggested. She claimed that way, way back, she owed parentage to Samuel D. himself. That explained her interest in power and adventure, the things that drew her to the police force, she said.

From the look of her skin, Marc would have been inclined to go with Ukrainian gypsy and Metis forebears. It had a coppery sheen that could have come from Indian parents on the prairies. Or perhaps she sunbathed in the nude.

He was still hungry after his muffin, so he went to the counter and ordered a soup and sandwich combo. This time, when he approached, Lise looked right at him.

"Hey, Lise," he said. "How are you?"

She didn't say anything. She had a small mouth and full lips. The left side of her mouth was twitching in a way that particularly bothered Marc because he didn't think she knew she was doing it.

He sat opposite her, sipped at the hot soup.

"So what's going on?" he said.

She turned her attention to the natives on her left. Two men, a woman, and a child, laughing softly.

"You know," he said quietly to Lise. "Some of our native brethren aren't doing half bad, given the oppressive nature of white culture— at least compared with what I saw in Ontario. I mean, we run stories about suicide and glue sniffing but still..."

Lise looked right at Marc, her large eyes an accusation. One of them was blue, the other a strange colour, blue flecked with brown. "What do you know about it, honky?" she said.

"Honky?" he laughed. "Nobody has more tolerance for other races than I do. And I know all about not belonging, not fitting in."

"Yeah?" she said. "A regular blockhead, forgetting his French roots. One of the cocks."

"Cocks? That sounds sexist to me."

"A Caucasian. What some of them call the cocks. They wouldn't trust you in a million years."

"Even though we send them all that money."

Her eyes narrowed. "There we have it."

"So why are you and I trying to solve the native question in Canada when there hasn't been an answer in 200 years?"

"Maybe so we won't have to talk about us."

"Us," he said.

"What are we doing here, Marc? God, I could use a drink. Get me another coffee."

When he brought it, her mouth was twitching, her face sunrise red, warning of a storm on the horizon. "Roll me a cigarette."

He did.

She inhaled, pushed the cigarette around and around on the ashtray, looked at the natives, her mouth twitching, twitching.

"Lise, what the hell is going on here?"

"You want to know, I'll tell you. No, let me ask you first. Always be fair to the witness. Do I mean anything to you?"

Marc looked away, trying to see where this was going, deciding whether to tell the truth.

"Yeah," he said.

"Okay, what?"

"I guess I mean you're a good time to me. You're interesting. I like the way you look."

"A good time. What the screaming Jesus does that mean?" Lise's fingers, holding the cigarette, trembled.

"We seemed to hit it off pretty well, physically. At least I thought so."

"I'll give you that. Anything else?"

"I don't know. Yeah, I think so. It's hard to say. It's only been a few months. And we agreed we weren't going to tie each other down."

"Except for fun."

A joke. Marc thought this might be a good sign. "Yeah, except for fun. I thought we were doing okay."

"So did I. So what's going on with this girl?"

"Girl?" Playing dumb. As if that ever did any good.

"I hear you've been hanging around with Teresa Basiuk."

"Well," he said. "Is that what this is all about? I'm not sleeping with her or anything."

"'Yet,' he failed to add," she said.

He ignored that. "She needs me. Needs a friend."

"And I don't?" She stubbed out her cigarette. It lay curled in the ashtray like a dead worm.

"I don't know. Do you?"

He couldn't believe it but a tear formed in the bluish brown eye, trickled down a cheek that was neither sunrise red nor coppery. It was pale. She rubbed the cheek, dug into the eye.

"I'm sorry, Lise," he said.

"People tell me things, Marc. You're spending a lot of time with that little Basiuk bitch. And the two of you are asking questions that aren't going to do anybody a whole lot of good."

"Are you jealous? Don't be."

"My poor little French fry. You don't know this town. And you don't know how much I need you. Right now."

"Oh, man," he said. "If only we could erase the past."

"Look, I understand how she's drawn to you. You're cute and you're 35 but you could pass for 28 and you've got eyes that tell every woman you understand her. If anybody knows all that, it's me."

"I'm not sleeping with her. She thinks we're onto something."

Lise got up quickly, found her purse, smiled sadly at him and kissed him on the cheek. "You've got to make your choices, babe. We all do. But listen to me and listen good. There's more than one way to be unfaithful to somebody and the physical kind ain't necessarily the worst."

She left him with that.

A Blackfoot man at the next table wore a rakish cowboy hat, black, with a circle of silver coins at the base of the crown. His brown eyes, shaded by the hat, followed her out of Tim Hortons.

"What are you looking at?" Marc wanted to say.

But he didn't.

He knew very well. He didn't need a broken nose to punctuate the fact.

CHAPTER 9

After the conversation with Lise, Marc drove downtown from Tim Hortons as if on auto-pilot. He wasn't thinking about traffic lights or the speed he was going. He was thinking about Lise and Teresa. Lise was right, he had to make up his mind about her. Never an easy thing for him when women were involved.

He was so caught up in his thoughts that he had parked in the newspaper lot before he realized what he was doing. In his auto-pilot mode, he had driven there out of habit. But since he was already at the paper, he decided to get a little work done.

Marc wandered into his office and found a note George had left on his chair so it wouldn't get lost among the papers on his desk: "Fiona didn't turn out the layout for the McLean grocery ad until 5:15 Friday afternoon. As far as I'm concerned, this is the FINAL STRAW. Hell could freeze over before I'm touching the ad on the weekend. I'll do it Monday morning and if McLean doesn't get a proof, that's Fiona's problem. Let her tits get her out of this one. George."

Fiona's breasts might get her out of some situations, but Marc didn't trust them to pacify a grocery advertiser already displeased with the newspaper editor. At 11:30, he began to labour at the Compugraphic keyboard and by 1:00 he had copy ready to paste up, enough to get a proof out some time Monday morning. He resented typesetting ads in his final days at the paper— and especially doing it the hard way, when a new computer typesetting system was planned for installation at the *Sun* within weeks— but he didn't need the frustration of dealing with Robbie McLean if the ad didn't get properly proofed.

Tense across the shoulders from the steady typing, Marc dialled Teresa's number. Time to sort out some of his relationship entanglements.

A little girl's voice said, "Hello."

"Who's this?"

Some breathing on the telephone. A cough. "It's, um, Suzanne."

"Right, Suzanne. Can I talk to Teresa?"

"It's Suzie."

"Right, Suzie. Can I talk to Teresa?"

"She's, um, sleeping. You want to talk to my mom."

"No, Suzie."

"I had Frosten Flakes for breakfast."

"You mean Frosted Flakes?"

"No, Frost-en Flakes."

"Tell Teresa that Marc called."

"Okay, bye." She rang off.

Marc line-taped the ad border, stripped in the items that weren't too horribly typeset, and shot the meat, broccoli, and carrot cuts to size on the long black process camera. At 2:00, he called Teresa again. Suzie answered. "She's having a shower. Did you have a shower?"

"No, Suzie, I didn't have a shower. And I'm not sure that's any of your business. Can you ask Teresa to call me? I'm at the office."

This time, Teresa got the message. At 2:07 according to the digital read-out on the black telephone in the composing room, she called. He almost didn't hear the phone over the buzz of the process camera.

"Hi, where were you?" asked a strained voice.

"Working. I let it ring until I figured it was you."

"Yeah? That's sweet. I think. So what're you doing?"

"Working, like I said. Not sleeping in like some people."

"Can you come get me?"

He hesitated, wondering about Lise. "I guess so," he said.

"Right away, okay?"

"Almost."

"Okay, I don't like waiting."

He corrected some of his typos and re-pasted the ad. Checking his desk quickly before he left, he recognized, among the junk mail, an envelope addressed in a familiar typewriter style:

```
MARC LEPAGE, PUBLISHER AND EDITOR
PERSONAL AND CONFIDENTIAL
```

Inside was a single sheet, folded, no letterhead.

```
THE CAR IS THE KEY
IT'S NO MYSTERY TO ME
YOU CAN'T BEAT THE BEAST
SO GO BACK EAST
```

"Jesus," he said, and looked at it again— the same IBM Selectric type, no other clues. "Messages from the poetically disabled," he muttered to the desk.

Checking his telephone set for the time, he said "Jesus" again and ran from the building.

Das Kapital had no clock, digital or otherwise, but he didn't need one to tell him he was late when his tires nudged the curb in front of Teresa's place.

She was on the front step, her body language telling him the time more loudly and accurately than Big Ben. Turned away from him without turning back. No smiles.

"Hi, Teresa," he said when he reached the bottom step. Swivelling part way toward him, she cocked one leg, gave him some bottom lip, and didn't say a word. Her faded blue jeans were ripped at the knee.

Little Suz burst through the front door and hid behind Teresa's leg as soon as she saw Marc. Moving away, Teresa slapped at the girl, but she persisted. Sitting on Teresa's foot, she clung to the back of her leg, riding it all the way down the steps.

Marc bent over and ruffled the little girl's hair. Brushing his hand away, she squealed and rode her sister's leg across the lawn. At the car, Suz grinned at Marc quickly and hid her face behind Teresa.

"Ready to go?"

"Half an hour ago. Where were you?"

"Pasting up the McLean ad."

"Pasting up the McLean ad?" she said. Her look said any man who pasted up a McLean ad while keeping Teresa Basiuk waiting belonged to an order of existence so low, it would look up at the snake in the Garden of Eden.

"Sorry."

Teresa peeled the little girl from her leg and the two of them did an elaborate kiss-hug-good-bye routine. Little Suz, pale except for the dark rings under her eyes, ran back to the house and waved pudgy hands at them until they were out of sight up the street.

"Where we going?" Marc asked. He rolled a cigarette, driving with his elbows. Tobacco bits flaked his jeans, the front of his shirt.

"Doesn't matter."

Marc considered Father Larry's suggestion that he had to start forgiving himself. Maybe he could start by thinking about somebody else before thinking about himself. "Can I help you? Is that why you called?"

"No, you called me."

"All right. But it was you who said to come pick you up."

"So?"

"So where we going?"

Pouting silence. Then, "You figure it out, okay? You're the grown man. Make a decision."

"Are you okay?"

"I'm..." Teresa stopped. The colour had drained from her face. She wouldn't look at him and then she forced her lips into a twisted smile. "How do I look?" She cranked the little Volkswagen mirror toward herself, fast, checked her make-up, frowned, and slapped the mirror back at a lopsided angle. "I look awful. I've seen day-old dog shit that looked better. Okay, let's just go somewhere."

"How about the RCMP station?"

"Sounds like a date with Mr. X. Citement on Saturday afternoon."

"Look," he said, losing his wonderful intention to think about her first, "I wanted to check the ownership of the Trans Am, okay? Like somebody suggested yesterday. And I don't know whether I trust the town cops."

"Finally. We're getting some place."

Nicky Kuchik shoved his way out the door of the RCMP station as they were coming in. Looking surprised when he saw them, Nicky managed a nod as he was leaving.

A tiny earphone in each ear, the RCMP receptionist worked behind a wall of security glass transversed by tiny lengths of wire. Her fingers hesitated between a bag of chocolate almonds and a computer keyboard. As they approached, she licked the tips of her fingers and rubbed chocolate off the keys.

Teresa paced. She stopped at a missing kid poster, then paced some more. She jabbed Marc in the ribs with her thumb. "Do something, numbie nuts."

Marc rapped on the glass. Startled, the receptionist glanced up, thumb and index finger arrested between the bag and her puckered, wet lips. She wore only one ring, on the thumb of her left hand. Each of her nails was painted a different colour. Her hands were very clean, except for the chocolate, which she licked with a wide pink tongue.

"Yes, can I help you?" The receptionist pretended to smile, the attempt shoving her wide cheeks higher, crimping the fat around her eyes.

"The staff sergeant in?"

"Sorry. Not back till Monday."

"How about somebody else?"

"We're real short-staffed right now. Two officers on holiday and Corporal Bradley, of course, the poor man is off until we get that case straightened around. I personally haven't had a day off in the last 21. But who's counting?"

She wasn't counting the almonds. Smiling briefly, she lowered her top lip over the candy they'd interrupted and began to suck back and forth.

"We're real sorry to hear that. I'm sure it's breaking my heart. What about you, Marc?" Teresa slapped his arm and frowned at him and managed a smile almost at the same time. "But we're here to see someone. Like the sergeant, if it's not too much trouble."

The receptionist glared at Teresa as if jeans that tight were an offence to cellulite and beamed at Marc. "I'll see if Sergeant Digby is off the phone." She turned with some effort and reached a telephone receiver on the desk behind her.

"Great, we get Dingbats," Teresa groaned.

"**M**arc," the sergeant said, hurting Marc's hand when he squeezed it.

"How's it going, Tom?"

"And Teresa Basiuk, if memory serves me?" His glance sawed back and forth between the two of them. Then he grinned, kissed the back of Teresa's hand and laughed a nervous laugh. "What can I do you for? Come with me. Back where we can have a little privacy."

As soon as Tom turned away, Teresa rolled her eyes and wiped the kissed hand on the back of her jeans. "Gross," she muttered to Marc.

Sergeant Tom Digby unlocked a steel door. Leading them down a narrow corridor to another steel door, he showed them into a room with dark wooden chairs around a dark wooden conference table.

"Coffee?"

"Thanks, half a cup, regular." Marc said.

"Nah, not for me," Teresa said. She chose a swivel chair, drew her knees up to her chin and spun herself around and around while the sergeant measured coffee and water.

As soon as the coffee was blurping through the maker, the sergeant pulled out a chair across from Marc. Tom squared a white notepad in front of him and placed a pencil carefully along the top of the pad. "Marc?"

"I'm doing a little more work on the Rose Hill accident."

"The one you wrote up already."

Marc pulled a spiral notepad out of his hip pocket. "We're working on a follow-up. A couple of new things have come to light. For starters, was there an autopsy?"

"Not to my knowledge. Are we on the record here? Usually, there's no autopsy unless there's a suspicious death. Not my case, but all the reports I've seen on this one make it pretty routine."

"So there was no autopsy. Is there an active investigation?"

"There was a file... There is a file. You have anything to add to it, we'd be glad to have it. Unless it's hearsay and gossip, which is about 90 per cent of what we get."

The sergeant had razor-cut hair, a thick neck and fingers the size of pork sausages. A fullback jammed into a cop's uniform, he pulled himself out of his chair clumsily. He fixed two cups of coffee and set them gently on the table, as if ceramic cups could be damaged by fingers as large as his.

"Sure you don't want any, Teresa?"

She frowned at her knees, ignoring Tom Digby.

"So you two together? Something going on here that the eyes and ears of Canada's Finest might have missed?" He laughed as if this were funny.

Marc smiled, didn't answer, sipped his coffee and rolled himself a cigarette. "Sorry, this is a non-smoking room." Tom pointed to signs on the walls.

Marc tucked in the ends of the cigarette, slid it into his pocket and said to his reflection in the dark, oiled table top. "So there was no investigation and no autopsy."

"What was there to investigate? This was an accident. Do I have to spell it for you? A-c-c... No, I don't. It was a car accident, for Chrissake."

Teresa frowned at her knees again and said, "You don't have to swear."

"No offence to the young lady."

"You boys checked out the car?" Marc asked.

The sergeant mashed the palm of one swollen hand with the thumb of the other. "Not sure... Yeah, we did check. Staff sergeant said the garage had to go over it with a fine-toothed comb. Brakes. Steering. The front end. The young lady's muscle car and the half-ton, just to be sure something didn't get balled up and that's why the two vehicles collided."

"And?"

"And it's like I've been patiently telling you. There was nothing. Some play in the front end of the half-ton, nothing to stew over. And nothing on the young lady's car. Christ, they were practically brand new."

"The young lady's car?" Teresa said to a blackboard along the wall behind her. The board was intersected by various lines. Abbreviated words in white chalk crawled between the lines.

"Beg your pardon?" the sergeant said.

"'Young lady's car?' I said. 'Young lady's car?'" Teresa's face had turned the colour of chalk. A bluish vein emerged in her forehead. "You know what's wrong with an asshole, man? It can't hear. It's fucking deaf."

Old sports muscles bulged under the fat in the sergeant's neck. In contrast with Teresa's, his face was as red as the maple leaf on the flag drooping on a pole in the corner. "You want to keep the young lady under control, or am I going to have to clear the room of spectators?"

Marc discovered a paste-up knife in his jacket pocket and pulled it out, clicking the precise blade in and out. In and out. He looked over at Teresa and said, "What's your problem?"

Teresa glared at him with eyes that were barely human, as if she were shutting out Marc and everything else in the room.

"It's okay, Tom," Marc said. "She'll be all right. It's been a trying time for her, her sister being killed..."

Nostrils distended, as if sniffing out the trouble in her life, the sergeant stared silently at Teresa.

"What about the glass?" Marc scraped the edge of his thumbnail with the thin knife blade.

"What glass?"

"The windshield of the Trans Am. The way it was cracked."

"Now that's news. That's the kind of thing makes the public glad we invest in community colleges, so journalists can do investigative reporting of such high calibre. Half the windshields in the province have stone chips. And the victim in practically a head-on hits the window with her skull and it cracks." The sergeant rolled his eyes ceiling-ward.

"But where did the crack start? Didn't you guys look at that? We did. It started on the passenger's side."

The cop studied his stubby fingers for a minute. This piece of information seemed to bring back his anger, as if he couldn't stand to hear another word contradicting the official news releases of the Royal Canadian Mounted Police.

"We followed procedure, Marc. Understand? The force has decades of experience in car accidents, and unless there's reason to suspect otherwise, what you see is what you get."

"We might have reason to suspect otherwise."

"Such as?"

"Such as, I can't say right now."

"Because you don't have anything hard to go on. You let yourself get pussy whipped— no offence— into certain opinions by this young lady— so-called— giving the benefit of the doubt. That's okay. It's a free country. But it's also a country that insists that its federal police work on evidence, stuff that'll stand up in court."

"So the window isn't evidence?"

"Maybe. Maybe not. Evidence of what? There are no safety check laws in this province. And there's a ton of gravel hauled between here and Edmonton every hour. That crack could've started a week ago or a month ago or two months ago. So her head hits and it appears to start from the passenger side."

"But can't that be checked? Wouldn't that be going over the car with a fine-toothed comb?"

"Maybe. We could also send it to GM, make sure it really is the year the dealer says it is. But we only have so much budget and so much time. Game of chicken. They're both dead. Staff sarge says the file's still open, but it's time to move on to other things."

"Couldn't you ask around? Check to see whether the windshield was cracked before?"

"We could, although we'd need a reason."

"But it wouldn't be that tough to find out. Check to see whether Stephanie Basiuk was the registered owner. And let us know?"

"That would be confidential. The Solicitor General decides the rules, not us. If somebody upstairs wants more done, trust me, we'll do more."

Marc was beginning to wonder how much Sergeant Digby could have accomplished in the amount of time he was taking to tell them he couldn't do anything. "So even though you know who owned the car and even though it should be public, you're not going to tell me."

"You have no idea what I know and what I don't know. And what I release is not up to me," Digby said.

Teresa muttered something to the wall.

"I beg your pardon," the cop said.

"Bobby's car, right?"

"Bobby?"

"Yeah, asshole. Don't try and snow me. It wasn't a young lady's car. It was Bobby's car. And the Bobby we all know and love wouldn't go around for any two or three months with a cracked windshield. He barely goes three times around the block without hitting the car wash."

"Bobby who?"

"You make me puke." Teresa looked like she might be sick. Her face was even paler, tinged with green, all hints of tan bleached by her turbulent emotions. "See ya outside, Charlie," she said. She stalked out and slammed the door shut behind her.

"A word to the wise, and it don't mean crap to me," the sergeant winked at Marc. "But those Basiuk girls are a long way from being good news."

"Thanks for nothing," Marc said.

CHAPTER 10

Marc found Teresa in the hallway and the sergeant escorted them out of the building.

"Bobby who?" Marc said, once they were alone on the steps.

She wouldn't look at him.

He grabbed her arm, shook it. "You said 'Bobby.'"

Her face contorted. "Town's full of ditch pigs," she said.

"What's that supposed to mean?"

"Nothing."

"Tell me."

"I can't," she said. "You don't understand."

"Can't tell me or won't?"

"Can't, okay, asshole? Can't. You got that? I said more than I should have already." She pulled her arm free and walked away.

Marc felt sorry for pushing her on the subject. Wanting to re-establish a feeling of closeness and companionship, he said, "Okay, let's drop it."

The RCMP station had once been a school. Junipers, mountain ash, and lilacs crowded the yard where students had once lounged in the sunshine. Teresa looked around and said, "He might be somebody I know. A rat, if there were any in Alberta. But I haven't got it all put together. It's like, if I can give you something solid, I will. Okay? You'll be the first to know. Deal?"

"Deal."

"So what are you doing tonight?" Teresa asked in one of the mercurial changes of subject that always caught Marc off guard.

Grabbing his elbow, she stumbled arm-in-arm with him down the steps past white lilac flowers, sweet and putrid in their late June dying.

"What is this, Saturday?" he said. "Tonight's the annual slowpitch banquet. Some time around 7:30 or 8:00, we get the piss tanks lined up against a wall for group shots. Ten photos all the same. You just change the faces. The whole thing has a certain Andy Warhol quality to it."

"The artist, right?"

"A strange cat who ended up in New York City and made Brillo boxes famous. Obsessed by the famous while trying to make fame ordinary. Remember his thing about everybody being famous for 15 minutes?"

"God, the things you know. Or think you do." They were inside the slightly musty interior of Das Kapital, waiting for a police car to pass so they could pull out. "So can I go?"

"Where?"

"To the banquet."

"You want to?"

"Maybe. It's awfully soon after the funeral. Is that what you're thinking? Like what are people going to say?"

"That's hardly the point. How are you going to feel about it?"

"It's so strange, like I was filled with such, I don't know... anger or almost hate, something like that. And I miss her like anything. But I'm dealing with it. Maybe later I'm going to have this really awful time. But right now, I watch myself do things, and as long as I'm watching, I'm okay. So it doesn't matter whether I go to some dance or not. You understand?"

"Yeah. I guess. The ability to distance the mind from the past and the future."

"If you say so, Mr. Weird or whatever we're being today. And I don't care what anybody thinks."

"You have a dress?" he asked.

Where was he now? Once Lise found out about this— and she would— dragging Marc to a coulee outside of town and letting the coyotes feast on what was left of his bones might seem like an act of mercy compared with what she would do to him.

Teresa didn't have a dress. She had tight jeans, washed a shade between process blue and white, and an imitation angora rabbit sweater— tangerine— serious distractions for the men's slowpitch league during the fast dances. Blue heels.

Marc wore his only suit— western cut khaki corduroy— with a string tie and cowboy boots.

The string tie lasted until dessert time at the buffet or his fourth vodka, depending on how he wanted to count it. Teresa stayed with beer during the meal, but when Marc came back from taking the last picture— the mixed league champions against the pale walls of the Moose Hall— she had a darker drink in a plastic glass.

"Diet Coke," she said, "With a little rum. Somebody bought it for me. One of my fans, I think." Hugging Marc around the neck, she wrestled him to his seat and kissed him with predatory frankness. "But don't worry." Her voice was in his ear, then her tongue, then her voice again. "He wasn't nearly as good looking as you."

Marc looked around to see who was watching. A man as bald as a melon winked at him and gave him two thumbs up. Marc decided he didn't care who was watching. "You're making me crazy," he said and pulled her onto his lap.

Later, Teresa dragged him up to join a wide circle of people who made clucking motions with their hands, flapped their arms like wings and wiggled their hips. "Bird Dance time," she said, "cool but dorky." After it was over, she made him slow dance. Marc swayed from foot to foot with Teresa's arms around his neck, her body flattened against his.

"Wanna polka?" she asked when the beat quickened, but the polka was more than he could handle. He stepped on her toes twice and she led him to their seats. Out of breath, sweating, Marc sank to his chair. His lungs burned in his chest.

"I'll get us a beer, honey," Teresa said and twisted her way through a group of men swaying arm-in-arm, singing "You Picked a Fine Time to Leave Me, Lucille," out of time and out of tune with the tape played by an Elvis wannabe disc jockey.

Somebody hit Marc's shoulder. He swung around. Behind him, Klaus Axel made rock and roll dance motions with his hands and shoulders, laughing at his wife. "We having fun, yet?" This to Marc, who polished off the vodka in his plastic glass and looked around for Teresa and his beer.

"Yeah," Marc shouted at him above the music.

Klaus moved his mouth close to Marc's ear, so close that the hairs on the back of Marc's neck felt electrically charged and he shivered. "That's some girl, our Teresa, eh?"

"I like her. You play slowpitch?"

"Used to. No time lately, is there, Anne? I still like to make the dance. These people know how to party." He went into the rock and roll motions again, a middle-aged guy's version of the twist, one leg raised. When he'd finished, Klaus grimaced, held his back as if he'd hurt it and laughed. "I'm surprised you're still on the job. What's the timing of the transition?"

"I'm doing one more paper. I've got some severance money coming. There are a few things I'm considering in Crooked Elbow. You do a paper in a town, the place starts to grow on you. Or you grow on it."

"A negotiated severance package can be a great thing in these circumstances."

"Yeah, I'll remember that for next time. So what's happening with the new Agriplex? I see that slipped through planning committee like shit through a goose, eh, Klaus? The day the anti-church delegation showed up?"

Klaus went into his little dance routine one more time and dodged the question. "This town is starting to rock and roll," he said.

Marc laughed at the performance: the guy doing his dance number to Randy Travis singing, "For Ever and Ever Amen," while half of Crooked Elbow society became incurably romantic for two minutes on the dance floor.

"Seen Bobby lately?"

Klaus gave Marc a look about as warm as the Crooked Elbow River in the middle of January. "You mean Robbie? He and the former Miss

Crooked Elbow Rodeo turned lovin' wife are here somewhere. Aren't they, dear?"

Klaus and his tall, bottled blond wife did a little square dance step, promenading on the spot for a look around the room. "Lot of people here, having a go-o-od time," Klaus said.

"Not Robbie, Bobby."

"There's a lot of Bobbies in this area, probably six here tonight."

"Forget it. I heard some Bob was a friend of yours and he was running into a bit of trouble."

The music seguéd back into a polka. Anne tugged Klaus's hand. "We'll do that lunch. Soon," Klaus said. The Axels polkaed across the dance floor, Klaus looking at Marc while he swung Anne around and around.

Teresa was dancing with the short, mustachioed man who had escorted Marc to his seat at the funeral home. The man looked dazed but happy to have a live body in his hands for a change, his belly rubbing her. Marc found a red liquor ticket and some lint in his shirt pocket and went looking for his own beer. Who knew when Teresa might be back, or whether she still had tickets?

"Hello, handsome." Lise was sitting at a long table, one arm over the shoulder of a man with big hands and a small suit. A county councillor in a dirty white cowboy hat slouched in a chair across the table from her.

"Lise," he said. "What're you doing here?"

"Wouldn't miss the social event of the year. Besides, I was invited." She leaned forward. "Like my date? Every woman's dream, 35 and in shape. Farms pigs between here and Rose Hill. I'd let him root for my truffles any time." She laughed, her eyes fixed on some middle distance between Marc and the disc jockey.

"You're that pissed off that you find a guy like him right away?"

"Whaddya mean right away? Me and Gord've known each other for years. I see you came with Little Miss Bitch."

"You're drunk."

Lise laughed at that or at Marc. "Who are you to talk? Least I didn't go robbing any cradles. C'mere. Sit down. We can still be friends."

He sat.

They drank.

Gord, Lise's date, talked to the county councillor.

People came, people went.

They drank some more. A couple of beers, three rusty nails, more beer, but who was counting? Lise stood, listing a little, and grabbed Marc's hand.

"Wanna dance, stranger?"

In her tight dress, ruffled around the bottom, Lise was rounded and warm and crisp in his hands. She was drunker, but still a better dancer than Teresa. None of the girl's hesitation— where do the feet go? Lise established the rhythm with her hips, her arms bounced, and the movement of feet became academic: they had no choice, they fell in line.

She pulled Marc's head down, his cheek against hers. "You dance good," she said.

"Good teacher, mamma."

"I like you. No, really, I like you. A lot. I think this thing with Teresa is just a passing phase. Or fancy. Or whatever. Though it is a little strange." A quick, impetuous kiss on the cheek.

"Stranger than pig farmers? Rooting at your truffles?"

"None of your business."

"None at all. None whatsoever." The "whatsoever" took some work to get out. "And Teresa's none of yours."

"Touché." Breathing hard, sweating, she exuded heavy, perfumed odours. Her thighs were relentless pistons churning against his.

"She's helping me out. She's a good kid. I like her."

"Yeah. If I could fit jeans like that, I bet you'd call me a good kid."

"Don't count on it. You're ba-a-a-d."

She grinned at him. "What's the difference between a woman and a sheep on the edge of a cliff?"

"I don't know. Can't remember jokes. You know that."

"The sheep gives better action. Or the sheep's more fun. Something like that. You hear they found two new uses for sheep in New Zealand?"

"No."

"Food and clothing."

"Hah!"

Circling and circling, Lise drew Marc into a poorly lit corner by the stage. Above them, the disc jockey imitated a rock star, playing an invisible electric guitar. Her fingers found the back of Marc's neck. "We had fun, didn't we?"

"Maybe. Somehow with you, I never quite remember."

"Well, believe me, sailor, this girl's had a great time. A great, big, great time. Maybe we can do it again."

They danced in circles in the dim corner. Her large eyes were hooded with mascara and a look that might have been genuine concern. She said, "You were the cutest one. So sweet. That's what I love about you. Just love. Could screw you silly and the next day, I'm talking to a monk. What's a hundred men at the bottom of the ocean?"

"Okay, here's my line... I don't know."

"A start."

He laughed and asked her what she was, some female version of a misogynist?

"Read my lips," she said, licking them. "Be careful, will you? This town needs more guys like you. Hell, I'd settle for one, since you're hung up on Little Miss Muff. You got me worried. Asking questions, looking in a couple of directions that aren't going to do you any good. Especially now that you're off the paper."

"Erase. Almost off the paper. Want to flesh that out, tell me what you're worried about?"

"Well, dancing with you won't do me any good. I don't think they have the balls to do anything about it, but you never know. I'd be safer, a lot safer, if I headed back to Arnold Ziffle or whatever his name is. Nice forearms, I'll give him that. I like the big-veined boys."

"Who's this 'they'? We're just dancing. It's a free country, last I checked."

"Thanks for the dance. I think he's getting lonely. I saw him turning around, looking sad. Just listen to somebody who cares about you, okay? Don't do anything stupid. And if you don't become a complete idiot over this fluff in your life, we'll get together again. Two ships colliding in the night."

Lise's pelvis collided with his leg briefly and she staggered away.

Teresa waited for him at the table, giving him the benefit of her lower lip. He set a beer in front of her and she chug-a-lugged it. "Christ," he said, "You were dancing? Why can't I?"

"With her? And don't swear."

"E-rase, what's bothering you? She's a police officer. I know her. We had a dance."

"There's nothing wrong with that, Marc. You want to dance with the biggest slut this side of Fort McMurray, that's your prerogative. Where'd you meet her anyway? Under some table? Where's my drink?"

"Where's your drink? Where's the drink you went for?"

"I drank it. Party hardy, man. Bring me something. *Garçon!*" She snapped her fingers. "More drinks. Drinks for the house."

"I'll get you a beer. Let's stick to beer."

She mimicked him. "Let's stick to beer, get sick on beer. Fuck the beer, let's have a drink. Double vodka and water, short. Two of them. To go."

When Marc came back with the drinks, she was out on the dance floor, writhing like a rock video groupie in front of some guy Marc didn't recognize. A young, good-looking guy with a mean, spoiled look.

Robbie McLean's wife, her aging Miss Crooked Elbow Rodeo face cupped in her carefully manicured hands, watched from her table, large eyes staring. Teresa wriggled low and then lower, limbo-style, until her legs gave out and she collapsed on the floor, laughing.

Laughing himself, the guy hauled her to her feet, tried to keep her dancing. Teresa was so drunk and was laughing so hard, she couldn't dance. Holding her sides, she bent over and fell again. This time, she slithered on the floor in front of him like a reptile.

Marc moved in above her. "C'mon, Teresa. I got my pictures. Let's go home."

Robbie McLean shoved Marc, a quick head-snapping push, one hockey player shoving another to see what he'd do about it. "It's up to her, Deadeye Dick. She wants to dance with him, she can dance with him."

Klaus and another man shouldered in beside Robbie, grabbing his arms. Robbie shook them off. "Leave us be, assholes," he said. "Leave me and Ace Journalist alone. Ladies and germs, presenting... Mr. Gotta Use The Names himself."

Marc stared at Robbie McLean.

"What're you looking at, eh, asshole?" Robbie taunted. "What's so interesting? I hate it when people do that." He moved in again, a shoulder against Marc's chest, and hit him, two quick rabbit punches to the stomach.

The punches bent Marc in two, the pain a surprise.

A crowd of men swarmed around Robbie McLean, a human circle of protection. "I'll see you outside. Later," Robbie said.

The opening strains of "Rock Around the Clock" brought couples to the floor within seconds. Out of the corner of his eye, Marc saw Robbie's wife take his arm and lead him out to dance. She looked thoroughly annoyed. Robbie grinned, made whooping noises. He threw his clenched hands high, like a victorious boxer.

Two heavy young men in high school jackets approached Marc from behind. "Time to go, sir," one of them said.

"And he stays?" Marc was still gasping for air.

"Let's be reasonable," the other said. "Let's just leave quietly." His sleeve patch said he was a linebacker.

"You got a steroid problem? Let me finish my drink."

"Okay," said his heavy-set partner. "But no trouble. I'll stay here with you, you don't mind."

"No trouble," Marc said.

He waited a long time for Teresa, a gladiator on either side.

Teresa's hands teased Marc on the way home to her place, her fingers drawing circles on his stomach muscles. "Thanks for helping me," she said.

Marc stuck to the back streets, feeling sleepy, driving without incident, but not trusting a Breathalyzer if they were stopped. "You're welcome. I'm not much of a fighter."

"Yes. You are. We got out. Didn't we?"

"Yeah. You could look at it that way."

"Yes."

"Who's Bobby? I still want to know."

"An asshole."

At the stop sign, she said, "What?"

Her head slid over and nestled against his shoulder, as if it had been made for that purpose.

She wouldn't wake up when he parked behind the cement truck under the street light in front of her house. "Teresa, we're here," he said softly.

Louder. "Teresa, we're home."

He shook her. Still no reaction. "Teresa."

Frustrated, a little panicky at the thought of going through this routine again, he shoved her away from him. She slid, a rubbery object, against the opposite door frame.

None too sober himself, he leaned over and kissed her cheek. It was cool and about as responsive as plastic. Inside him, something warm and alive and dangerous smouldered. He looked around, checking the street to see whether anyone had seen him. No one that he could spot. The booze moved in his muscles, with him, like a phantom beast. He imagined his fingers moving lightly down her unconscious body, imagined his hands cupping her breasts, and stopped, ashamed. He leaned over and cuffed her cheek lightly, shook her, called her name. "Teresa. You've got to wake up. We're here."

She snapped to some level of consciousness and lashed out at him, the back of her hand hitting his nose. "Get the fuck out of here. Dweeb. Asshole," she said.

Banging her door open, she staggered out. She leaned against the rounded front fender of the Volkswagen, rubbing her eyes, yawning up at the street light. Marc was worried that she would pass out and go to sleep on top of his car. Then where would he be?

He opened his door. Confused and mad, he moved around to give her a hand. Why did things always happen when a guy was half in the bag? He had his arm around her shoulder when she straight-armed him in the ribs, harder than he thought possible for a girl her size.

"Get lost, you lousy prick. You didn't have to do it," she said.

"It's Marc, I'll help you to the door," he said.

"Pleased to meetcha. I'm gonna be a star." A boozy, lopsided grin. "No pants, they all look the same. Let me go."

Teresa fell on her way to the front door, forced herself to her knees and then swayed to a standing position. Measuring the distance to the front step, she lurched her way toward it, determined not to fall again. Going to make it, as a point of pride, or die trying.

CHAPTER 11

The ringing of a telephone woke Marc at 2:00 in the morning. He'd gotten to sleep about 1:30 following the slowpitch banquet. The telephone rang a long time, persistently, gave up, started again. After an equally long time of trying to ignore it, Marc flopped out of bed and stumbled to the kitchen in rumpled T-shirt and sweat pants.

"Hello."

"Dust wanted to hear duh sound of your vocal chords," a man's garbled voice said. It sounded as if he had something in his mouth or was deliberately mispronouncing some words.

"Who is this?"

"She better nod be dere. Nighty night."

"Who are you?"

The line went dead. Marc sat in a chair in the kitchen. His fingers trembled. He shook his head once, violently, and went back to bed.

At 3:00 in the morning, just after he'd drifted back to sleep, the telephone rang again.

"Christ," he said, tossing back the bedcovers. On the way to the kitchen, he banged his little toe on the couch. "Christ," he said again.

He picked up the phone. "Yeah?"

The man's voice was still muffled and stupid-sounding. "She dere?"

"How's the party?"

"No pardy. Dust you and me, bud. She dere?"

"There's nobody here, what's wrong with you? Can't a guy get some sleep?"

The man laughed in his muffled way. "Nod you. So she's not dere? You wouldn't wanta lie to me. We don't like wad you're doin'."

"Who is this? You're pissing me off. Is this Robbie McLean?"

"Who? We be over dere do see you." The man rang off.

Marc checked the door to make sure it was locked, unplugged the telephone from the wall and went back to bed. He couldn't sleep, so at 3:40 a.m., he got up and made a pot of drip coffee and rolled a smoke and thought about things. At 4:00 a.m., the upstairs doorbell to his apartment rang. So tired his chest ached, he levered himself out of his chair and pulled on jeans, a jean jacket, and running shoes.

The doorbell rang again. "Yeah, yeah, *tabernac*, keep your shirt on." He ran up the stairs to see who it was.

Waiting for him at the top of the stairs were a porch lamp with a 60 watt bulb and a driveway and his aunt's compact car and a moon the size of a spoon in June that was rapidly losing to the dawn threatening the dark grey buildings of Crooked Elbow. A man walked to a car. It squealed its tires away from the curb and stopped.

Marc opened the door and ran for Das Kapital, parked by the curb in front of the house in the strange pre-dawn light. The Volks started immediately— it was a night for surprises— and he took off after the car, now a block away. A big car, Ford LTD from the shape of the tail lights.

He followed it through the downtown residential area where the bourgeoisie snoozed on a Sunday morning. Cotton candy clouds began to show blue and pink in the eastern sky, ushering in the day. Birds chirped and cawed to each other outside his car window. Their cheerfulness was depressing.

The LTD passed a 7-Eleven. Marc thought about a coffee and the smokes he'd left in his apartment. In the 7-Eleven parking lot, an idling police car blew exhaust at flattened pop cans and empty chip bags. A cop leaned against the counter inside the store, paying attention to the coffee in his cardboard cup and the brunette leaning against the till, and no attention to the dawn outside.

A right turn and they were on the main highway through town, Marc speeding a little to catch up. His heart was pounding and not just because he needed a smoke. Who was in the car? Robbie McLean? Thugs hired to get him out of town? There had to be a reason somebody sounding like an idiot would goad him into following a car at such an ungodly hour of the morning.

A stoplight turned amber as the LTD went through. The light was red when Marc got there, but he ignored it, counting on the brunette to keep the municipal cop occupied.

In his rear view mirror, the dawn display was so fascinating, he just had to yawn, a long, mouth-stretching, tear-wrenching yawn, the car running in third gear at 80 kilometres an hour into mist wafting from the river.

He opened his eyes and a truck was coming at him. The truck had huge front tires and a grill the size of a small building. Its front bumper was aimed at about windshield height on the Volkswagen.

Downshifting, Marc steered the car left, hoping to run around the truck on the far side. His hands trembled, although he wasn't thinking about the trembling. He was thinking about those lights relentlessly approaching at just about windshield level, just about brain level.

The lights moved with him, tracking the path of his car. "Damn," he said. "What's wrong with you, man?"

Marc took a chance that there would be no traffic on the highway at this hour. He steered further left into the oncoming lane. The truck, stalwart in its mission, followed. Holding the car steady, Marc played his own game of chicken, and the truck never faltered, give it that.

At the last possible moment, he cranked the steering wheel, hard, to the right.

"Damn, *tabernac*, *estis*, piss." The car wobbled, crossed the highway, righted itself and ran up on the sidewalk, where it touched the steel guard rails and bounced back to the street.

And stalled.

The truck, round in his rear view mirror, a ready-mix concrete delivery truck, screeched to a stop, pneumatic brakes belching air. A large man tumbled out of the truck.

The LTD backed out of the mist and blocked the road in front of Marc. He tried the ignition. No smoke, no burning rubber smells from the engine, but it wouldn't start.

Three men got out of the LTD. Three car doors slammed. Two redwinged blackbirds flitted off the guard rail, flew away and came back for another look. The three men weren't big, but one of them carried a tire iron, another a cattle whip.

Marc cranked the starter over, rah-wah-wah-wah. No luck.

He opened the car door with his shoulder. The men were running now and Marc knew he didn't have enough time to get away. It was stupid to try. But he tried anyway.

As soon as his running shoes hit the pavement, he was sprinting. Cowboy boots and running shoes slapped the pavement behind him. Grunts. Breathing.

He looked over his shoulder as somebody grabbed his arm. He shook his arm free, but it slowed him down, threw him off balance. Somebody else grabbed the same arm. Marc staggered.

"Time you was leaving town," the one with the tire iron said, breathing heavily.

"Fuck you," Marc said. "What'd I do?"

"Not very nice language," somebody else said. "You don't listen, is what you don't do. Hold his arms."

The men spun him around. They wore Zorro-like Hallowe'en masks—black, covering only half of their faces. The one with the tire iron had the most hair. One of the others still had on a cowboy hat after all that running. Marc struggled, shook his arms. He was almost free when the tire iron hit his gut. He groaned and went down. His face scraped the pavement. Boots kicked at him, avoiding his face, concentrating on his gut, his chest. He moaned and tried to cover himself, like a rabbit curling up to protect its soft underbelly.

Somebody pulled his sweat pants down, raised his T-shirt, lowered his shorts. Somebody held his legs, somebody his arms. He lay on his belly, stretched out by a human rack.

Crack.

The whip lashed his buttocks.

Crack.

He cried out in spite of himself.

"That's enough, boys," the man with the cowboy hat said. "I think he got the message. There's buses and highways out of town and we want you on one."

A Cadillac swept behind Marc in the mist, braked and swerved into the middle of the road between the cement truck and the huddle of men, a white limousine with smoked glass and a Bristol board sign bordered by remnants of tissue paper flowers. "COMP HIGH—Summer. Let's Party," said the sign. A window glided down and a teenaged boy shouted, "How's it going, eh?"

The boy lobbed a beer bottle like a grenade in the general direction of Marc and the men. It missed and shattered on the sidewalk. "Ye-e-e-s," he wailed. The redwinged blackbirds took flight from their cattail perches.

The men returned to the LTD.

Marc lifted his head, tried to see the licence plate of the LTD. He couldn't make it out in the mist. The licence of the cement truck was only partly visible— most of the characters were obscured by cement dust. But how many cement trucks were there in Crooked Elbow?

Marc pulled his pants up, his shirt down, brushed himself off.

It wasn't a long walk to the 7-Eleven, three or four blocks, up the rise from the river, but it took him a while. Marc could almost straighten up by the time he got there. His face burned from its contact with the pavement, his butt from the whip. His belly ached where he'd been kicked, but he didn't have trouble breathing. Nothing seemed to be broken.

The police officer was gone, the brunette still there. Her face looked like it had trouble surviving an all-night shift at the 7-Eleven. Her body was holding up.

"I saw a cop here a while ago, talking to you."

She eyed him suspiciously, arms folded beneath her breasts. Her cocked hip said the breasts could be weapons or pillows depending on his intentions and her mood. "Yeah? What happened to you?" she said.

"Nothing. I need to see him."

"You might check next door." She went back to stacking cans of cola in the middle of the aisle in front of the microwavable food counter. He watched her do it— mesmerized for a couple of minutes by the clean simplicity of her movements— and left.

Next door was a Tim Hortons. A green and white Crooked Elbow police car idled in the parking lot. Its officer's broad back was parked at a table inside.

"Can I help you?" asked a sad-eyed waitress, one of several Guatemalan refugees who'd emigrated to Canada under the sponsorship of the Catholic church in Crooked Elbow. The rings under her eyes were nearly as dark as her hair.

"Coffee, cream and sugar, to go."

Coffee in hand, he eased himself into a chair at the cop's table. Marc asked him for a smoke. "Good morning," the cop said, looking up from the comics section. From the veining in his neck and hands, he looked as if he had an off-duty love affair with free weights.

"Morning." Marc peeled back the plastic lip on the lid of his cup. "There's been an accident."

The cop slammed his cup down on the table and reached for his hat. "Looks like it. Did you get pictures?" He smiled at Marc. He had teeth so straight and white, they belonged on a television commercial.

"So you know me?"

"Who doesn't? Where's the accident? There's nothing called in yet." He flicked a thumb at a black radio sitting on the table.

"There wouldn't be. I was the accident. Some dude tried to run me off the road, then he and these other guys came after me."

"Get out of town! Let's take a look."

"Can I ride with you?"

The police car roared down the hill, fast, and parked behind the Volkswagen, four-ways flashing. They got out. The cop walked around, jotting things down in his little notepad, asking Marc what he knew.

"So this truck started where?"

Marc showed him.

"There's no skid marks. I mean, you have a close call with a vehicle the size of a cement truck, there should be skid marks."

"Unless he wasn't trying to stop."

"Or the vehicle was experiencing mechanical problems."

"Yeah," Marc said. "Always a logical possibility. The driver finds he's got no brakes. Without brakes, how can he steer? The Volkswagen acts as a magnet, pulls him into the wrong lane. They narrowly avoid a collision, the car ahead stops and its occupants beat up the Volkswagen driver for his carelessness."

"You get a plate number or anything, smart guy? Any markings on the suspect vehicles, a sign or anything?"

"No. I tried. Too much fog off the river. There's one skid mark from the truck." He pointed to it.

"I see it and I noted it. But that could be anything. Lots of trucks take this highway to Saskatchewan."

Marc shifted his feet and something inside let go. He winced. "The only crimes that happen in this town occur right outside the doughnut shops in broad daylight. The ideal perpetrator is a resident of Saskatchewan, long gone. Is it in your job description to toady to the police commissioner? Or does that just come naturally to you boys?"

"In your condition, I'm going to ignore that for the moment. Is there anything about this truck that you'd like to add, Mr. LePage?"

"It was a cement truck and I know a cement truck driver."

"Yeah, who?"

Marc told him. The cop wrote something in his fat little pad and said, "With a mouth like yours, it doesn't take a rocket scientist to see why you're leaving town. I'll measure this off. I've recorded the truck tire marks and some skid marks from what could be your vehicle on the other side of the highway. Now just for the record, I'm going to have to ask you to blow."

"What?"

"The Breathalyzer, Mr. LePage."

"Somebody tries to do serious bodily harm to me and my vehicle and you think I should be taking the Breathalyzer?"

"Yes, sir."

The officer unravelled the equipment from the front seat of his cruiser and held the mask over Marc's face, like an anaesthetist. Marc blew.

"Nice and steady, that's it. Okay, thank you sir." He jotted down the results and asked Marc to do it again.

"I'm sorry, sir, but you're over .08, the blood-alcohol limit while in operation of a motor vehicle. I'm going to have to write you up."

"But you never saw me driving."

"No, sir, but you admitted you were driving when you first approached me. That and the alleged incident with the cement truck, without evidence, would suggest to me a driver who's legally impaired."

"That's impossible. I haven't had anything to drink since the slowpitch banquet. I've been to bed. I was asleep when the bullshit started."

"When was your last drink?"

"Midnight. Maybe 1."

"Or maybe 2 or maybe 3. It's now 5:16 a.m. Maybe only a couple of hours since your last drink."

"You give me the ticket, I'm going to fight it. I'm not drunk, you can see that."

"You have the legal right to plead however you like in a court of law. I've seen lawyers get people off. Don't ask me how, extenuating circumstances or something, but usually with the Breathalyzer, it's all over but the shouting."

The Volkswagen started, but the cop wouldn't let Marc drive it. He could arrange to have the car picked up later, once the detailed police inspection and towing were out of the way. Marc felt like calling the cop an asshole, but he didn't. Instead, he asked for a ride home. The cop took Marc to the station to repeat the Breathalyzer, confiscated his license, and drove him home. Marc slept in his bedsitting room until early afternoon.

He dreamed that he and Teresa were putzing along in the Volkswagen. A huge truck rolled up beside them, a fat man driving. Teresa gave the guy the finger, then promptly parted her legs and rolled her tongue over her lips at the fat man. The truck scraped the car, squeezed them into a fence, and the driver lifted Teresa out between his thumb and forefinger.

"At least he's a man." Small and wan, Teresa smiled down at Marc.

Marc looked over. Big shoulders hunched at the steering wheel, his stubby nose snorting, the pig-man leered at him. With his left hand, he massaged a huge erection which Marc could see, now that he was in an elevator looking down through the roof of the truck. The erection was thick, closer to the phallus of a stallion than a pig. The truck squeezed closer, closer, and the Volkswagen's frame crumpled.

Throat dry, heart pounding, Marc woke and listened for noises. A break-in, maybe? Somebody in the kitchen? He checked the small apartment, all the closets, the doors, up the stairwell, outside. Even when he was satisfied there was nobody, it took some headache pills and an hour with the *Critique of Pure Reason* before he started to relax.

He tried three times to phone Teresa at her house and failed. If he believed Mr. Kant, maybe that didn't matter. Her house was not a thing in itself. It was only an appearance. The transcendental object it represented was unknowable, easily as unknown as the reasons for the punishment inflicted on Marc's body.

By 9:00 that night, after a couple of drinks, a hot dog supper and a video, he was starting to feel like something that resembled a human being, in form, if not content. Going through the motions.

He was reading the Second Analogy in the *Critique* when the call came. "Marc?" Teresa's voice was low, almost a whisper. Music in the background. Country rock. The sound of running water.

"Yeah," he said. "Where have you been? They got me on an impaired."

"Marc?" Still the raspy whisper.

"Yeah," he said. "I'm here. What's going on?"

"Come get me."

Somebody shouted behind her. A scream or a squeal. A door slammed shut. "Where are you?" he said.

"They made me and I hate it. God, I feel awful. You can hate me. I do."

"Where are you? I'll come and get you. Shit, I've got no car."

"That's okay. It's okay." Her whispery voice was beginning to slur.

"No, I'll get you. I'll find a car. Where are you, in town? At friends'?"

"Friends? Very funny."

"You don't sound good."

"Thanks very much. Fuck you, too. I got to go."

"No, you can't. I have to talk to you."

"Yeah?" Her voice was depressed, distant, fading. A chasm opened in the floor at Marc's feet and in it writhed snakes and rotting intestines. He took a deep breath, let it go, then another, let it go. He closed his eyes and the chasm spiralled; when he opened them again, he was still dizzy but the snakes were gone.

"You still there? You sound stoned, not good," he said.

"Course," she murmured, her words slow and spaced. "Course. I'm in ecstasy."

"Where are you? A party?"

She laughed and started to cry, and her voice scraped savagely in his ears. "What the fuck are...? The fuckin' club... maybe you'd like to join us. What do you care? It's not my fault. I tried to call you. I didn't..."

A man's voice in the background called her name. "Teresa." Harsh laughter. Marc couldn't hear anything else he said.

Teresa shouted at the man without covering the telephone receiver. "It's my mom! Okay? She told me to call, so I'm doing it. Okay, nerd face?"

A pause. Marc could hear Teresa breathing. "It's over. Okay, Marky Marc? I love you, but it's over. I thought I could stay away, specially after she, like... died... but I can't. Don't blame yourself."

"Don't go."

He pleaded with her, but he knew she was going to hang up on him long before he heard the click in his ear followed by the steady, annoying Alberta Government Telephones hum.

CHAPTER 12

The Sunday night receptionist at the municipal police station answered the telephone as if talking were painful: "City police. Roxanne speaking." No matter what the caller's problem, it was nothing compared with hers.

She said she'd try to leave a message, sir, for Lise Champlain to call you, sir, when she got off at 11:00.

"You're positive she's off at 11:00?"

"It's on the schedule. A police department couldn't operate without a schedule."

Lise got the message and called him at 11:05.

"Can we talk?" he asked.

"Long as you'll buy me a drink. And something to eat, babe. Somewhere not too conspicuous. The 'We Hate Marc' club is growing even as we speak."

Marc took a taxi to the Viking Motor Inn on the highway at the west end of town. Marvelling at the lingering evening light, he waited for Lise outside in the gravel parking lot. It was what? 11:30? And not quite dark. In the greyish blue light, he could still discern waves of barley in a field behind the lot. Vast Alberta farmland stretched beyond the barley field, meeting a yellow glow above the distant hills. Dotted stars competed with that glow and were beginning to succeed.

Just before midnight, Lise arrived, out of uniform and into blue jeans, wearing a red jacket and low red heels.

She led him inside, to a booth in the Saga Lounge. The backs of their vinyl seats were laced with alternating coloured stripes as bright as the sails of the Norse model ship stationed just outside the lounge door.

"Love the shoes. I could see them a mile away in the dark," he said.

"A true romantic."

"Looks good, no, really."

"Thanks, babe. Wish I could say the same for your face. I'm glad you called. Believe it or not."

Lise ordered a toasted clubhouse and a beer. He had an orange brandy. A double.

"Where's your little girlfriend?"

"Who knows? Maybe with your little pig farmer."

She tried to give him a surprised look, but it didn't work, so she smiled and bit her lip. The lip wasn't twitching tonight. She finally said, "I can't believe I did that. Anyway, what's up with Little Miss Trouble?"

"I don't know."

"You don't look so good and I don't just mean whatever happened to your face— like you're down and you don't know how to get up."

"Some guys beat me up. Early this morning."

Lise looked angry. "Who was it? I tried to warn you."

"I don't know who it was. But I am going to find out."

"Even if it kills you. I know the feeling, and it's never done me any good. You have to look after yourself, Marc. You're good with words, but words won't protect you from sticks and stones."

The waitress brought the clubhouse and asked if they wanted anything more. Marc asked her to hit him again from the same bottle and turned to Lise when she said, "Let's get back to Miss Trouble. You said you didn't know where she was."

"She called me tonight. From a party or something. With other people. Guys, I guess. Party interference happening in the background. I could hear water. And then somebody notices she's on the phone so she starts pretending I'm her mother."

"And she sounds, how?"

"Drunk, maybe stoned."

"This surprises you?"

"Yeah, well." Lise was making him mad and he didn't want to get mad. He swirled the liqueur in the water glass the Viking used for brandy, watched it tear on the sides and drift down. Angry with her. Angry with himself.

"Babe, there's brandy at my place. Good stuff."

He had to think about that for a minute. "I've got to work tomorrow, put my last paper together."

"We could have a great time, get a little drunk."

"That doesn't sound like the Lise I know."

She smiled at him and licked a blob of mayonnaise from the corner of her upper lip in a way he couldn't help but admire. "You're so right, it drives me crazy," she said. "So do you love her? Is that what I'm up against?"

"Who?" He sipped the brandy. It was starting to do what the first one had promised: going down slow and warm, hinting at untold vistas to be explored.

"Elizabeth Taylor, you jerk." Lise reached over and cuffed his chin where it had scraped the pavement. Marc flinched but Lise did not look sorry.

"Love," he said, swirling the brandy, bringing the glass up for a sniff and tilting it at her.

"You shouldn't fall for her. That's old, old advice, but it's good. You know why?"

"No."

"Never mind May and December. She's a whore at heart. And you can't change that, no matter what you think. You can't save her."

"What makes you an expert?"

"I saw too many when I worked Edmonton vice, and you know why they're terrible at relationships? They're lazy bitches for starters. They get some idea what men want, but no idea what they want for themselves. Unless it's a fix, then they know."

"Unlike some women. Who do know what they want."

Lise smiled as she brought a napkin off her lap and wiped her lips with it. "Jesus, you've got it bad. All right, let's talk about the little slut. Better yet, let's talk about me."

There was an edge to Lise's voice as she kept talking. "Can I get another drink? What does a person have to do to get some service around here?"

She ordered a rusty nail and "a double brandy for my friend." Before the waitress left, one corner of Lise's mouth twitched, and she was talking again. "What man would stay with me? I mean, what if I had a shot at a promotion, had to transfer?"

"I thought you didn't want a husband."

"Other people's are okay. Don't look like that— I'm joking. At work, it's perfect. I get along with the guys and I don't have to give anything up. But you know what happens when I try to see somebody full time? I either can't stand him because he's a sensitive dink and he wants me to run his life, or he's not a dink and he goes for his little controls over me. His stupid little controls."

"So which am I?"

"You're a dink," she laughed. "Look, I'm joking again. Life is compli-cated."

"I know."

"You know diddly."

Their drinks came. She swallowed hers and ordered another. That seemed to wake up the waitress. Outside, a livestock truck rumbled past the window, its tiny side lights warming the coming night like Christmas bulbs on a lonely country store in December.

"They're trying to close," Marc said.

"Let's get a bottle. Let's get a bottle and a room."

"And make the world go away?"

"I can make anything you want go away. Long as you leave before breakfast." She laughed again, the laugh so hollow it sounded as if it could break from its own reverberation in the room.

"God, why do I believe you?"

Her foot stroked the inside of his leg. Toes massaged his inner thigh. She must have slipped off a shoe. He said, "I have to know something... God, what am I doing? No, it's okay, I have to know... what you know about Teresa and her sister."

"I know a little. I can't tell you much."

"Okay, don't. Give me your 'off-the-record' routine."

"Excuse me for living. I am a cop, a good one sometimes. It may surprise you, but we have professional ethics that I stick to when I can. So I can't tell you if there's anything in a file. But I guess I can tell you what I think about those girls. Remember tonight's word, 'whore?'"

"The word I tried to ignore?" He could feel his upper lip curl, taste sour bile in his throat, as he said it.

"I noticed."

"So you're saying she does it for money. What? A drug habit or something? Is that what you're saying? Because I don't believe it."

"I'm saying there are many forms of prostitution. And your little Teresa knows some of them. You trade anything for sex and you're walking the line, you ask me."

"So don't we all trade something for sex? Which makes us all whores. Either I'm missing something or you haven't exactly helped me out here."

"Like us, you mean? Like the whole world's rotten, so what difference does anything make? Look, with her, it's serious shit. Take the word of somebody who knows." Her foot trailed down the inside of one leg and up the other. "She's bad news. She'll pull you under. You're into saving her, but you know what I think? Nobody can."

"You're wrong. And I am getting out of here."

Lise looked away. "Forget it, okay, jerk? You taking me home?"

"I don't have a car. They got me on a pretty questionable impaired."

"So I'm taking you home."

"You can't stay. I'm not ready for that."

"You mean, 'not yet?' Or 'never again?'"

"I mean, if you hear anything about Teresa, you let me know, okay?"

She refused to say anything, including good night, when she let him off in front of his aunt's house.

CHAPTER 13

Marc LePage woke in his cool, stale bedroom with Teresa's phone call from the day before worrying his mind. The red digital numbers on his bedside clock said 6:35 a.m. Feeling confused, he rolled out of bed and sat on the edge, trying not to think about anybody. It didn't work.

He showered, wiped the steam off the bathroom mirror with a bulky white towel and stared at his reflection. With a day's growth of beard and no razor, a moustache that needed trimming, hair too long for a man well into his thirties and a bruised face, he looked more like an aging outcast from a Grateful Dead concert than a newspaper editor.

Calling Lise's place, he left a message that said he cared for her— which he didn't that morning— and took a taxi to the office. The press foreman stopped him in the hallway before Marc got to the editorial area. "You still in charge around here, LePage?"

"For a couple more days," he said.

"That new shopper out of Stettler?"

"Yeah?"

"The one we're starting to print today?"

"Yeah?"

"They don't know their ass from putty. I'm getting pics in here, says shoot 'em a certain percentage, but we shoot 'em at that, I know they ain't gonna fit."

"So what are you going to do about it?"

"What I'd like to do about it would probably cost us the job. You're leaving the paper, I know, but could you give 'em a call, get this thing straightened around?"

"I can try."

The press foreman frowned and went back to work. Marc called, but nobody was yet at work at the shopper in Stettler.

Barb Zelnak had been in the office when he'd arrived that morning. Between them, they had pages rolling to composing ahead of schedule. This was his last paper before she took over as acting editor and publisher or whatever she was going to be. Apparently she knew what was going on, even though nobody from Brownrigg had said a word to Marc. If she— and Klaus Axel and Jordan Hamm— knew about her promotion, that would mean half the staff also knew. Resentment burned in Marc and it was worse than the burning his skin had taken on the pavement early Sunday morning.

At 10:30, Barb poked her head inside his office door. "What am I supposed to do? I can't finish B1 until that new guy, Kenneth, finishes his story. And where's your film from the slowpitch banquet?"

"Welcome to the joys of meeting deadlines. I turned my film in yesterday. So are you running this paper before I get a chance to clean out my desk?"

Ignoring most of Marc's question, Barb rolled her eyes at the condition of his office. "A bulldozer and a week should look after the housecleaning in here. Why's Rollie so slow souping the film?"

"Ask Rollie. Probably drooling over weekend shots of girls suntanning in Beaver Park."

"God," Barb said and left. Marc laughed at her, famous for missing deadlines, changing her tune now that she apparently had a shot at his job.

Marc dialled Teresa's house as soon as Barb had gone. Teresa's mother answered, sounding depressed or hung over or both. Marc asked whether Teresa was there.

"Who?" the woman asked.

"Teresa. Your daughter."

"Just a minute." Marc could hear her yell the name away from the phone. Silence, before Shirley Basiuk came back on the line sounding like a teacher under whom Marc had suffered for a year in elementary school. She had hated him almost as much as she hated her job. "Not here. Maybe she's at school."

"School's out for the summer."

Silence, then her depressed voice. "Oh, yeah. There a message?"

"Tell her to call Marc when she gets home." No answer. He could hear the telephone receiver being hung up at the other end.

He went back to dummying pages. Fifteen minutes later, Carmen paged him: "Marc, line one. Marc."

"Marc LePage, can I help you?"

He could barely hear the voice on the other end of the line.

"Who is this?" he asked. "Teresa?"

"Can you come?" she croaked.

"I'm finishing the paper."

"Can you come?"

"Where are you?"

"The hotel."

"What hotel?"

"They're all gone."

"What?" he said. "Are you stoned?"

"They did it to me."

"Who's 'they?'"

"Can't move..."

"Where are you?"

"Rose..." Teresa said, and for the second time that morning, a Basiuk woman left Marc hanging on the phone. The line was still open. He called Teresa's name. She wouldn't or couldn't answer. Drunk or stoned, he was pretty sure, and now she expected him to do something. Maybe Lise had been right about Teresa and there was nothing anybody could do, but he hated that thought.

The day went downhill after that. Rollie, the darkroom tech, complained about focus problems with a couple of Marc's slowpitch pictures. Page dummying slowed to a crawl. The press foreman wanted to know what to do about the shopper pics. Marc had just settled that when Lise telephoned him. It was early afternoon and Marc still hadn't eaten lunch.

"Babe, there's something you might want to know," Lise said.

"You still love me, after all?"

"Besides that. You better get somebody to drive you to Rose Hill."

He had a premonition of what was coming, and it wasn't a good premonition. "What's happening?"

"Remember how you wanted me to tell you if I heard anything about Ms. Basiuk? There's a report of an overdose. The ambulance is on the way and the Mounties are next."

"Nothing came in here." He corrected himself. "Nothing on the police radio, but maybe everybody's so worried about getting the paper out on time, they turned off the scanner."

Marc made sure Barb could finish the paper and borrowed a Toyota pick-up from one of the men in the pressroom, without mentioning his licence dilemma. The truck didn't protest at going flat out. It was a clear day, little traffic, a perfect day to rev a Japanese four-cylinder to the maximum.

The highway ran due east through grain country— barley and wheat and the occasional canola field bursting with flowers of a violent Vincent van Gogh yellow. He turned south on the road to Rose Hill, the grain broken occasionally by rolling cattle pastures.

Neither the grain nor the canola flowers nor the cattle nor CBC Radio— none of it— could deflect Marc's mind from the guilt gnawing at his belly like a caustic chemical. Why hadn't he done more to find Teresa? He was an idiot. There was always more a person could do.

An ambulance roared by, heading north from Rose Hill. On a hunch, Marc pulled a sharp U-turn and followed it back to Emergency in Crooked Elbow.

As the attendants rolled the stretcher out of the ambulance, Marc saw a mask over Teresa's face, an ambu-bag attached to the mask. She looked young and frail and dead, but he assumed she was still alive or the attendants wouldn't have left the mask over her face.

They wheeled her into Emergency and he followed.

"Excuse me, sir," said a nurse with a white uniform and a pear-shaped body. "Do you know her?"

"Teresa Basiuk, I'm pretty sure."

"Are you part of the family?"

"No. Well, sort of."

"Can you go to the desk, give them information?"

"What, about her?"

"Yes. And if you go to the waiting room, we'll get back to you."

He told the receptionist that he didn't know Teresa's Alberta Health Care number, but he gave her all the other particulars he could think of. She called the number he supplied for Shirley Basiuk. No answer. She said she'd keep trying.

The waiting room had *Maclean's* and *Chatelaine* and a year-old *Parenting* magazine. He tried to read, but the antiseptic smell, the bustling atmosphere, the frail patients in bathrobes panicked him.

Marc became feverishly hot, sweating, his heart hammering in his rib cage. He rubbed at his chest, but he couldn't calm his heart. He had such trouble breathing he left the waiting room.

Shirley Basiuk, wearing too much lipstick, came in as Marc was leaving.

He pretended he didn't see her. His breathing eased as soon as he left the hospital, his sweat cooling in the dry Alberta air.

CHAPTER 14

"You look awful," Barb said when Marc returned to the office from the hospital. Her lipstick that morning had been deep purple, almost black. It was soft pink in the early afternoon.

"I feel worse."

"What happened?" She sounded concerned— and her concern might have been sincere— but she moved quickly to the topic of deadlines. "I did front, but George's been all over us, looking for that dummy you were working on for the B section. Can you see him? The man's wanking out."

"They found a girl. In Rose Hill, I think."

"So?"

"Maybe dying. Maybe dead."

"Whoa! So which is it?"

"I'm not sure... she's probably still alive."

"Anybody we know? Can we get it in this week's paper?"

"I don't think that would work. Somebody said it was a drug overdose."

"Yeah? Let me talk to George, see if we can get it in the front section. We know who it was?"

Marc looked away, at a wall where politicians' photographs had been pasted somewhat randomly among headlines and pictures of animals, interspersed with tabloid clippings. Klaus Axel's head nestled between the thighs of a tabloid starlet. Robbie McLean's face smiled above a dog's body. "Sexual liberation of the grey generation," announced a headline clipped from a newspaper. And from a supermarket tabloid, "Midgets possible."

"Teresa," he said.

"Your little friend? The one who works here? God, I'm sorry. That was... I mean, I heard."

"Why would you care? Especially now."

"Why wouldn't I care?" Her hand found his arm briefly before she moved it away. Her fingers flopped ineffectually in mid-air for a few seconds. "I am sorry. And don't forget George needs you. He's turned into Hyde, the deadline monster."

Marc escaped to his office, lowered the camera bag to the floor, and called Carmen on the telephone intercom. "Can you hold my calls?"

"Sure," she said. "You have messages. Your mail's on your desk. Sorry about the girl." Word travels like a bullet in a newspaper office. Thoughts have wings.

But not Marc's thoughts. His thoughts were weighed down by heavy, pedestrian boots. He moved around his desk to the familiar padded contours of his chair. Resting his elbows on the desk and his forehead in his hands, he closed his eyes, exhausted.

Alberta was sucking the moisture out of him, drying his tear ducts. Or was it simply too early for the tears to well up and spill over, relieving him of his guilt and grief?

Motion might be good, better than sitting in a state of depressed non-grief. Beyond his office, the building hummed with deadline pressure. People hurried. Press units rumbled, ready to print some area weekly newspaper. Press bells rang an urgent message as deadline approached: "You're going to be late. Time to give 'er." How could anyone, with so much to do, give in to grief?

Tobacco and papers bulged from his shirt pocket. Marc worried out some tobacco, rolled a cigarette, went through the lighting motions and inhaled. The cigarette tasted sharp and strong.

The awful thing was, Marc was glad to be alive. That was guilt trip number one, as they had said in his college days.

And guilt trip number two: after so many years in the business, Marc couldn't help himself— he had been tempted to let Barb talk the Mounties into giving her the story. Teresa was an adult, technically, under the laws of the province of Alberta. The paper didn't normally do domestic violence or attempted suicides, if that's what this was. But there was a powerful news angle: two violent incidents in the same family in the same month. "A

Crooked Elbow girl– sister of Stephanie Basiuk, recently killed in a game of chicken near Rose Hill– was discovered in that village..." Reason enough to dust off the First Commandment of the newsroom: "News is what the editor says is news."

Marc was sure somebody or something had gotten to Teresa– perhaps because of her involvement with him. Teresa's attempts to reach him hadn't been the telephone calls of a party animal. They'd been the calls of a desperate young woman. If the paper ran the story of her overdose, maybe somebody would call with more details. That information might help Marc pry loose another chunk of the dirty glue holding this puzzle together.

He groaned and beat the desk with his open palm over and over, pummelling until his hand hurt. Moisture formed at the edges of his eyes. The moisture was close to tears. Damned close.

Too close to finish the paper right now. Let George stew in his own rancorous juices. Marc needed ordinary things to do, things that required no thought and were devoid of emotion. He turned to the mail on one side of his desk, press releases in one pile, dregs of correspondence in another.

"M. LePage, Managing Editor: The 4th Crooked Elbow Scout Patrol would like to express our sincere appreciation..."

Routine misspellings... "Mark Lapage, Publisher: The Optimist Club of Crooked Elbow is hosting its 43rd anniversary banquet and election of officers Saturday July 4 at the Optimist Hall. Would a photographer..."

Buried among these missives were two letters Carmen hadn't opened.

One envelope, he recognized– all upper case, typewriter-style– with a salutation on the outside that was all too familiar. Inside was a single sheet of paper:

```
IF YOU DON'T LEAVE THE GIRL ALONE
YOU'LL FIND TROUBLE CLOSE TO HOME
IF I WERE YOU, I'D BE WISE
AND LEAVE TOWN WITH CLOSED EYES
```

He didn't know what to do with the note. He called Carmen on the telephone intercom, asked her if she'd seen the letter or how it came to the office.

"It was in the overnight mail slot," she said. "Is that okay?"

"Yeah. Sure. No problem," he said.

The other envelope was pink with purple handwriting, addressed to him— Marc LePage, Editor and Publisher, *The Crooked Elbow Sun*— in loopy, regular handwriting. "Personal, Personal," said the bottom left corner of the envelope. This one bore a cancelled stamp of the Queen of England and Canada in the upper right.

Sunday morning

Dearest Marc,

You don't know how much these last few days have meant to me. You can't know. I know your very busy at work and you really don't have time for this, but I wanted you to know that YOU are the BEST THING that has ever, ever happened to me.

How was your head today? I'm starting to feel pretty normal. At least as normal as I get!! I didn't even get out of bed till ten. It's my summer schedule— sun, sand, and sleepin' in. (Maybe a little sin, but only with you, my darling)!

Please don't worry about my drinking, although I know that you do. I only do that once in a while. And it is only for fun.

I'm going to "a party" tonight. You are not invited. So I don't want to go, but "they" say I have to. I just want you to know for sure that I DO NOT WANT TO GO. I'm going because I have to and if I can ever blow this Popsicle stick town, there'll be no more of that. I may not be able to phone you, but I'll be thinking of you.

This is pretty weird, you know, writing to somebody who's a writer for a newspaper. I hope it is all spelled correctly and I'll see you next week.

No matter how you spell it, I KNOW that I LUV U.

Come see me when the paper gets out.

A thousand kisses

XXXXOOOO
Teresa

Marc folded the letter and stuffed it in his shirt pocket behind his tobacco. He tried to make a connection that added up to something. How did the tone of the letter fit with the phone call from Teresa and what he'd witnessed outside Emergency?

He couldn't make sense of it. Marc wandered in his sideways fashion into the composing room. George glowered at him from behind his steel desk, arms folded in front of him.

"Spare me, George," Marc said. "I know we're running late. Something came up."

"Seems like certain people always got something coming up. Something's been coming up every week for years and it got no better when they brought you in. If it ain't the grocery ad, it's the dummies being late. But I guess that's about to change, when, next week?"

"Sorry."

"Sorry don't put papers on the street."

Marc turned his back on the man and bent over a layout table, checking the front page. "THE 'BIGGEST MAN IN CROOKED ELBOW' WANTS THE BIGGEST JOB" said the lead headline. The story said Klaus Axel had announced his intention to run for mayor that fall.

Reporter Adrienne Brindall had asked Klaus whether he was announcing early so he could ward off any potential competitors.

"The early bird gets the worm," Klaus was quoted as saying. "But I've never been one to stand in the way of the democratic process. I look forward to, indeed encourage, people to get in on the action."

And did he know whether the incumbent, Mayor Person, was running again?

"I can't speak for the mayor, but I understand he's making progress with the cure in Sweden."

Barb had composed a front-page editorial which was nothing like the outline Marc had given her: his last newspaper, and the editorial in it was a piece of gutless fawning.

"Good for the community," said the headline.

"The agricultural society is responsible for the new Agriplex, including its operational budget," Barb had written. "The society, the province, and the city are jointly funding the capital side. That's over $5 million being pumped into the local economy in the coming year.

"There's a commitment of over $2 million from the city alone.

"This is the kind of financial involvement and leadership that will put Crooked Elbow on the provincial map in the years ahead.

"The project has been discussed for 10 years. The speed with which it has recently moved is a credit to the leadership of people like planning committee chairman Robbie McLean and recently announced mayoralty candidate Klaus Axel.

"If this marriage of private and public enterprise is the kind of thing we can expect from our civic leaders, more power to them."

"This is one flowery piece of crap," Marc told George. "Hold the flat until I find Barb."

Barb was in the coffee room, sitting with Tony, the Mountie. Fiona sat opposite them. "God," Fiona said to Tony. "Poster boy at the academy? Doesn't surprise me."

"Nice editorial, Barb. I'm pulling it."

"You can't. We're past deadline," Barb said.

"I gotta go," Fiona said, smoothing her purple skirt back down over her knees. "Places to go. People to see."

Tony and Fiona left together. Marc said, "My name is still on the masthead. And as long as it's there, we're not running that editorial."

"Then I guess we'll have to pull your name."

"What?"

"Look, Marc, I used to work for you and I respect your journalistic integrity. But not your judgement. Your name may be on the masthead for one more week, but you don't own the paper."

"What the hell does that mean?"

"One call to Edmonton will settle this. They warned me that you might react exactly as you are."

"What's the use? Forget it," Marc said. "Save the company the long distance call to Edmonton. I don't suppose any of this is the result of a friendly chat— or one of those famous lunches— with Klaus Axel?"

"Fuck off and die, okay, Marc? I work for Brownrigg, not you. My loyalties lie with the company, not with some lefty and his misguided ideas about what a community newspaper should be. What was it you used to say when you were mad at a local politician who didn't meet the Politburo's standards? 'Don't argue with a man who buys his ink by the pail.' Maybe you should take your own advice."

Marc called the city police station and asked for Lise. In a voice that wasn't any improvement over the last time he'd called, the receptionist agreed to page her. While Marc waited, he sorted some news releases and gave them to the new reporter, Kenneth, to edit so he wouldn't have to talk to Barb.

"Marc, line one," said Carmen's voice over the intercom.

Punching a button, he said, "Marc LePage. Good afternoon."

Lise's voice. "Hey, big guy, what's shaking?"

"A few things," he said. "Can I see you?"

"I'm on duty. You fit better in my off-hours' calendar."

"Yeah, well this is important."

"Okay, I'll ditch my partner, old Dougie the sluggie here, and we'll do coffee. You and me, 20 minutes, the wrought-iron chairs of the Emporium."

Marc admired the way Lise took on a room when she was in a good mood: the sharp thud of her boots hitting the floor, the authority in her hips, the way she looked everybody in the eye, throwing out a challenge: okay, I'm here and what're you going to do about it?

"Coffee. Cream, no sugar," she said. Marc got it for her, plus one double-double for himself and a doughnut. Lise didn't want a doughnut. She was watching her weight.

"Somebody new in your life?" Marc asked.

"Yeah, a 19-year-old bodybuilder with a passion for Mahler. I like my Romantics with stomach muscles that ripple."

"You serious?"

"What do you think? Anybody besides you and me in this town know

Mahler, lover? And I didn't, till I met you. By the way, your face is healing, but I've seen you look better."

"You were right about Teresa. I followed the ambulance back to town."

"So she tried sleeping pills, the coward's way out. You want sympathy? The poor thing. You're better off without her."

"You're pissing me off. I'm low on sleep."

"Sorry." Lise didn't sound sorry.

The mention of sleep made Marc more tired. He was losing it. Lise was Lise. Why lose his temper at her for being herself?

"When I got back to the office, Barb Zelnak was running an editorial extolling the virtues of Robbie McLean and Klaus Axel, under my name. I can't believe anybody would stoop so low."

"Couldn't you stop it?"

"I tried, but Barb apparently now reports directly to Jeremy Brown in Edmonton. All I have to do is be a good boy until Friday. God, I wasn't thinking. I should have taken Barb's advice— told George to take my name off the masthead before they sent the editorial page to press."

"Those bastards," Lise said.

"Yeah. Do you know any more?" Marc asked. "About it?"

It. His upper lip trembled. He was dangerously close to letting it out.

Lise's coffee cup was in front of her face, a barrier between them, when she answered. "Off the record. Very unofficially. Somebody... you know that guy who's only half there and walks all over Rose Hill with a cigar he never lights? He found Teresa lying behind the Wild Rose Cafe and called it in from a pay phone in the lobby. I didn't know he had the brains."

"So what's the word on Teresa? Is she going to be okay?"

"Hard to say. It's one of those teen things."

The remains of Marc's doughnut littered his plate. "One of those teen things. But there'll be an investigation. Unlike Stephanie," he said.

"What's that supposed to mean?"

"It means 'unlike Stephanie.' It means that nobody checked out Stephanie."

"She got in a car half snapped, and she crashed into some guy in the same condition. What's to check out?"

"Who was the car registered to?"

"Pierre Trudeau? I don't know. To what car might we be referring, lover boy?"

"Stephanie's car."

"Stephanie Basiuk, far as I know."

"I don't think so. We went and had a look at it, Teresa and I. She pointed out a couple of things. The crack appeared to start on the passenger side of the windshield. And Teresa said Steph didn't have the money for a car like that."

"Maybe somebody gave it to her. Maybe she blackmailed it out of them. Lots of people in Crooked Elbow owed Stephanie, or might have thought they did."

Marc lowered his voice and leaned toward Lise, catching her perfume. "We're not talking people here, are we? We're talking men."

Marc looked away. Afternoon coffee time. The Emporium was filling up. Farmers in caps and cowboy hats and jean jackets. Business people in suits. Seniors wearing whatever they felt like wearing that day. A man in a business suit carried a laughing little girl on his shoulders between the chairs and tables, set her down in a booth and sat beside her.

Lise looked through Marc, staring at the man and the tiny girl so hard that Marc turned to look.

"My cousin, Janet, was only a little kid when she came to live with us. My mother had this man, this 'stepfather'... He never had a job. He stayed home and 'took care' of Janet..." Lise's words tumbled into space, half mumbled.

"Lise."

"I was 15. I got out. I didn't have to take any of that shit. I never will." Her voice came back, shakily. "Will you love me forever?"

Marc didn't answer. The room looked harsh in the summer light; across the street, the sky was impossibly blue above the false fronts of stores, bright with awnings.

"Will you come away with me again? Soon?"

Marc didn't answer that, either.

"Will you do something with me? Anything?" Lise sounded slightly hysterical, not like herself. "Buy me a drink?"

"Yeah, I'll buy you a drink. I'll buy you a bucket and we can both drown in it. Now will you do me a favour and look up the registration on that Trans Am?"

"You do like me? Note that he didn't say 'No.' Which is almost 'Yes.' I don't have to look it up. It was registered to a McLean. And I should not be doing this, lover."

"*Robbie* McLean? So why wasn't this reported?"

"You didn't hear it from me... It was Bobby."

"Who is?"

"Who is Robbie's son. Which is... still chicken. She was the driver. Two people dead. Nobody at fault. Case closed."

"'Prominent local politician's son owns car that kills two people.' That's something for our doughnut shop cops to check out."

"Sure, pump me for information, then insult me and my hard-working partners."

A very old woman with a black dress, black shoes, black hat, black veil, and a black, bitter expression pulled out a chair to sit down. Bumping Marc, she told him, "Some people are trying to eat a bite in peace."

"Sorry," he said, and to Lise. "So why didn't the locals do more to investigate the accident?"

"It was a rich boy's car. So what? Stephanie had tried out more cars in town than the GM dealer. Who, by the way, might challenge our friend Klaus for mayor. Robbie McLean sits on the police commission, which Klaus Axel happens to chair. We're not going to start making accusations unless there's pretty solid evidence to go on. Half the people in town are in hock to those two."

"Even you?"

"Maybe." Lise's eyes darted around the room.

"What's that mean?"

For a space of time so small that he almost missed it, Lise looked sad. The sadness turned just as quickly to anger and she lashed out at Marc. "Nothing. I'm a cop..."

"So what?" he objected. "You are supposed to uphold the law. If you knew about the car, you had to act on that knowledge. And if you had, maybe Teresa would still be all right."

"Keep your voice down," Lise hissed at him. "Everybody's looking at us."

"I don't care. You make me so mad, I could..."

"Come outside with me." Lise picked up her hat and shoved it on her head. "C'mon," she said when he wasn't getting up.

Marc stood and followed her outside to a bright, hot 50th Street. His mind was in a still state, a place of insensible rage where he didn't care what people thought or what he did. They were near her cruiser, but he didn't notice it until she said, "I can't help what happened to Teresa."

When Marc didn't reply, Lise gave him an order, as if this were a routine arrest. "Get in the car."

He followed her command. They drove to Tim Hortons. She parked and said, "I'll instruct Dougie to cool his heels and drink coffee till I get back to him. I like him. He does exactly what I say."

"And what are we going to do?" Marc's anger was less intense, shifting from that still, inner place which he didn't trust back toward irony and self-pity. More usual states for him.

"We're going to my place."

"While you're on duty? What happened to Ms. Champlain, the professional?"

"I'll leave Dougie the portable radio and my phone number. What are the chances of somebody robbing a bank in this town in the next hour?"

"About as high as a murder being reported. Or a rape called in."

"There's a bigger chance of that," she said. "You wait and see."

With the air conditioning on high, she drove the police cruiser to her apartment. Heat waves shimmered on the asphalt as the car drifted toward her parking space. When the car had stopped she said, "Come with me."

Marc's answer was to get out, follow her lead, up to her apartment. He was neither happy nor sad to be doing it. It was numbness he felt, coupled with sorrow and guilt over what he'd seen at the hospital and what Lise had told him.

She ordered him to get in the shower with her. He did.

When she told him to follow her to the bedroom, he did that, too. And laid himself face down on the bed when he was instructed to do so. She massaged him vigorously— his back, his legs, his hips, his feet— like an athletic masseuse, reducing him to putty in her hands.

When she told him to roll over, it was a new experience for him, being naked with her when they were both sober. She slapped his face, his chest, emitting tiny sounds with each slap. Fitting him with a condom, she rammed herself on him in a strangling embrace, smothering him with her breasts. The ebb and flow of his anger was overtaken and negated by some terrible rising need of hers— to dominate and to connect with him. At first, Marc resisted. But resisting was no good. Lise was so strong and his own need for human contact so great that he lost himself in her.

At the height of their wild, angry ride, right after he allowed her to take complete control, his mind and body found simultaneous release. Tears— the ones that had refused to come at the office— discovered unblocked paths and streamed from his eyes. He cried out, and the final shreds of his anger washed out with his tears. His throat and ears ached, but he welcomed the aching as symbolic of the pity and sorrow he felt for himself and for Teresa. It was like the passionate encounter a newly widowed man might share with his wife's best friend the day of the funeral. A helpless grappling with the knowledge that his beloved will never again share a moment like this with any man on this earth.

CHAPTER 15

Sex with Lise had solved nothing for Marc. The next morning, at his own place, he felt renewed tuggings of responsibility toward her. But he also felt uneasy stirrings in another direction. His sad, hedonistic time with Lise felt like a betrayal of the 18-year-old languishing in hospital.

Wednesday, July 1, Canada Day, Marc was in anything but a holiday frame of mind. As the morning wore on, his guilt sharpened until it was eating at him so strongly, he knew he had to make an effort to see Teresa.

Marc walked to St. Jude's Hospital, built in 1911 on a grassy piece of property sloping down to the river, and entered through front doors massive as a church's.

He was asking the receptionist for Teresa's room number when his heart started thumping in his chest— loudly and with alarming speed. He was so suspicious of what this malicious organ was up to that he stopped in mid-sentence. The receptionist instantly developed the face of a young woman about to help a disabled person. "Yes?" she encouraged him. "Are you okay?"

"I'm okay," he said as calmly as he could. "Need some air."

"Are you a reporter? Is that it?" she asked, nodding to Marc's camera equipment.

Barely managing a nod in reply, he hurried out the doors and down the steps, where he sucked in huge, sweet gulps of air. Somewhere on the long walk between the hospital and downtown, his heart reestablished its normal rhythms.

Downtown was choked with people for the Canada Day parade. Leading the procession were thick-thighed girls doing cartwheels. Marc shot film. Their sequined panties sparkled like nickels tumbling from a Vegas slot machine.

More of the parade swept past him, loud and commercial. Marc pivoted to get a picture of a girl in a wheelchair clutching a balloon in one hand and her mother's hand in the other.

As his shutter clicked, a wave of water struck Marc's back. Turning awkwardly on his heels, he confronted a float filled with county politicians dressed as Maritime fisherwomen and perched in a long, white fishing boat. "What the Jesus!" Marc said, hunching his shoulders against a second wave of water. It never came.

"Gotcha," shouted the county reeve, dipping another bucket of water and hurling it at somebody else in the crowd.

A black Model T Ford rattled by, then six classic cars, the last one a red 1965 Mustang convertible. Its top was down and the sides of the car were decorated with signs that said: "Support the Agricultural Society and the New Agriplex." In smaller type: "Car Donated by the McLean Family & Driven by Bobby McLean." The convertible swerved side-to-side on the parade route, parodying the Shriners who followed on miniature bikes.

The Mustang swerved at Marc, its front fender brushing his pant leg. "Need to see you later, man," said the driver through the open driver's window. He'd been the one limboing with Teresa the night of the slowpitch dance.

Marc rolled away, slamming his palm against a fire hydrant so he didn't tip over. Righting himself, he ran after the car— camera bag and jacket over his shoulder— and vaulted over the passenger door of the convertible into a bucket seat.

"You're Bobby, right?" Marc said.

The driver looked at him and grinned. "What the fuck are you doing? You'll get the seat wet, man. I said I'd see you later."

"A new angle... the crowd from a parade entry. Just what the *Sun* needs, man." Marc grinned at Bobby, catching his breath, shivering a little.

"Hey, get the fuck out. You're ruining the upholstery, that wet shirt," Bobby said, smiling the whole time at the crowd, waving.

Marc waited until the convertible had swung right up to the crowd before he took a picture, using the wide angle for easy focus, people jumping in his lens. Girls in fringed leather jackets and tight jeans screamed at Bobby as if daring him to come closer. When he did, they crammed into each other, laughing and shouting and crowding the people behind them.

"Foxy little bitches," Bobby said. "Looking for a good poke."

"This driving strike you as a little dangerous?"

"Nah. They love it. Now why don't you get your ass out, old man? I'll see you after the parade. Cruising with hippie peace freaks... not my style."

A girl about 13 thrust her breasts, barely contained in a red halter top, at the camera. "Wanna get laid?" a friend of hers screamed. Marc could hardly believe his ears, but he was sure that's what she'd said.

"What's the world coming to?" he asked Bobby.

"Yeah, ain't it great? My advice? Get 'em before they're 16. 'Fore they start thinking."

Bobby waved to three old people slouched in aluminum lawn chairs in a vacant lot. An old man in brown shirt and black pants, face jaundiced by age and bad health, wearing very dark glasses, raised an aluminum cane in return. Bobby waved again, smiling, the politician's son.

Lowering his arm, his hand a fist, Bobby clubbed Marc on the shoulder. "You like to bother people? Or you got something else up your ass?" he said, grinning the whole time.

"That hurt." Marc rubbed his shoulder. A man in sunglasses and a fez, driving a mini-bike, puttered up, waved to them and dropped back to join his Shriner buddies.

"Yeah?" Bobby hit him again on the same shoulder, harder. The parade swung away from downtown, toward the elevators. A Palomino horse danced past them, hooves clopping hollowly on the pavement. A woman in white buckskin bounced on the tooled saddle, her leather pants smoothly clearing the horse on the downswing of each trot.

"Want to tell me about the car?"

"'65 Mustang. Red with white interior, my daddy's pride and joy. Next to me." Bobby stared straight ahead, at the woman and the horse.

"You don't sound too happy about it."

"Yeah, well, there's a Mercedes parked in the driveway. Why do I get this piece of junk? It don't fool me, this classic car shit. The babes, they relate more to a Mercedes. Not that I blame 'em."

"What about the Trans Am?" Marc kept on shooting with the camera, pretending this was an everyday occurrence, riding around with BM2's son, taking crowd shots.

"What're we talking about? This is a Mustang, dude, proud member of the Ford family."

"Not this car, the other one. The Trans Am. How'd the chicks respond to the Trans Am?"

"The chicks? Can't say, daddy-o. But I'd say the babes go for a Trans Am. I've done okay. But they could say the same, the way they act. You might say we sometimes get mutually lucky."

"Especially if they're under 16. I don't suppose you know or care that women were declared persons by parliament over 50 years ago?"

"You know what I learned from women in my history class? Never say never." This was a big joke. Bobby laughed, his mouth gaping open.

The parade entries got tired and wound themselves down, heading toward the elevator grounds to be dismantled. A man in a white cowboy hat, blue official's ribbon flapping on his chest, waved at Bobby and Marc, "Keep left. Left."

Bobby squeezed past the cowboy traffic guard on the right, grinning, flicking a middle finger at him. Narrowly missing the man, he slid the car through a shallow ditch and pumped the gas pedal. The engine roared, tires spun. They fishtailed back onto the road and turned down a quiet side street, bypassing the rest of the parade.

"You going to get anywhere, you got to do things a little different. That's what my daddy always says."

"So what happened to the Trans Am you had?"

"Totalled."

"You driving?"

"Don't be an idiot. Me, I totalled a car, they wouldn't let me drive for a year. You seen the insurance on this stuff?"

"So who was driving?"

The Mustang slammed to a stop on the grass in front of a high wire fence protecting a concrete mix factory on the edge of the wartime housing. A loader ran its bucket along the pavement, heading for a gravel pile. Stones squealed between the metal bucket and the pavement.

"How'd you like to get the fuck out?"

"Stephanie was at the bar in Rose Hill. So were you. You let her take your car. She'd been drinking. And pow, no more Trans Am."

"Good for the car industry, right, man? They should pay us for action like that. A major purchase program every time somebody trashes one. Yeah, I like that idea a lot."

"So you let her take your car. How'd you get home?"

"Dear old dad. Later. He and some of his buddies ended up at the Rose like they always seem to on the weekend. I hitched a ride with him."

"Have I got this right? You lent a new muscle car to a girl that's not your girlfriend or anything?"

"Muscle car?"

Marc was getting tired of Bobby and his mouth. "Okay, erase. What-ever. Why'd you do it?"

"I don't know. She was a girl you could cut a deal with. Had a thing about fast machinery. With her, opportunity knocked fairly regular, know what I mean? Wing nights at The Victoria, I've seen her in and out of the parking lot two, three times. Guys with cars, guys with bikes. Stephanie was like that, and Teresa, well, birds of a feather, peas in a pod, what can I say? A favour to one was guaranteed nooky in the bank in other directions."

"Teresa was nothing like that. And you're a jerk for saying it, especially now that she's unconscious in a hospital bed."

Bobby grinned at Marc, the grin of a conspirator. "Cool your jets. Think what you like, dad— nobody forced nobody here. They decide to repay favours, great. They don't, no problem. That's their loss. They never get to know Bobby McLean, what a sweet ride he can be."

Bobby worked one knee up to the console, hooked it half across the gear shift, stretching his jeans, a cool cowboy ready to head uptown.

"So what about the windshield?"

"You lose me, dad."

"What about the crack, starting on the passenger side?"

"I don't follow you. My daddy buys the car. A demo with a little stone chip. Half the cars in Alberta got one. The babe borrowed my car and got herself dead. End of story."

Marc thought he might get more from Bobby, if he had the stomach to sit around stroking his ego until it ran out his mouth. Instead, he asked for a ride back.

"Yeah, I'll give you a ride." Bobby looked at Marc with dead eyes. Straightening his legs, Bobby bent over, groping under the seat.

"I got more than a ride for you, pal." He came up fast with a tire iron. Rubbing the metal bar gently against the soft part under Marc's chin, Bobby grinned at him with blank coyote eyes. "Funny coincidence, you jumping into my car back there, 'cause I was supposed to pick you up. You got a lunch date and the man don't like it if you're late."

Clawing at the arm that held the iron, Marc moved it away, but not far. The kid was strong. Marc held on tight, the iron a couple of inches from his Adam's apple. If he let go, he was afraid the tire iron would snap back, puncturing his throat. Bobby might get a kick out of that.

"All right," Marc said in a strained voice. "I give up. Let go."

The kid grinned at him, lowered the tire iron to the bucket seat and left it there as a threat. His crotch bulged in his tight jeans. Marc noticed that and was sickened by the idea that Bobby found bullying and violence stimulating.

"You like this, don't you, you little bastard?" Marc said.

"We're outta here," Bobby yelled, grinning. "Rip them signs off."

They ripped the parade signs from his car, leaving them in the ditch. The back tires spun gravel and burned rubber when the car hit pavement, Bobby laughing like a kid who's found a fresh fly with wings he can slowly peel off.

CHAPTER 16

"**W**ait'll you see this... man's home is a castle," Bobby shouted. Hot air whipped around the convertible's windshield, fluttering and growling in Marc's ears.

They breezed past spruce and pine and poplar posted at regular intervals with signs that read: "No Trespassing. Violators Will Be Prosecuted." The pavement ended. Bobby drove fast and the dust followed them just as quickly. What did he think, that if he slowed down, Marc would jump out? No chance of that: as nervous as he was around Bobby after the tire iron incident, Marc wanted to see where this was going.

Through the trees, a meadow-sized lawn appeared, the road oiled in front of it. The edges of the lawn were neatly clipped right up to a one-sided ditch, with weeds in it, running down to the road. In the centre of the well-trimmed meadow stood a large, white fountain with a basin. Near the top of the fountain, the concrete penis of a concrete cupid spouted water into the open mouth of a concrete fish.

A guard dog patrolled a pen near an entrance on the far side of the property. Thin lips white with slobber, the dog barked at them from behind heavy wire fencing of the sort normally used to enclose school children and hydro installations and prisoners. The animal ran at the fence as if it could get through, hit it, bounced off, whimpered and started over.

"Shud up, dog," snapped a man polishing the Jaguar, parked in front of a hut beside the dog run. The man looked as if he'd stepped out of a sumo wrestling match and into pants as black and shiny as the pants of a funeral director having a bad year. His polished shoes were black, his ruffled shirt white and his tie bright, bright red. A scar, running from one tiny eye to his jutting jaw, spoiled the left side of his face. He lumbered toward the Mustang, a chamois balled in his fist.

"Mr. Axel here, Jeeves?" Bobby asked over the door of the Mustang.

The man leaned against a free-standing sign engraved in Olde English type: "K. Axel Enterprises: Anybody Can Be Ordinary." Large enough to raise questions of hormone problems in his youth or steroid injections later, the guard made the Jaguar and the guardhouse and Marc LePage seem small. "He's here and expecting you. Missus, she's out. The maid, she's here, and some broad. Shud the fuck up, dog. Sid. Lay down."

The dog didn't like it, but it lay down on the dirt and licked a front paw. It eyed Marc as if daring him to jump out of the Mustang, fence or no fence.

Bobby said, "Open the gate, Jeeves," and the man did. "Thank you. Carry on," Bobby said insolently, and the man's eyes narrowed until no pupils showed under the bony protrusions he had for a forehead. His right fist clenched and unclenched on the chamois.

The driveway, like the front ditch, was defined by two inches of manicured grass edge. The lawn flowed from this edge, blue-green, over a slight rise where sprinklers pulsed. Opposite the fourth sprinkler, the asphalt widened and curved toward a five-car garage designed more like a riding stable than a building for housing vehicles. A tan Cadillac flecked with gold raised the value of the neighbourhood in front of the garage. The real riding stable was in a field behind all this, and beyond that stretched dark brown fences and clipped knolls where horses grazed.

The main house erupted from a grove of poplar trees off to the left, on a high piece of land with lawn and bush behind it.

"I've been moving in the wrong circles," Marc said.

"Not bad, eh, for a guy who started bootlegging in high school. Axel's a positive role model in my life."

The building materials for the British-style mansion were neither indigenous to Alberta nor cheap. Flat grey stones, or a good imitation, covered the outside walls. Long, narrow windows, bordered by intricate shutters, broke the monotony of these walls. A turret rose in one corner.

"You coming in?" Marc asked Bobby when the car stopped by the front door.

"Been here before, man. I got things to do, so I'll just drop you off. You and Santa Klaus can work it out your own selves about the ride home. I'm no fuckin' cabbie and you can tell BM1 I said so."

Marc slammed the car door shut behind him. "If you're not a cabbie, what are you?"

"A waste of skin." Bobby McLean grinned, popped the gear shift into drive and tore around the circular lane by the house. He roared past Jeeves at the guard house in less than 15 seconds.

A pair of concrete lions defended each side of a heavy wooden front door boasting a large brass knocker in the middle and an ordinary doorbell off to the side. Marc pressed the doorbell and chimes rose and fell inside— bong, bong, bong, bong— like the bells on Parliament Hill in Ottawa.

An old woman in a black dress and white frilled apron answered, her hair white, her face rouged. "Ye-e-e-s?" she said, drawing the word out in a question.

"Hello. I believe Klaus is expecting me."

The maid looked at Marc's camera equipment. "You must be that nice young man who's been doing such a good job with the paper."

"Nice young man, that would be me. Thank you, I think."

She swung the door wider and swept a hand to one side, inviting him in. The front hallway was as wide as a church vestibule, the floor covered in linoleum patterned after Italian tiles. Marc and the maid padded past various doors opening onto assorted rooms— a study, a children's den, a room with a pool table and a stuffed buffalo head. Just past the buffalo room, a staircase wound its way to a landing topped by an enormous, curved skylight.

The old woman hop-stepped ahead of him in time to slide open an aluminum and glass door, ushering him into a hot, fenced area. A woman bounced on a diving board, dove into a pool. An inner tube and a water mattress rocked in the wake of her dive. She swam to the end and jackknifed herself out of the pool, slick as a seal.

Marc smiled. "Hello," he said.

"Hi." She had equine teeth, the kind orthodontists give people with fat cheque books or excellent insurance plans. Her bikini bottom slanted above the tan line of one saucy cheek, but she didn't bother to snap it back down.

There was enough time for Marc to appreciate this and no more before she paused at poolside, thrust her hands in front of her and again dove into chlorinated depths.

She stayed under a long time. Marc thought of Teresa in a hospital bed and wondered whether the poor girl was still breathing.

"Pshaw," the old woman whispered. Her false teeth clicked wetly.

"You don't like her?"

Instead of answering, the maid pasted a smile on her face and led Marc to Klaus Axel's table. Klaus wore a white velour robe with a dark K/A insignia embroidered on the pocket. He was scanning a newspaper, or pretending to, under a white, mesh umbrella that shielded him— and three white chairs and a white table and a sweating beer in a tall slim glass— from the sun.

"Mr. Axel. Your lunch guest is here."

Klaus didn't look up from his paper. Marc balanced his jacket on one arm and stood near the table, sweating.

"May I join you?" Marc finally asked, keeping the irony out of his voice. Pulling out a white plastic chair, he flipped his jacket over the back and sat down.

Klaus set the paper on the table. He'd been perusing the comics page of *The Edmonton Sun*.

"A beer? Of course you will. Emily, would you be so kind?" Klaus smiled. He seemed friendlier than at any other time Marc had seen him, his voice steady, his words carefully enunciated.

The woman nodded and shuffled away.

The diver crept up on Klaus from behind, wrapped her arms around his neck and, leaving wet patches on his velour robe, exhaled in his ear. Nipping one of Klaus's earlobes between her too-white teeth, she wiggled her head back and forth. "What about me?" she murmured. "Don't I get a beer?"

Pulling her forward until the back of his head rested against her bikini top, Klaus raised her arm, studying her waterproof wrist watch for a few seconds. "You know how you get when you drink. And we have to get you out of here by what? 3:00?"

The woman put a little pout and a lot of little girl in her voice. "Can't I stay?"

"Yeah, and get me divorced, then see where we're at." Klaus winked lewdly at Marc and slapped the woman's buttocks as she padded away, retracing the wet spots she'd left on the tiles with her tiny perfect feet.

"Ain't she a doll? I just love her. Our little secret, okay?"

Emily brought beer bottles in a champagne bucket jammed with ice. Marc's glass was frosted and the beer in it so good it made him shiver.

"Cheers," Klaus said and smiled. The woman cleared the side of the pool again. "I suppose you wonder why I brought you here."

"Hadn't occurred to me. I'm used to being scooped up suddenly and transported to strange places."

Klaus loosened his robe. Unruly greying hair matted his tanned torso like the coat of a lynx. He wore a single strand of gold around his neck. Slurping a mouthful of beer delicately, he let it roll around in his mouth and swallowed. "A-a-a-ah," he said, picking up the thread of conversation. "Astral projection. Teleportation. Peter's had similar experiences."

"Who?"

"Peter." As if any rational human being would understand the reference.

Marc let that pass. His beer glass was empty, and he refilled it from one of the bottles sweating for him in the netted shade of the white umbrella. "Nice place you have here."

A muddy shadow floated across the cream-coloured tiles. A hawk, gliding on currents of air above, swooped down for its prey.

Watching it dive for the kill, Marc repeated himself. "Nice place you have here."

"We like it. It's comfortable," Klaus said, with a long wink, his attention returning immediately to his beer. "I sometimes have trouble believing it myself, how we live now. Anne's father started us, of course; it was his land got me going. And a lot of good people helped along the way. That's all it takes to build something— hard work and good people."

Marc nodded toward the woman smoothing suntan lotion on her legs and lowered his voice. "Isn't she a threat to all that? Your wife's not here, you've declared your intention to run for mayor and your mistress..."

The index finger of Klaus's right hand rose. Demanding silence. Marc quit talking and went back to his beer. "You suppose a lot for a journalist. She might be my mistress, old-fashioned word. Or she might be my niece, or a friend of my wife's from the club. These things, guy, you suppose, but you do not know. You may also be ignorant of how it is for a man when he marries an older woman. But I bore you. Yes, we have done well. And I have done well, not least of all to control this..."— he raised his glass to the sky where the hawk had reappeared— "...in ways my father never could. The war destroyed some men, you know. And our lunch is here."

Lunch came under a stainless steel cover, on a platter which the old woman placed carefully on a side table. She served Klaus first, then Marc. Steak, medium rare, on a slice of thick garlic toast. Baked potato heavy with sour cream and chives and bacon bits. Caesar salad, the dressing whipped up by the woman while they started their steaks.

"What about her?" the maid asked, jerking a salad spoon toward the short woman stretched out on a lounge chair, eyes obscured by dark glasses.

A wink again for Marc's benefit. "She's dieting. Not a bad idea for petite people, though I think she'll go for some salad. People who don't eat, they end up with flat stomachs and bad breath. I hate bad breath in a woman. She'll work it off. Go on, take her some. I gotta pee."

Klaus stood to walk toward the house, and Marc knew then that his host was very drunk. Klaus' movements were as carefully articulated as the words he'd been using, occasionally with unpredictable results. The tie for his robe swung loose as he walked. Try as he might, Klaus couldn't quite swing it back into position before he reached the sliding doors to the house.

When Klaus returned, seeming steadier, the two men ate quietly in the white glare of a timeless afternoon, eons removed from office routine and small city politics and girls lying drugged and helpless in hospitals.

"That was good." Marc shoved away his plate. He didn't mind if he tried another beer. Klaus had eaten very little and was already drinking again.

"Something you could get used to? The way I see things, enjoy them while they last. You never know. They can come crashing down pretty fast."

"I decided a long time ago I was never going to be rich. Didn't even want to try. Hope I wasn't kidding myself."

"Admirable, I'm sure. But do you have any plans? I mean, you're an editor, but that's coming to an end." Klaus belched as if big burps were a joke and wiped his mouth with a white cloth napkin.

Marc looked away. The woman's salad seemed to be attracting more flies than attention. One bronzed knee bent, she relaxed in spoiled, ripe contentment, a hand across her forehead. "I have no idea. Maybe I'll get another job at a newspaper. Or I'll try freelancing, and if worse comes to worst, PR."

Sweet, iced, after-lunch liqueurs arrived without Klaus signalling for them. "There you are, guy. I'd like to follow up on that, get you to think about something. We're a growing organization. Axel Enterprises is a lot more than insurance and real estate."

"I've noticed." Marc sipped a liqueur. It was so sweet, his back teeth ached.

"We're into land acquisitions and the gasohol thing and the Agriplex.

Thanks for that editorial, by the way. The land and the organization, that's where I come in, it seems. The organization."

"Yeah," Marc said, sleepily.

"That'll be all, Emily," Klaus said.

The old woman bowed and left. Marc finished his liqueur and noticed there was a full glass beside it. Tiny feet slapped the tiles behind him. A hand cuffed the back of his neck. "Just relax," a cool voice whispered. Strong fingers massaged his trapezius muscles. The massage, bringing back memories of the day before, felt so good, he closed his eyes.

"The publicity side has been my short suit. That's where I'd like you to come in. Specially now that I'm going to be mayor." Words, slurring slightly the more Klaus drank, hummed around Marc, lazy locusts devouring a neighbour's field. "Cigar?"

"Thanks." Marc leaned forward and the woman's fingers leaned with him, kneading, kneading. When Marc settled back, his head moulded itself to some hot, comfortable part of her body. "Let's me and you go swimming some time," he said.

Klaus exhaled cigar smoke, slowly, and watched it drift toward the pool. "You got your journalistic principles, I understand that. I'm part of the Watergate generation. We know what journalism did for the States. We'd never ask you to compromise your principles. And there'd be benefits. There's a nice suite above the garage, near Brian's, two bedrooms. Brian, you probably met out by the gate. There's parties, women, booze."

Klaus winked at Marc and Marc winked back, a big one, scrunching up the left side of his face, wondering if even Klaus Axel in his cups could miss sarcasm so broad. "I thought his name was Jeeves. And I don't think so."

"What?"

"Thanks for thinking of me, but I can't see myself in your organization."

"Think about it some more. You wouldn't have to leave town." Klaus swallowed his second liqueur at a gulp and stood, steadying himself by grabbing the stem of the table umbrella. His efforts sent a liqueur glass crashing to the tiles.

"Shit," Klaus said. "Leave it. The help will get it... Don't be stupid. You want your crummy little apartment or you want this?"

Opening his robe like the wings of a huge bird, Klaus stumbled around the pool area, spinning slowly in a circle, so Marc could appreciate the house, the pool, the woman. And the land and buildings and horses and automobiles beyond the pool fence. A skimpy black bathing suit was all that Klaus wore under his white robe.

"Thanks for lunch." Marc stood, picking up his camera bag. The woman padded away from him, toward the pool.

"Don't be stupid," Klaus said again.

"I'm not," Marc said.

"Then you better get out. You piece of..." Klaus's mind searched for the proper insult, but after exploring different options, the best his befuddled brain could conjure up was "...reporter shit. Staying in this town could be dangerous to your health."

"I'll take my chances." Marc surprised himself when he said it. It sounded much braver than he felt. "You wouldn't happen to know anything about what happened to Teresa Basiuk? She was helping me with some things and now she's in the hospital."

"Who?" Klaus snarled at him. "Get lost, you asshole. Get out of here. You're lucky, you know... that guy, Jeremy Brown, likes you."

"I'm one of his favourite people. He likes me so much, he fired me."

"Connie," Klaus roared out of the blue. "Take this young man home."

"Aw, Klausy, get Jeeves to do it."

In his intoxicated state, Klaus spaced out each word of his answer, loudly, as if instructing a child. "His name is Brian. And he has to take me to a meeting. Don't you understand anything, you bitch?"

Connie looked hurt, didn't say anything.

Marc said, "Don't call her a bitch."

"I'll call her whatever I want. You wouldn't understand 'cause you don't even have a house. Or a woman you can control."

"What's that supposed to mean?" Marc asked quietly.

Klaus's eyes narrowed and he grinned. "That lap dancer you're hanging around with? What's her name? Lise? I wouldn't mind if she sat on me and lapped at my nipples."

Marc grabbed Klaus by his necklace and twisted until he saw his eyes go huge. Without thinking about it, he up-ended him into the pool. A good thing he did it quickly. When he stopped to think, that always impeded action. They were two different things, one pure, one practical, as Immanuel Kant argued so well.

Connie chuckled, gave Marc a glance which he interpreted as appreciative, and padded toward the house. Marc followed her, taking his camera bag. Klaus's robe and his soused state made for a slow, clumsy and sodden attempt at exiting his pool.

As soon as Connie had gone into a bathroom to change, the maid whispered to Marc, "Come with me. Quick."

Marc followed her to the stairway under the vast skylight. Looking both ways furtively, the old woman said, "I got something for you. You have to promise me you'll never, ever reveal where you got it."

"Okay," Marc said, whispering in the spirit of secrecy. "Whatever it is, it's safe with me."

Emily slipped a video cassette out of her apron pocket and passed it to Marc. "It's a copy. There's more where that came from. It's not right."

Marc heard a bathroom door open. He quickly unbuckled his camera bag, laid the cassette on top, rebuckled the bag and said to Connie, "Ready to go?"

"Yeah." Connie had changed into shorts, a halter top and sandals. A large bag hung from her shoulder. "Let's take the Cadillac. God, he pisses me off when he gets like this."

CHAPTER 17

Back in his own apartment, Marc locked both the upstairs and downstairs doors, closed all his curtains and had a cigarette and a coffee to counteract some of his alcohol intake at Klaus Axel's. Only then did he pop the video into the VCR, hoping to see some damning evidence about the Agriplex or a confession about the sale of land for the new complex.

Instead, when he pushed the "play" button, he got a long stretch of fuzz and snow on the screen, followed by an amateur video— or more accurately, a copy of an amateur video. The film was grainy and often obscured by the kind of horizontal lines familiar to Marc from fast-forwarding rented videos. Sometimes the colours held, sometimes the movie switched to black and white.

Marc watched it twice, trying to figure out why the maid had slipped him the cassette. The action took place in a hotel room, in different segments and at different times. It started with a standard porn routine— a woman performing oral sex on a man— but whoever was running the camera had little experience with the zoom feature. The camera careened in for an intimate close-up and found focus just as the operator decided to back off for a more panoramic view. The man on screen seemed to have difficulty standing at attention for great periods of time. That problem— and the protrusion of his pot belly— were distracting. The requisite spasm finally came after the woman had given up on fellatio. Grabbing her hair, the man turned her around and rammed at her from behind.

Marc thought about man's inhumanity to woman, and how the materialist fantasy of woman as property had never left the capitalist system. But he also couldn't deny his own measure of prurient interest in this amateur production. Taking a sip of cold coffee, he reconciled the two positions with a sneer. "The guy's faking it," Marc said to himself.

Later video segments were marginally better in quality but little improved in performance. Men were tied up by a woman in a dominatrix outfit who did various things to them using condoms and an assortment of paraphernalia. The climax of the movie was a group effort involving a middle-aged man and two women— one much younger than the other, from what Marc could tell. Midway through the threesome, the camera was fixed in one position, and a man who seemed to have a lot of hair on his back came trotting over to offer his contribution— apparently the camera operator had decided to get in on the action.

The poor video quality worked against identifying any of the *ménage à quatre*. To further frustrate identification, the participants wore black masks, without slits for eyes. One man seemed to be wearing a gold chain, another a watch. One mask slipped during the ultimate congruence of anus and penis and hand and mouth, but try as he might, using pause and rewind, Marc couldn't get a picture sufficiently clear to see who the man was.

After he'd watched the video a second time, crying "Focus, focus" at appropriate moments, Marc cracked a beer and called Klaus Axel's house. Emily, the maid, answered.

"I, um, watched the movie," Marc said, feeling awkward about broaching this topic with a senior citizen.

"Isn't it a shocker?" the maid whispered into the phone.

"I guess so, although I didn't see anything that's patently illegal. Maybe when the woman's hair was grabbed, but she didn't protest."

"If it isn't illegal, it should be."

"I was hoping for something incriminating against Mr. Axel, maybe the tape of a meeting about the Agriplex."

"Oh," Emily whispered, "I wouldn't know anything about that. But he's in the video."

"Who?"

A pause. "Mr. Axel."

"How do you know?"

"I found it in his study when I was cleaning his desk. I was so shocked, I almost told Mrs. Axel. I never saw anything like it in my life. And he's running for mayor!"

"The tape wasn't the clearest. Do you have an original?"

"I don't think so. There's somebody coming," Emily whispered, adding in a louder, stagey voice, "It's been really nice talking to you. I have to go start the supper now. Bye."

Marc's noon-time drinking on top of a general Canada Day lethargy made him drowsy. He slept for two hours and woke with a picture— Teresa being wheeled into Emergency— so vividly on his mind that he knew he'd been dreaming about her again. To hell with the panic attacks— he had to see her.

Marc walked back to the hospital. Without allowing himself any time to think about it, he approached the first-floor receptionist and started talking. In a pink striped uniform, she looked like a hospital cheerleader. Part time, covering Canada Day, Marc assumed.

She wouldn't let him see Teresa. "Sorry, nobody but immediate family. She's still in intensive care."

"But I saw her yesterday," he lied.

The receptionist checked her chart. "Somebody bent the rules for you, I guess."

"How's she doing?"

"Sorry, sir. We're not allowed to say."

"Thanks for nothing. Can I check with the second floor?"

The candystriper looked a little offended. "Certainly, sir. The elevators are down the hall, to your right. You'll see the desk as soon as you get off."

The elevator seemed almost as ancient as the religious order that ran the hospital. It made ghostly noises as it lifted him.

The reception desk was directly in front of the elevator doors. "May I help you?" asked a frazzled-looking woman. Her bottle-bottom glasses gave her eyeballs a wide, spacey look.

Marc inhaled two quick gulps of antiseptic hospital air and said, "I'm here to see Teresa Basiuk. How is she?"

The woman glanced at a clipboard in her hand and pulled at her hair. It was thin, as if she'd been pulling at it for a long time and the roots were losing their resistance. "She's stable, last I checked."

"What room's she in?"

"Intensive care. Can I ask your relationship to the patient?"

"Marc Basiuk. I'm her uncle."

"Down the hall and to the left. Room 225. Policy doesn't usually allow more than one visitor, and I believe her mom's with her. But I can't say it'll make any difference in her case."

Down the hall and to the left, Marc saw Teresa as soon as he entered the room. She seemed like a wraith of indeterminate age. Pale as marble. A tube in her mouth, running to a respirator. A long tube running from a bottle into her arm. Another to a bottle near the floor. At the foot of the raised hospital bed sat her mother. Fixing a look on Marc when he first came in, Shirley Basiuk didn't say a word. After a time, she went back to staring at her daughter. Near her on the window ledge sat a water glass nourishing a single wild Alberta rose, browning at the edges.

"How is she?" Marc whispered.

"How she looks. Not too good," the woman said. "Why are you whispering?"

"Don't know," Marc said quietly. "Has there been any change?"

"Only the tubes and the bedpan. Not her. She just lies there sleeping like a little girl who don't want to wake up. It's hard on me."

"Do they think she's going to be all right?"

"They don't know. Or they're lying to me." She began to pull at a thread on the white bedspread. It unravelled as she picked at it, like the threads of her life.

"She wake up at all yet?"

"No. That's the scary part. Can I see you?"

"What?"

"Can I see you? Not here." She glanced toward the wide open door, her eyes flicking about as if she didn't trust this room and its tubes and its single wilting flower in a water glass.

"Yeah, I guess so."

"Well, let's go, then. I been here all night and nothing's changed. I'll get them to call me if it does."

"Could you have stopped her? I don't think so. Nobody could. She wouldn't listen to nobody," Shirley Basiuk said as they drove from the hospital in her car. She had insisted that Marc drive her rusting compact. He didn't want to explain his recent impaired driving problems, so he acquiesced. Shirley Basiuk sucked on a long cigarette and coughed.

"Sorry about what happened," he said, wanting to talk to her but not knowing what to say. The afternoon was hot, the sky a wide-angled blue. The white trails from two jet planes intersected on the horizon. It seemed impossible that someone he cared about was shut up in a hospital room, unconscious.

"I needed to get away," she said. "The place was making me crazy. I work there. At the hospital. Cleaning. So they let me stay all night, no problem. Kept drifting off, so I ain't tired. I need somebody to talk to. We can go home. He'll be gone."

"I'll take you home."

"They..." she tossed her head angrily at a few people standing at a bus stop, "... don't understand."

She repeated the thought as if it justified her state of mind. "Not at all."

The route signs for the Canada Day parade were still taped to the light standards on 50th Street, but the celebration had shifted to a small municipal park down by the river. A fast bass guitar beat throbbed up from a riverside bandshell. A few cars on the main drag were scattered in careless holiday fashion in front of a coffee shop.

"Mind if I stop by my place and pick something up?"

The woman shook her head and asked with a sly smile, "Something for me?"

"Maybe," he said.

He parked in front of his aunt's house and returned with a brown paper bag with the usual black-lettered Alberta Liquor Control Board warning. Shirley stared at it, her eyes red, occasionally nodding. Maybe she'd been crying.

"What's this?" she asked, frowning and smiling at him at the same time, as if he were a teenager whose behaviour confused her. Her tongue roamed her lips. Her fingers combed her hair.

"Scotch."

A disapproving tone. "Not my drink. Got sick on it once in high school."

"Okay, I'll drink it. Your place next, after I pick up some soda."

"Yeah," she said. They turned in at the Safeway parking lot— "Closed for Canada Day," according to a huge banner in the front windows— and drifted back through downtown to the 7-Eleven for club soda.

"But I might."

"Huh?" he said.

"Take a drink, if you join me. There's not much of anything up at the house. Not after the wake he had." She emphasized "he" and wrinkled her nose, as if the word smelled bad.

As soon as she saw Shirley and Marc coming up the walk, little Suz hopped down the steps from the bungalow and ran to them, clinging to the woman's leg.

"Hey," Shirley whispered. She rubbed the child's hair and pushed her away so she could move. The two of them walked apart from him to the house, the child trying to get back on her leg.

They were halfway to the house when little Suz asked, seriously, as if the question had been bothering her for a long time, "When I die and go to heaven, how will you find me?"

Shirley Basiuk lifted the child and buried her nose in her hair. The woman's body shook. Tears fell unprotected on the girl.

"You know what my mommy told me?" Marc lied to the child.

Suz turned her large eyes to him and the eyelids blinked seriously. "What?"

"She told me that when we get to heaven, we're with God and we'll know where to find everybody. We'll all be part of the mind of God."

They sat on chrome and plastic kitchen chairs at a chrome-legged kitchen table. Shirley found two glasses and Marc poured hers a third full without comment. Scraping a tray from the humming white refrigerator behind him, she added ice.

The first sip made her shiver.

"More soda?" he asked.

"Less," she said and drained the glass.

"Scotch on the rocks?"

"Maybe," she said. "Skip the rocks. Not usually my drink."

He poured for her again. "That's better," she said. Jiggling the bottle closer to her side of the kitchen table, she pretended she was studying the brand name and the label and didn't move it back.

Little Suz swished through a curtain that divided the kitchen from a cluttered dining room. A television set murmured from somewhere in the house. She brushed the hair, shiny as corn silk, of a naked Barbie doll missing one arm. "What can I do, nana Shirl? I'm bored."

Shirley grabbed the child's small forearm and shook her. "Quit it. How many times I told you to mind your manners when we got company?"

The child ignored the shaking and grinned at Marc. "My mommy's gone to heaven." The sing-songy voice had come back.

"Go watch TV. Play with your friends." The look Shirley gave Marc said she was at the end of her rope and the fibres were fraying badly. "Kids today."

Marc tasted his scotch and soda. He liked the way it melted the inside of his mouth. If he had a couple, he wouldn't have to think about what kind of man brought alcohol into a household like this.

"Nana? I thought Suzie was..."

Shirley took a drink carefully and carefully set her glass back down on the table. She scanned the bottle's label again. Her restless hands, showing traces of black in the cracks, sought the bodice of her black dress, moved to pat her hair. "A lot of people do. I think I'm the youngest grandmother in Crooked Elbow. I used to be something, you know, before him."

"I can see that," Marc told her, and there was some truth in what he said. He calculated quickly. She might not be all that much older than he was, a thought that scared him.

"You mind?" she asked. He shook his head, but she didn't bother to wait for that. Lutescent scotch gurgled into her glass.

"I'm not really a grandmother. They... They wasn't ours, you know?"

"Excuse me."

"The girls wasn't ours, the twins. We got them when they was nine."

"Does that matter?"

Shirley wasn't paying attention. Her eyes were glazed from booze and the memories it stirred up. "Foster kids. We would of adopted right away but we needed the income. I always thought of them as ours, right from the start. They was a pair of beauties, I'll give them that. And we did our best. But it's hard, raising kids."

"Tell me about it." He thought of his own daughters and took a long drink.

"There's problems no matter what you do. There's how their lives could of been better and from the look of their real mom's apartment, that's possible. I drove by one time, had a look. But then it could of been worse, if their mom didn't want them in the first place."

"Uh huh. And you did."

"That's what I was always saying to myself. I wanted them. They weren't babies. We didn't have a baby around here until little Suz. But they was such beauties. I'd forgot about that, how beautiful little girls are, until they come along to remind us. Or remind me, at least."

"It's hard to adopt." Marc poured a soda water, straight, into his glass, in the interest of slowing himself down. Little Suz squealed from the living room. The television was louder now. A music video blared. Shirley was either beyond hearing it or adept at shutting it out.

"It is damned near impossible unless you fork over ten thousand for a baby from one of them Third World countries, which we didn't, let me tell you. So we took them in as foster kids. And they come up for adoption when they was 12. Johnny was working. We didn't need the money so bad by then. And now one's gone and one looks like she's goin'."

"But you gave them eight or nine good years."

Shirley's glass was empty. Slumping at the table, she twisted strands of hair around her fingers like an aging cosmetologist trying to restore life to split ends. She resembled a woman in her fifties, 15 years older than her actual age. "Tried to," she said. "But there was trouble. Men."

The mention of the gender seemed to rouse her from her stupor and she picked up on the trouble she'd introduced. "I wonder how much different it would of been if we could of had our own kids."

She smiled at Marc, her lips twisting and bitter. "Johnny was a man in those days, as good as they come at anything you wanted to name. Most of that bunch went on to be pretty successful in this world."

"You think maybe time might be obscuring your..."

Shirley didn't let Marc finish. She was sitting straighter and she had some of her younger body back— breasts and a waist and hips— the body's memory awakened by old dreams. "You know, it's funny, how we was as hot as could be, and when I got pregnant, I thought it was a huge scandal. Hard to believe, now that everybody and his dog's a single mom, but there you go..."

She poured again, waved the bottle in Marc's direction and set it down carefully this time when he said no. "Where was I? Oh yeah, the family scandal, the shock of it all. So we make these quick wedding plans and before the wedding, I lose the baby. So did I tell him?"

Marc didn't answer.

"Well, did I?"

Shirley's glass banged the table. Whisky sloshed and wet her hand. She slurped at her fingers with her lips, her tongue. Marc thought about leaving. He couldn't trust a woman this tired and this drunk to tell the truth. She'd lie, and then insist her lying was his fault.

He didn't move— couldn't until he'd heard all the lies she had to tell him— but he had trouble looking at her.

"Goddamn you. Goddamn you to everlasting hell fire, you and the rest like you, Johnny, did I tell you?"

"No."

"Right fucking on. I didn't tell you. I couldn't. The plans was all set. We had the mixed stag. My dad had the hall and everything. And I thought you were Mr. Wonderful, but I knew, even then. This tiny, tiny little voice inside me said…"

Some old film was playing for her, louder and more violent than the long-haired muscle boys with the guitars little Suz was watching on television. "What did you know?"

Shirley looked at Marc sitting in Johnny's chair, and hatred inflamed her face. She screamed and it must have hurt her throat. "You prick!"

A door slammed. Marc went to the living room and little Suz wasn't there. The top of her hair showed over the screen of the poorly fitted aluminum door, her body rocking back and forth, back and forth, bumping against the aluminum. He went out to join her, reached out to touch her. She recoiled from him, shrank away, ran down the steps.

Marc went back to the kitchen. "So you married him."

Shirley seemed calmer, as if she had realized the liquor was in control. She chose her words carefully, shaping her lips before she would allow them full release. "I married him without telling him, and then I acted like I had a miscar… a miscarriage later. I told him one night after we made love and…"

"And?"

"I can't blame anybody but me. His life came to nothing since then. Nothing. He tried things, but they never worked out. Not like when he was with the guys in high school, everybody's hero."

"Some hero."

She nodded her head in agreement and drifted off somewhere. "Some hero," she said and yawned. "But it's also their fault."

"Who?"

"The other guys, the Four Horsemen."

"The what?"

"The club. The Four Horsemen. The two guys and Robbie and the Ukrainian. They was bosom buddies and I was the one breaking them up. You know? I never really thought of that before, but here they were barely out of high school. I took him away from them. Breaking them up."

"So what?"

"So the club kept going anyway. They was in the same 4-H Club, horses, in high school. They called it Happy Harry's Whore House for a while and now it's the Four Horsemen. Big deal."

"The Four Horsemen?"

"Yeah." Shirley looked at Marc as if he were incredibly stupid.

"What is it?"

"It's their club, dingle-arse. They get together, the four of them, like it's boys' night out or some goddamn thing."

"What, like a service club? What do they do?"

"Here, I'm drinking all this. I think this'll be 'nough. Not bad stuff." She poured herself a full glass and slid the half empty bottle toward him with the back of her hand. "It's been a hell of a day... I shouldn't be doing this..."

Her elbow slipped off the table and she rubbed it as if wondering how she'd hurt herself.

"The Four Horsemen, what do they do?"

"Damned if I know."

"But they do something."

"Know what I call it? To myself?" She waved a finger in the air, directing the visions in her mind. "I call it Three Horsemen and a Pup."

"And a pup?"

She laughed, almost a cackle. "Yeah, a pup. 'Cause he follows them around like a little dog trying to keep up with the horses, eh?"

"I don't get it."

"They get together at the bar. I did tell him once, I said that about the dog."

"And?"

"Johnny didn't think it was very funny. Not at all." Shirley paused, staring into her glass as if the liquor could help her form her next sentence. "That's when he hit me. The first time. Maybe. I'm not sure. He doesn't like things that aren't funny."

"So they get together all the time? Once in a while? What?"

Shirley moved an index finger to her lips and formed a sh-sh sound at him. That took a while. "Every weekend. At least," she said, "They plan what to do. But we're not going to say what, are we, Shirley?"

"They meet in Rose Hill?"

"We can't say any more. We said too much already. Johnny couldn't keep up, that's what I think." Shirley paused, tilting her head. For a moment, Marc thought she was going coy in her drunkenness. Her face drained of colour, she seemed suddenly sober.

"I heard him." Shirley spoke in an urgent whisper as if the man were already in the room. "I know Clem's car. Johnny always rides with somebody else since the liquor laws got so stupid. I was you, I'd get outta here."

Chapter 18

Shirley changed her mind about the Scotch. As Marc got up to leave, she cradled the bottle protectively, like the baby she'd never had. He left it with her. She seemed to need it more than he did.

"See ya," Marc told her.

Shirley didn't answer him. Eyes downcast, she backed through the curtains into the dining room, following a path battered into the carpet by years of people trailing in and out to watch television or drink or abuse each other.

Marc chose not to follow her. He decided to go down the back steps and out the back door. It made a lot of sense right up to the moment when a ham-sized hand seized Marc's bicep and half shoved, half carried him back up the stairs. At that point, his decision made no sense at all.

The hand came with a voice. "Who let you into my house?" the voice roared.

"Nobody."

The voice seemed unhappy with that answer. "Who let you in?"

"I let myself in."

Johnny Basiuk forced Marc into the kitchen, backward step after backward step. Strong for an overweight man, he was using his belly as a battering ram. "Bull," Johnny said, and then he yelled, "Shirl!"

The yell was loud in Marc's ears. His heart raced and it wasn't from exercise. He started to tremble and sweat and it wasn't from exertion. It was from fear, the emotion he'd been too stunned to feel when Johnny first grabbed him. He had it now, in spades.

No answer from the living room.

The bull coming home to his own pasture didn't appreciate the silence. Johnny let go of Marc's arm, and Marc ducked, but not fast enough or far enough. As ideas go, ducking wasn't any better than his original plan to leave by the back door. It allowed Johnny to grab Marc's throat and mash it between his thumb and his fingers, squeezing as if this were a hand grip test for cement truck drivers.

"Shirley Basiuk!" Johnny bellowed, and his roaring seemed to add to his strength. Marc thought about strength, about women in emergencies who lift trucks off their children. Then he thought about Kant's Categorical Imperative, about acting in universal accord, about kneeing the man in the groin or gouging out an eye or two, but he didn't have the strength. Marc was light headed, floating. He stopped breathing and that was fine, because as long as a person is floating, he doesn't need to breathe. He becomes New Age man, absorbed in an out-of-body experience.

A near-death apparition glowed in the dimming, reddish light. A ghostly presence, it drifted in from Marc's right side, coming to take him away, *sacre main*, down a tunnel of light, far from this vale of tears.

But he didn't have time to follow it. The pressure around Marc's neck eased and he slumped to the floor. He sucked in one long rasping breath and coughed it out.

"Shirl," the voice said, quietly, above Marc, slumping on the grimy linoleum near a droning refrigerator motor.

Shirley, no longer pretending to be an apparition or in any way concerned with the choking mass of flesh littering her kitchen floor, said the obvious. "Johnny."

"Where you been?"

Offering her bottle like a gift, she said, "You want a drink?"

Marc coughed and it hurt. He didn't want to breathe. He coughed again and some obstruction cleared. He tasted oxygen as fresh and sweet as a wild rose in June. Mental memo for the lead on that one: "Noted local editor Marc LePage decided to quit smoking recently. He began to value his lungs after he was found half-strangled..."

"Scotch? Where'd this horse piss come from?" Johnny sputtered.

"I..." She looked away— fluffing up her hair with her fingers in a drunken parody of flirtatiousness— and wiped sweat off her forehead.

"Him?" Johnny hooked a thumb at Marc, the bug taking up space on their kitchen floor.

Shirley screwed up her face at Johnny, moved to the kitchen counter and opened a small cupboard door over the sink. Clinking three nearly empty rye bottles and some vodka out of the way, she tried to hide the Scotch.

Taking two steps, Johnny came up behind her and grabbed the fleshy backs of her arms. Squeezing until the flesh turned pink and white, he turned Shirley around and asked her a question, slowly and quietly. "He feed you this fag lawyer piss?"

She averted her face.

"And you drank with him when our daughter's laid up in the hospital?"

Her lower lip trembled and tucked itself inside her top teeth.

"And what else?"

"Nothin.' Where you been?" she said.

Shirley's eyes widened and flinched shut. She doubled up. But she couldn't double up all the way because Johnny had a fistful of her hair in his left hand.

"Nothin'," she said, grinding the word from her mouth, then taking a quick breath. "Nothin', nothin', nothin'."

Shirley flinched again. Her voice tried to grate more words at Johnny, but they came out as exhaled breath, the wordless sigh of an injured animal.

"Stop it," Marc protested. "She didn't do anything."

Johnny let her go and turned back to Marc. "Yeah? So why'd you bring the booze here, Mr. Editor? Why you keep sniffing around the women of this house? Seems to me there's... Did I say you could get up? Seems to me there's been nothing but trouble since you started hanging around... I said not to get up without you got my permission."

That was good advice. So, naturally, in his drink-besotted, oxygen-deprived, stubborn way, Marc couldn't take it. He needed to get up off the floor and abuse the abuser. Time to punish this relic from the 19th-century working classes who used his fists to keep his wife in her place.

"I warned you," Johnny Basiuk grunted and raised a black, polished, go-to-church shoe. It swung like a wrecking ball into Marc's midriff.

Either Johnny Basiuk knew what he was doing or it was a lucky kick. The toe of that shoe exploded in the soft unprotected place where the ribs meet. Marc felt himself lifted by the kick. His hands moved reflexively and far too late to protect himself. When he hit the floor, the brunt of his 165 pounds was taken by his left cheek.

He didn't care about that.

He didn't care about anything except, for the second time that afternoon, the most basic element of life: taking a breath. Curled on the floor, he expelled a long groan. He knew it was his after it was out. His lungs burned for air, he groaned some more, and at last, he inhaled.

And tasted blood.

Too weak to get up, his fury and his desire for revenge spent by the kick, he lay on the linoleum and listened. A dog howled down the block. Other dogs yapped. Kids screamed outside. A car rumbled by. A tinkling bell invited children to come out for cold, sweet ice cream. Marc's mouth tasted as bad as it ever had, the mouth of a man waking from a short sleep to a terrible hangover. He heard a voice. He heard a thud. He heard a cry sucked back into a woman's mouth. He heard one crash followed by another and the shattering of glass against metal at the kitchen sink.

"Bitch," a man's voice said.

Footsteps faded into the next room. A cry rose and fell, an animal in heat or pain. More thuds. A living room chair creaked.

"In my house," the man's voice said. "I got to teach you. You know beans."

Movement, the slap of flesh against flesh.

"Please," moaned a low woman's voice.

Silence.

"Not here," the woman's voice said again.

Footsteps.

An interior door slammed. Marc rolled over and sat up. He would know he had abdominal muscles for a few days.

An outside aluminum door creaked open and eased shut. Footsteps scratched the linoleum. A wet nose nuzzled Marc's cheek where he'd fallen. He shivered and discovered he still had a voice. "Get lost," he said.

The dog liked this attention. It licked his face and sniffed him for traces of canine delight. Shoving it away, Marc saw the little girl, half hidden behind the refrigerator. A child's drawing of a Canadian flag was secured to the refrigerator door by small fruit-shaped magnets. In the drawing, a very large man and a small woman and a girl about the same size as the woman stood to one side of the flag. There was no sun in the picture. "Canda Day. Suzie. Croked Elbow. Alb. Canda," it said at the bottom of the drawing.

"Did you... make that?"

Suzie stared at Marc and blinked.

"Did you... make the drawing?"

"Where's mommy?"

"I think she went... down the hall."

"You mean heaven. That's what nana Shirl said, she's gone to heaven."

Marc wanted to get up, just to be sure he could still do it, but he didn't want to frighten the girl. "That's right. I forgot. She went to heaven."

"And auntie Teresa is going there, too."

"Maybe she'll get better."

The child wisely ignored this. "When are they coming back?"

"You mean nana and grandpa?"

"When are they coming back?"

"Soon."

Suzie stamped her foot. "Mommy and auntie Teresa?"

"No, nana and grandpa. You have to come with me. I'll get you away— some place safe."

"No. I hate you." Suzie stamped both feet and marched back to her television. When Marc peeked in at her, Suzie had crawled up on a living room chair with an old piece of blanket and was rocking herself back and forth, back and forth to the rhythm of game show music on television.

Marc left by the back door. There were no hands to grab him this time, no voices to tell him what to do. Next door, a Latin American man, hair so black it bordered on blue, hosed down a station wagon badly rusting in the rear panels. Two dark-haired children swarmed around him swinging soap-saturated sponges.

Leaning a little to one side, nursing his lower belly, Marc slowly approached the man. "Hello, " he said. "*Comment ça va?*"

The man showed white teeth, one front incisor repaired with gold. He wiped his brow and the children hugged his legs, splattering wet soap on his pants.

"You know the people next door?" Marc indicated the Basiuk house with an open hand.

Still smiling at Marc, the man extracted a cloth from his pocket. Reaching up, he brushed gently at Marc's cheek where it had met the floor. Marc blinked and pushed the man's hand away. "Never mind that. You know the people next door? Your neighbours."

"Yeah." The man looked at his running shoes.

"They ever do anything to you?"

"Sad," the man said. "Uh, very sad." And he pointed an index finger at his temple. Spinning the finger in a circle, he crossed his eyes and then closed his thumb on his finger, firing a pistol, the universal symbol for craziness.

"I know what you mean," Marc said.

CHAPTER 19

The next morning, before going to work, Marc took a taxi to Phil's Petro-Can on the highway for breakfast.

"What happened to you?" asked a waitress. Her smile said displays of facial damage weren't all that unusual at this gas station and restaurant. Marc smiled back. His cheek hurt. He had tried to cover the scrape under one eye with a Band-Aid but it wouldn't stay on.

"Ran into a shoe in the dark."

"High heel, I hope."

"No such luck."

"What'll it be?"

"Coffee. One egg, poached, on brown toast."

A man in work clothes darkened by grease and oil stains set down a newspaper, paid his bill and left. Marc slid over and took his vacant stool at the counter. The man's *Edmonton Sun* lay folded in front of him. A three-word headline, all caps, blared at Marc from page one: COPS COLLECT CORPSE. And in smaller type: "Page Two."

The page two headline was almost as strong as the banner headline on the front. BRUTAL HOLIDAY SLAYING: WOMAN DEAD, it said, followed by the sub-heading, "Mother makes third victim in family!"

> "She never stood a chance.
>
> "Shirley Basiuk was savagely pummelled to death near her home in the quiet, rural city of Crooked Elbow, Alberta, before midnight on Canada Day. Husband Johnny Basiuk is being held as a suspect.
>
> "That makes Tragedy Number Three for this accident-prone family. Crooked Elbow police admitted last night she's the latest Basiuk woman to be injured— fatally or otherwise— in the past three weeks.
>
> "Teen daughter Stephanie died earlier this month in a freak car accident involving a game of chicken on a rural back road. Second daughter Teresa is in intensive care, following what appears to be a drug overdose.

"Now their mother is dead.

"Crooked Elbow police denied any connection between the three incidents. 'The first death was an accident,' said Crooked Elbow Police Chief Paul Bjenson. 'It's being handled under RCMP jurisdiction, since it happened outside city limits. The girl with the overdose is getting proper medical attention in hospital. We have no reason to suspect foul play in her case.

"'The latest death looks like murder. But there is nothing to connect the three,' he said.

"John Albert Basiuk, once a well-known local athlete, was picked up by Crooked Elbow police shortly after midnight outside a local hotel.

"'There appeared to be blood on his hands,' said the chief. 'He seemed to be in a confused state, possibly intoxicated. The arresting officer recommended a Breathalyzer, and Mr. Basiuk hit the ceiling.'

"'It wasn't me,' Basiuk told police. And later, 'I hit her,' according to reports filed with the police chief by the arresting officer, *The Sun* has learned.

"'This is not a confession. He's entitled to the full protection of the law. And a fair trial,' the chief told *The Sun* in an exclusive interview. 'If he can't afford a lawyer, we'll help him get one. In fact, there's one interviewing him right now.'

"Formal charges had not been laid at press time."

Marc called the city police from a pay phone between the men's washroom and a candy machine with a sign that said the proceeds were going to help find missing children.

"I'm sorry, the chief's not in. Not expected till noon," the receptionist said.

"How about Lise? She in?"

"Maybe. Let me check."

"Hi," he said, when Lise came on the line. "Busy night?"

"Yeah, you might say that."

"That's my impression. Too bad I had to get it from *The Edmonton Sun*, since nobody called me while it was all coming down."

"Sorry. I guess I better check my contract. I missed the part where I have to call the local rag every time a police officer goes for a leak."

"Yeah? Even when a woman's been beaten to death and you have her husband in custody? Doesn't happen every day in Crooked Elbow. A little media consideration might be in order."

"You can't do anything with it until next week anyway. And by then, you're gone. I figured I'd let you get your beauty sleep."

"This is the kind of story I like to hear about. You know that, Lise."

"You're too personally involved. Maybe somebody just about solved the Basiuk problem in town. Or maybe the family solved it for themselves. Which, the way things are going, I'd pretty much say was a good thing."

"I don't need to hear that."

"I keep forgetting. I'm supposed to be in mourning." Lise lowered her voice. "One of them was so good in bed, she almost stole my guy."

"Fuck you."

"Not a bad idea, sailor."

"You're pissing me off."

Lise's voice turned soft. She said three words and they were frosted with sugar and ice when she exhaled them.

"You've got a mean mouth," he said. "You know for sure Johnny killed her?"

"No. Either all those blows to the head and body led to internal injuries and death, or it was alcohol poisoning, but that seems unlikely given her tolerance and the other damage."

"Where'd you find her?"

"I didn't. They found her out behind her place. Half in and half out of a garbage dumpster at the end of the alley. Those Basiuks are a class act all the way. We got the call from some kids who were down there doing whatever it is kids do these days. They saw a leg sticking out and figured it was a real life horror movie."

"And you arrested Johnny."

"Yes, sir, and off the record— you need to get the story from the chief—

he's probably guilty as sin. A history of priors for alcohol offenses. Occasional domestic violence. He starts drinking after his daughter's suicide attempt and disappears into the place guys like him go so they can really cut loose on the gender they love to hate. Starts blaming the little woman for all his troubles. Knocks her around. Once he draws blood, he likes the smell of it, can't stop."

"Any evidence? Any witnesses?"

"The lady'd been violated. We're getting semen samples, pubic hair, anything we can. And we're probably going to need it. He babbled on about hitting her. But he says he doesn't remember anything else. The man's not in good shape. No witnesses, unless you count one scared little girl... The Mexican neighbour isn't saying shit. We're trying to locate a translator."

"Lise, it's not easy for me to admit, but I was a little out of line when I first called. I appreciate you telling me this."

"Yeah, well, you were partly right. I should have called you last night... Look, there's something bothering me. What's going to happen to the girl?"

"Little Suz?"

"Yeah. What happens to her now?"

"I don't know. You know where she is this morning?"

"Somebody's keeping her, pending the outcome of the trial and so on. I'm more worried about her long-term future."

"What happened to Lise the cynic?"

"I'm just saying somebody should help her if they can, okay?"

"Okay, settle down. I'm glad somebody cares."

"When can I see you again?" she asked.

"Soon. I... don't know what I'm doing, yet."

"We got to get together again. I'm... Look, call me."

Marc returned to his egg, congealed over the piece of toast on which it had been planted. Ringing it were lumps of cool, onion-flavoured hash-browns. Three half slices of toast— imitation butter slathered in the centre of each slice— cooled on the side. None of it was as cool as the coffee or his thoughts, as the implications of the story in *The Sun* began to sink in.

As he tentatively took a bite of egg and toast, it occurred to Marc that he wasn't very satisfied with the answer to the question he'd posed on the telephone— why hadn't Lise called him as soon as she knew about the murder? And another thought galloped in almost on top of that question— why did bad things keep happening to the women who were close to him?

His mother had left and never come back. She could be anybody— he wouldn't recognize her now— the woman gassing up her car outside, say, or, dressed like a man, the fat truck driver coming through the door. He would never know. His memories of her were both so naive and so painful that he had wiped them out. Except for the picture of an angel. And the thought that sometimes came reeling down a tunnel of darkness at him like a pervert pursuing him in a sewer: maybe he and his dad had driven his mother away.

His daughter had died; his wife had left him.

His lover slept with a pig farmer; Teresa lay unconscious following a drug overdose; her mother had died after talking to him.

Marc thought about his flirtations with Kant's philosophy, his clinging to Marxist ideology and its implied feminism— all poor props, dodges, ways of avoiding a central truth— he was bad news for women. Why hadn't he seen it clearly before? He was cursed and this curse was the root of his self-destructive behaviour, his bitterness, his irony. But he wasn't content to keep the curse bottled up inside. Oh, no. He had to share it. No woman was safe near him.

Including the waitress, who could have been his mother, for all he knew. When she came around offering coffee refills, he berated her for the condition of his breakfast.

"It's my fault you been on the phone 10 minutes? Blame me for the friggin' weather while we're at it, why doncha?" The woman tucked her free hand into the front of her apron and balled it into a fist.

"Think we could give them the truck stop microwave?" Marc asked, nodding toward three red heat lamps glowing above other breakfasts on a shelf between the dining area and the kitchen.

The woman shook her head at Marc and took his plate away. Fresh coffee came and in five minutes, the kitchen's second stab at poaching an egg. This one was also runny, but it was warm. The waitress didn't say

anything and neither did Marc. If athletes could eat raw egg, so could Marc
LePage.

As the gelatinous mess slithered down his throat, Marc came to a
conclusion. He knew a condition of low self-esteem when he saw it; he
could recognize depression when it stared him in the face; he was familiar
with the urge to slide out the razor-sharp blade of the little utility knives
from the office, the temptation presented by idling vehicles in enclosed
places.

He also knew one way of dodging that bullet. A trip to the Alberta
Liquor Control Board outlet would do wonders for his state of mind. There
were only two problems with that idea— in his current condition, he was
not absolutely certain of its effectiveness, and the outlet didn't open until
11:00 a.m.

All right, there was another direction his life could take, he thought.
Things had been pointing to a new course of action but he hadn't been
paying attention. The men in masks might have been right in their own
way. Klaus Axel was on the right track. The typed notes to his office were
right as rain. Marc obviously had no idea what was really going on in this
town, and he was a risk to others, if not himself, just by being here.

Ergo, he should leave town as soon as he collected his final cheque
from Brownrigg.

He would call the office, let them know he was taking a sick day. He
felt sick enough to qualify, and, besides, he didn't know what he'd do if he
went in to work with only today and tomorrow left. If he stayed away, he
could spend the day packing, getting a bus schedule— east or west, it didn't
matter. Maybe he should see Vancouver again. He could reinvent himself
in a place more tolerant of left-wing philosophers and depressives and fools.

CHAPTER 20

Friday morning, Marc could tell that the janitor had been busy in his absence. The garbage basket near his desk had been emptied, the papers on his floor carefully vacuumed around. Marc wished the janitor had kept going, sucking all the papers up, so he didn't have to deal with them on his last day at work.

Throwing two large pack sacks and his guitar– all his wordly possessions except for his car, some books, his television and the VCR– on top of some papers beside his desk, Marc called the bus depot and confirmed 1:00 and 5:00 departures for Edmonton. From there, he could go east or west, and he was still favouring west. Maybe he could get a job at an alternative newspaper. That was how he'd gotten his start in the business. Time to go back to his roots.

He dialled his aunt and took minor pleasure in letting her know that he was vacating without notice.

"Typical," was his aunt's comment. "I wondered, when I saw you walking away with the bags and the guitar. What am I supposed to do with the TV and the VCR? And the rest of the books?"

"Let the next tenant use them, I guess. Or maybe I'll come back for them." He had a good idea how his aunt knew that some books were gone and that the TV and VCR were still in his apartment. Old people get curious. She had a key.

His aunt didn't sound enthused about the prospect of Marc coming back. Without saying good-bye, she rang off, grumbling about him and his father.

Leaning back in his chair, Marc congratulated himself for packing the previous day and watching movies all evening. Instead of going to the bar. His eyes felt gritty from the endless viewing, he still ached from the beating two days before, and he had trouble dealing with the reality that he was leaving the paper. But he felt relieved to be putting this small Alberta city and its problems behind him.

Packing, he had thought about telling Lise his plans and had rejected the idea. He could do that when he reached his destination. He'd check on Teresa at the same time. The less contact with anybody, the better for him. The safer for others.

Out of habit, Marc leafed through the "in" pile on his desk. A yellow carbonless sheet from the Crooked Elbow police reminded him that his licence had been temporarily suspended pending his court appearance on the impaired driving charge. He might not be able to make that, now, he thought with some satisfaction. Among the other correspondence, no letters expressed love, no typed foolscap warned him about the future. He tucked the yellow charge sheet from the police into his shirt pocket and went to see Barb.

"Management going to your head?" he asked, glancing at the clock. At 9:15 she was at her desk, make-up applied, a coffee going.

"Don't be smart. I'm always on time. Lately. What happened to your eye?"

"Keyhole surveillance on a husband with a spike."

"Very funny. You saw yesterday's *Sun*?"

"Why do you think I'm here?"

"It wouldn't have something to do with a final cheque, would it? I've got a call in to the chief, who's being a jerk and will probably give us a glorified press release since he's given the dailies all the juicy stuff. Here's the chief's attitude to crime and the media in Crooked Elbow..." Barb stood, shoved her chair under her desk and turned her back on Marc and the two reporters in the room. A very nice back it was too, Marc thought. She wiggled her hips slightly, turned around again with a huge grin and said, "It's a bitch."

"Good," Marc said.

"Good? You are losing it."

"The outside media'll have half the town pissed off before noon today. Which means, if you're decent to the other half, they might talk to you. By the time you're out next week, all the big city guys'll be gone, and this'll be old news anyway. I'd go for backgrounders. Family, old pictures, people Shirley Basiuk went to school with. Religion."

"I've got a call in to Basiuk's lawyer," Barb said, flipping the pages of her notepad with long fingers further elongated by red nail extensions. "And the funeral home, for names of relatives."

"Good start. Johnny Basiuk's lawyer might talk to us if he thinks he can control the slant of the story. But don't let him manipulate you into trying the guy in the paper, or he's got a mistrial. Not that I care."

"Lots of 'allegeds' and all that."

"That's right. Heard anything about the little girl, Basiuk's daughter?"

"No, is she part of the story?"

"Probably not. If she's out of that family, that has to be good news for her. So, tell me, has the Brownrigg Corporation put any restrictions on your coverage this time?"

"What's that supposed to mean?"

"Don't get huffy. I was just thinking about your Agriplex editorial."

Barb's face coloured. "That was a business story, and we handled it like one. This is a news story and— not that it's any of your business— I happen to have the green light from Jeremy to give it the full treatment. I'm a big girl, and I can handle it."

Carmen's voice came over the telephone intercom. "Marc, line one. Marc."

He took it in his office. "Marc LePage, good morning."

"Good morning to you, Marc. It's Jordan Hamm."

"Yes, Jordan, what can I do for you?"

"I'm involved in the Basiuk case. And we're wondering if we could solicit a few minutes of your time."

"Well, Barb Zelnak's handling the story. Can I put you on hold and find her for you?"

"That won't be necessary. We're not on the record, per se. We'd like to talk with you in a more perfunctory fashion."

"This is my last day. I'm leaving town."

Jordan chuckled at that, although Marc missed the joke. "My client is currently incarcerated, as you may know. He's insisting on seeing you. The city police are holding him until there's a preliminary hearing and a choice of venue and all that good stuff."

"You don't mind me saying, this is a little weird. I'm not sure I can talk to him if we're not on the record."

"It's my client who's outlined the perimeters of this meeting, so I can't say what sort of eventuality we might anticipate," said Jordan Hamm, the word mangler. "But we'll see. Soon. Meet you at the jail in half an hour?"

Jordan hung up before Marc could tell him that Mr. Basiuk could do hard time for all Marc cared. On the other hand, Marc had to admit to a certain ingrained reporter's curiosity about what Johnny had in mind.

He found Barb talking to the press room foreman, who scowled and left as soon as he saw Marc.

Marc said he was leaving and didn't know whether he'd be back. He didn't tell Barb why. Barb said the paper seemed to be under control and it was okay if Marc left. But she wasn't as sure about the front page and editorial page dummies. They wouldn't be ready until Monday.

"You'll figure them out," he said. "You're a big girl."

Marc passed Fiona on the way back to his office. She was selling on the phone, the way some men liked it, hints of little girl softening her voice. "I know it's the holidays, Mike. Everybody knows that. But I need an ad... What will I do for you if I get one?... I don't know, what will you do for me?"

Marc waved to Fiona, left her working on the ad and returned to his desk.

Pretending he was Teresa's uncle, he rang the hospital for information about the 18-year-old. A receptionist put him on hold. When she came back, she said Teresa was still in intensive care.

Letting Carmen know he'd be gone for a while, Marc walked out into dazzling sunshine, his jacket over his shoulder, heading for the police station to meet Jordan Hamm.

British Columbia had the most Missing Children pictures posted in the police station lobby. Some of the children had been gone for 11 years. Marc wondered what they would look like if they were still alive, and then he imagined what they would look like if they were dead. The thought was so morbid, he was ashamed of himself. He flipped through a pamphlet called Preventing Shoplifting until Jordan Hamm showed up, after about 10 minutes that seemed like an hour.

"Sorry I'm late." The lawyer wore an expensive grey two-piece, tie and puff, and he wasn't sweating at all.

The receptionist set down a crossword puzzle magazine and asked Jordan what he wanted. He said, "We're here to see my client."

She glanced at the lawyer and paid no attention to Marc. "I'll see if the sergeant's in, Mr. Hamm."

The sergeant was in. He led them through a long hall and down cement steps that echoed to their footsteps. They passed a desk not manned by anybody. Against the wall were three cells, only one of them housing a prisoner. With a key that looked like any ordinary house key, the sergeant unlocked a steel door, and waved them into the cell.

It resembled a small room in a cheap hotel, except that the two beds were bolted to the cement floor and there was no carpet. The television was encased in a steel frame that looked like a safe; plexiglass reinforced with thin wire covered the TV screen.

A toilet bowl sat between the beds. The television was on, but Johnny Basiuk wasn't watching it. He was lost in his own snoring, huge, veined hands rising and falling on his plaid shirt. His upper lip sank in and fluttered out with each breath. When the cell door banged shut, his eyes flew open and he rolled over to face the wall. After a minute, he rolled back and sat up, staring at the bed across from him.

"I brought the editor, as per your request. How're we coping?" Jordan Hamm put a hand on Johnny's shoulder as if Hamm were a night nurse preparing to administer medication. "Are you ready to confrere with him?"

"Got a smoke?" Johnny turned red animal eyes on Marc and Jordan. His skin, the colour of whitewash, was broken by tiny magenta veins clustered around his nose.

Marc rolled him a cigarette and dug out some matches that offered a training course in electronics on the cover. Johnny lighted the smoke and tossed the spent match at the open toilet. It was none too clean and the match missed it.

"Will I leave you guys?" the sergeant asked, his voice carrying the lilt of the displaced Newfoundlander. He treated Jordan Hamm as the one in charge.

"Yes, please. I believe we require some innate privacy. Don't you agree, Mr. Basiuk?"

"How'd you like to go play with them big words somewheres else so me and him can have a chat?"

"I beg your pardon?"

"You heard me. Go find a little girl's room to spy on while me and the editor enjoy some privacy, eh?"

Jordan laughed in a nervous way at the sergeant, who didn't say anything, so Jordan ventured, "This is highly unregimented. Couldn't we have the interview room?"

The sergeant didn't think so. "Sorry about that, sir. Some jeezly staff training session." His eyes bored, unblinking, into Jordan's.

"You wish to speak with this man without the beneficence of counsel," Jordan said to Johnny.

"Your hearing seems to be improving."

"I absolutely do not recommend this. As your lawyer, I think you should be concupiscent of that."

Heaving himself to his feet, Johnny gave the lawyer the full benefit of his red animal stare. "Get lost, four eyes," he said, although the reference was lost on Marc. Jordan wasn't wearing glasses. The sergeant's fingers slid toward the gun snapped shut in a holster on his right hip.

Jordan's hands waved apologetically in the air, palms open, fingers twitching. "All right. If you want your lawyer to leave against his own advice, it becomes a problem he can no longer expedite."

Johnny drew on his cigarette, gummed in the smoke. Marc watched, but he didn't see any smoke exhaled. The lawyer dropped his hands and didn't know what to do with them, so he put them in his pants' pockets and nodded to the sergeant. The officer quickly patted Marc for weapons, taking his pens, his wallet, his belt, and his running-shoe laces. Opening, then slamming the steel door shut behind them, he locked it, walking away with Jordan.

Johnny sat, hunched up on one bed, Marc on the other. "It ain't the Hilton, but it's all I could afford," Johnny said, a sick grin on his face, but with a trace of the spirit Marc recognized in Teresa. Johnny reached for the upper plate of his teeth floating in a cup on top of the toilet. As he slipped them in, a line of spittle trailed down his chin. It glistened on his stubbly chin, but Johnny didn't move to wipe it off. With his teeth in, he looked almost human.

"Don't feel great," he groaned and rolled onto the bed in the position he'd been in when Marc entered, this time putting one hand above his head, tucking the other inside his shirt.

Marc felt like a teenager abandoned to the mercy of a brute. To compensate, he spoke loudly, with a panicky edge to his voice. "Somebody thinks this conversation can happen off the record. That's the most ridiculous thing I've heard in a long time."

"'Less you just listen to me, and then decide whether you or some other bunny is going to write up the story."

"Why should I listen to you?"

Johnny stared at the ceiling and didn't answer, so Marc stood and made as if to bang on the steel door. The bars by the door were stainless steel, but compared to Johnny, they didn't look all that tough.

"Don't do that." It was more of a threat than advice from Johnny Basiuk.

"Why not? My previous experience with you wasn't any joy ride. You're the last person I'm interested in helping."

"Or the first."

"Yeah?"

"Why did four eyes leave?"

"You kicked him out."

"Right," as if that answered some unspoken question.

"Erase. I don't have time for games."

"I could use a drink, you understand. Look at this." Johnny moved his right paw from behind his head and held it in front of him, meaty fingers jerking in mid-air. "I'm doing pretty good since I came here." He smiled at his accomplishment, but the smile was pasted on.

"Can you fill me in on what brought you here?"

"That's not why I invited you. How's Teresa?"

"Still unconscious, far as I know."

"I don't remember much from that night anyways. You spare another butt?"

Marc tossed Johnny his makings. "I'm surprised they let you smoke in a government building."

"I been thinking what I wouldn't give for a drink, but I'll beat it yet. She never thought so, but I will. I done it once before when she said she was leaving, and I'll do it now. But what am I saying? That don't mean I'm not done like a Thanksgiving turkey."

"Done how?"

No answer.

"Okay, let's move to the open-ended part of our seminar. What the hell is going on inside that working-class, low-rent, jailbird mind of yours?"

Afternoon soap opera music rolled majestically from the television set. Johnny Basiuk watched a very pretty woman tell another woman she thought she had breast cancer. "Turn off the noise, will you, bud?"

It was Marc's turn not to say anything. Prompting the man didn't seem to help. The front of the steel box had a switch. He pushed it and the actors disappeared. Johnny swung his legs around, sat up and looked at the cigarette dying between his thumb and forefinger. "TV and everything. It ain't going to be so bad."

"Not that they'll leave you here. You'll probably go to Edmonton for the trial."

"So they say."

"You confessed?"

"Something like that. They wanted to hear things, so I told them. Too late for me. I don't remember nothin' so they're prob'ly right, eh?"

"I was there. I heard you start in on her."

"You was there? Ain't that a notion? You prob'ly remember more than me. Sometimes a woman gets out of hand, you got to do something. They bring it on themselves. But I don't remember killing nobody. What kinda man's going to do the cow that's givin' him milk? That don't make no sense." Johnny crushed the cigarette between thumb and forefinger and threw it in the toilet, hitting the water this time. "Somebody else done her," he said angrily.

"It might have been you."

"Who knows?" Johnny lowered his huge head and shook it slowly from side to side. "They got me anyway."

"But you've got the biggest lawyer in town."

"Sure, bud, and who's paying the shot? It ain't old Johnny B., cause he ain't got the scratch. So let's guess who it is. Maybe somebody keeps Mr. Hamm on retainer?"

"Klaus Axel?"

Johnny coughed into his hand and wiped his palm on the heavy blanket that covered his steel bed. "BM1. An' what's the lawyer doing here?"

"Trying to help you?"

"Maybe. I don't give two ounces of sheep shit about that. I get off, there's nothing but the wrong end of a bottle. But I go down, some of these hoity toity assholes is comin' with me. I got to play along with that lawyer. 'Cause there's not a soul can help me on the outside. 'Cept maybe you." Johnny endured a coughing fit at the end of that speech, bad enough to make Marc think he might throw up. But he didn't, and when it was over, he sat on the edge of the bed, a beaten hulk, his head swaying. He spit and hit the toilet bowl.

"You're asking me for help? The guy you half strangled and kicked and tried to run over with the truck? I liked it so much, I'm dying to give you a hand."

"Did I? Sorry. I got a temper. I was thinking you'd help 'cause you're a newspaper man, and I've got a story that'll curdle your biscuits."

"Offer's only good till the end of the day. I've already got my walking papers and they made it worth my while to stay clean until I leave."

"You leaving *The Fun?*"

"Their choice, *monsieur*, not mine."

"Yeah, well, then there's Steph and Teresa. You might hate my liver, but you was some sweet on my Teresa. Not to mention how I feel about Stephanie."

"Yeah. Shirley's dead, Stephanie is dead, and Teresa's in hospital," Marc reminded him. Saying this brought back buried hurt and blackness. Marc's ears ached and he had difficulty swallowing.

Johnny rolled his head, as if trying to free it from the alcoholic longings inside. "Don't that make you curious?"

Marc shook his head and wondered what the man was driving at. "I was once."

Reaching over, Johnny pinched the sleeve of Marc's shirt, pulling his arm. "You know who's got little Suz? Klaus Axel. Jordan tells me the bastard moved for custody this morning. Somebody should have done Klaus a long time ago. Maybe I'd still have a family. I got Klaus's lawyer working for me. And Klaus has the only thing left of my family. Which leaves me next to nothing. And when you got nothing left..."

The sentence hung in the air. A fly, ignoring the bars, entered the cell and buzzed in circles until it landed on Marc's cheek. He swatted at it and it landed on his sleeve. Johnny killed it with a slap that jarred Marc's teeth.

"Jesus," Marc said. "Look, you expect me to feel sorry for someone who drinks himself stupid and then has bad things happen to him? Man, I drink myself, but it never..."

Johnny cut him off. "You got nobody. That makes it easy."

Was that true? Marc didn't want to bring his own past into this. "What's the point, Johnny?"

Johnny ran his fingers through his thinning greasy hair several times and said, "I'd start with the registration."

"Yeah?"

"On the car that killed Steph. That fancy muscle car." He spat out the reference to the automobile with contempt.

"I did. It was Bobby McLean's. So what? He says she borrowed it."

"Did I say registration? I meant insurance, check the insurance, eh? Maybe he didn't have none."

"But his dad's best friend owns an insurance company. And you can't drive without insurance."

"Wrong."

Marc stared at Johnny, wondering how many brain cells the alcohol had killed.

As if he knew what Marc were thinking, Johnny rolled back on the bed and stared at a second fly's slow progress across the wall. "You can't drive without a pink slip."

"And?"

"Bobby had a pink slip and nothing to back it up. Bobby thought he had insurance because he wrote good old Axel Agencies a cheque, you understand? But that don't mean the money made it where it was supposed to go. Maybe my old buddy was skimming the till."

"Even though he's rich?"

"Look, the biggest man in Crooked Elbow badly *needs* everybody to think he's rich. Sometimes he has been rich. That don't mean Klaus's got two pesos to rub together at any given moment. All he invested in that gasohol scheme, going down the tubes once the oil lobby got wind of it. And him sitting on that Agriplex land and having trouble putting the deal together. All the time, he's got expenses, and the clock's ticking. Old Indian saying: Man with too many irons in the fire, liable to get privates burnt."

Johnny stood up and there was no room to pace so he sat down. He leaned against the wall, his hands on the bed to give his back a rest.

"How do you know this?" Marc asked.

"Man's married to his wife's sister, man spends time with a guy for over twenty years, he's got to learn something. Some of that's family and that's private. But Shirley's gone and these others turned on me like hungry wolves."

Johnny bounced a little on the bed and his eyes gleamed with envy or hate. "I could get done just for talking like this, but I'm willing to take the chance. Maybe I done the wife, I don't think so, but maybe I did. But I didn't do them girls any harm. I loved them girls like they was my own, temper and all, and I never meant to hurt them. Or my wife. It's them other guys got after the girls. You understand?"

"Are you saying you pimped for your own daughters?"

Johnny leaned forward, his breath thin and rancid behind the tobacco odour. He grabbed Marc's shirt front, not roughly, but firmly so he had Marc's attention and there was nothing Marc could do about it. The hands closed on Marc as relentlessly as clamps.

"Fuck you," Johnny said. "I'll be so old when I get out of here, it won't make no difference. You follow the trial and you'll see old Jordan using them big words in such a way as to guarantee me a long stretch in maximum security."

Marc tried to squirm away, as much from Johnny's breath as his grip, but the squirming did no good. "So get another lawyer," Marc said.

Johnny laughed gusts of bad breath at Marc, and his coughing started up again. After a while, it stopped and he let Marc go.

"So you want me to check the insurance?" Marc said.

"Check the insurance. And there's more, this other little morsel I been wondering whether to leak. Was I a newspaper man, I'd get out to The Wild Rose Friday night. That's tonight, isn't it? I'm all screwed up on time in here. Anyway, Friday night. Room 4, ground floor, about 11:00. And I'd bring a camera. And something else..."

"What?" Marc said, deciding to prompt the man again, now that he was on a roll.

"There's a set of keys to my place and the hotel and my truck and stuff. Little Suz's got them in her purse, for emergencies, you understand?"

"And this might be an emergency."

Marc banged on the steel door. Jordan Hamm was gone. The sergeant stood up slowly from the desk down the room and walked over at a leisurely pace to let Marc out, as if he had all day.

"Not a word to anybody," Johnny hissed at him from the bed. "They'd do little Suz soon as look at her. I couldn't stand that, eh?"

CHAPTER 21

"Is Klaus home?" Marc asked Jeeves late Friday morning.

"No. Mr. Axel not here."

The dog lifted its head, whined a couple of times and decided it was stupid to charge the fence in this heat.

"I'm expected," Marc lied, showing Jeeves a business card. "I've got something Mr. Axel asked me for. Why don't you let me drop it off at the house?"

"Why doncha leave it here?"

"It's confidential." Marc flashed an Axel Agencies envelope he'd picked up when he slipped into the *Sun* office after leaving Johnny Basiuk's cell. The envelope had recently contained an invoice for newspaper advertising. There were occasional advantages to a messy desk.

Either the envelope satisfied the guard or Jeeves was too hot to argue. He shrugged, shuffled over and opened the gate. Marc puttered through, waving one hand.

He could afford to put on some airs, having just gotten Das Kapital out of the garage. With $513 worth of fender repairs and a new back window for his car, he could visit the *haute bourgeoisie* any time he wanted. Licence or no licence.

Halfway across the lawn, water arced over the grass, droplets glinting in the sunlight like streams of costume jewellery. Marc parked in front of the house.

Little Suz knelt on the clipped lawn, playing with another girl in the bright, bright sunshine. Dressed in shorts, halter tops, frilly hats and over-sized high heels, they manipulated dolls inside a large pink and white plastic house with a pink plastic roof. Their running shoes were carelessly strewn across the grass. They paid no attention to Marc.

The big door to the house opened a crack and then shut again. The girls looked up at the door, over at Marc, and went back to their dolls. Marc strolled across the grass to them and hunkered down on his knees. The other girl seemed shy, but little Suz looked boldly up at him.

"Hi," he said.

"Hi," Suzie said.

"What're you doing?"

"Playing Barbies."

"Who's your friend?"

"Jennifer."

Marc didn't try to figure out how far a person would have to drive out here to find a little girl for Suzie to play with. "I saw your daddy today."

Her eyes widened. "You did?" she said.

"Sorry, your grandpa. He said to come with me."

"No." She started brushing her doll's hair with hurried, clumsy strokes.

"He said you *had* to."

"No. He's gone. Uncle Klaus and Auntie Anne told me. He's in prison."

The front door of the house re-opened a crack, and Marc tried another tack. "Yes, he is. That's where I saw him and he wants you to come see him. I'm supposed to take you there. He's got something to tell you. A secret."

"Can Jennifer come?"

"Sure she can."

"Okay, you want to?" Suzie smiled a bleak, false smile at Jennifer. Continuing the pretence that Marc didn't officially exist, the girl returned the smile and rocked her small body back and forth, which seemed to mean yes.

"Let's go," said little Suz.

"You got your purses?"

"I brang mine, but Jennifer didn't bring one."

Each girl was allowed to bring one Barbie doll with her into the dusty back seat of Das Kapital. He made them leave their hats on the lawn and exchange their high heels for the running shoes he quickly gathered from the grass. Once they were in the car, Marc checked to make sure little Suz still had her purse. That part was easy.

The tough part would be getting his passengers past the man in the butler suit by the road.

Das Kapital started back down the lane. It was even with the fancy garage when Marc made up his mind. He slammed the steering wheel hard right, shifted into second gear and accelerated onto the lawn, ripping a slick patch of grass as he went.

Jeeves had lumbered into action. A rifle barrel poked around the corner of his hut, and the dog bounded from its cage, barking furiously, so eager for the chase that it forgot all about the heat.

The little car tracked smoothly across the lawn until it reached the irrigation pipe. Marc cranked the steering wheel left and followed the pipe. The car was soon washed by wet zircons from the sprinkler. They were dangerously close to Jeeves' hut, but Marc didn't dare an earlier crossing for fear he'd crush a pipe and blow a tire. Just past the sprinkler, he rammed the little car right.

Marc accelerated, tires spinning on the wet grass, away from the gun and the dog. As soon as the tires touched dry, unirrigated grass, he rocked the car side to side, hoping to dodge bullets if they came his way.

"Whoa," one of the girls shouted as they bounced around in the back seat.

"You kids got your seat belts on?" he yelled at them.

"Can't find them," Suzie said.

The gun cracked, but the bullet came nowhere near its target. Unlike the dog. As Marc slowed for the one-sided ditch sloping down to the road, the dog caught up, slobbering and running at the tires.

Marc took the ditch on an angle, violating with two tire treads the clipped effect of the lawn above the wild grasses and weeds. It was steep but Volkswagens make good dune buggies. The car teetered, righted itself, and his tires ripped into gravel, leaving the dog to whine at stones flung at its nose. In the back seat, the girls laughed at his crazy driving. "It's like the fair!" one of them said.

The girls' excitement had evaporated by the time they reached town.

"We're hot," little Suz complained when she saw the 7-Eleven in Crooked Elbow.

"I'm thirsty," her friend joined in, looking out the side window at the convenience store.

Marc bought chocolate ice cream for them at the Burger 'N' Cone and left Suzie and Jennifer sitting on the cement curb while he used the pay phone. The police receptionist told him Lise wasn't working this shift. The answering machine at her place wasn't any more instructive, so he went back to the girls and immediately regretted buying the ice cream. Chocolate smeared their knuckles and rimmed their mouths. Wet chocolate stained their halter tops.

He ignored the stains and asked them if they were ready to get back in the car. "No," little Suz said, but they got in anyway.

"Where's grandpa? How much longer is it?" she asked, wiping at her mouth with the back of her forearm.

"Almost there," he said, turning left into a side street lined with cars and skinny trees. The girls finished their ice cream while he drove through an older residential area to the Catholic church and parked. "Stay here for a minute. You can't leave unless *I* say so, you hear?"

Little Suz didn't say anything and then she said "No" quietly as if she were scared or angry. "No," she said again. "Let us out."

"Okay, c'mon." Marc swung himself up out of the car, pushing the back of the driver's seat forward for them.

"I'm still thirsty," little Suz said, squinting out the window into the sunlight.

"Let's go talk to the priest, see whether he's got any nice cold lemonade."

A car drifted by. A wrinkled man with a crumpled fishing hat gave them the once-over. "Hurry up, you guys. Let's get inside."

Marc rushed the two girls through a door into an office. A receptionist who looked as old fashioned as the church said the girls could wait on a couch while Marc knocked on the priest's door.

"Come in," Father Larry yelled from inside.

Marc opened the door on a haze of cigarette smoke. The priest was working at a computer on his desk. "Am I disturbing you?"

"Hard to disturb a priest. I get interrupted all the time."

"I can imagine. How've you been?"

"Fine. But I'd say you're not here because of my health."

"Maybe somebody else's health. Maybe a child's, from the wrong side of the tracks."

"We remain committed to the health of children," he said formally.

"I'm working on a story, and..." Marc hesitated over how much to tell Larry and decided, not much. "And a couple of girls are in trouble. I brought them with me. Can you keep them for a while?"

"What kind of trouble?"

Marc talked very quietly, as if he didn't trust the office walls, though they looked innocent enough with their crucifix and picture of Jesus in prayer. "I don't know exactly. I think it might be... one of the girl's uncles. He..."

"Enough said," the priest answered, his mouth set. "There are too many of those cases. We can provide temporary shelter. Any idea how long?"

Marc calculated quickly, wondering what his next move would be and how much time he needed. "Overnight?" he asked. "Please."

"Okay, but no longer than necessary. It can get messy when you're interfering in child custody."

"I may be back for the other girl, Jennifer, sooner," Marc said, getting up quickly before the priest changed his mind. "But little Suz, at least overnight."

"Last names?"

"Sorry, no can do. Not a good idea. The less said, the better."

"Do I know them?"

"Not that I know of."

"Did they bring their pyjamas?" the priest asked.

"Haven't you got something?"

Father Larry's eyes narrowed and glinted at him. "I guess. What are you up to, Marc?"

Marc looked at a small plaque on the desk, with the message "Let go and let God." "Nothing," he said. "Just trying to help a kid who's lost a mother. Thanks for looking after them. Give me a couple of minutes, I'll bring them in, do the introductions."

"Fine," Larry said, the lines in his forehead showing how much trouble he felt and how little of it was out in the open.

Little Suz scrambled up when Marc opened the door, and the other girl immediately followed. "We're still thirsty," she said, her whiny tone returning.

"Okay," Marc said. Almost whispering, he knelt in front of little Suz. "This church is going to look after you for a while. And I'm going to see your grandpa and set things up. Okay? He said he wanted your little purse, so you give it to me and I'll take it to him. You stay with the nice priest and he'll give you a drink."

"What's his name?"

"Father Larry."

"He's not my father or her father."

"I know, but you can call him that. He's a priest. Now, can I have the purse, please?"

"No." Little Suz shrank from Marc, cowering as if she could hide in a corner of the couch. One finely veined hand clung to the purse.

"I just need to borrow it."

"No, I can't give it to nobody. I'll get the belt."

Her voice was rising. The little girl stared at him. Without saying another word, she raised her arms as if her hands could protect her from belts or any other bad things that might be coming her way.

The gesture was pathetic and it touched Marc's heart. "I'm not going to hurt you," he said. "That's why you're here, so people won't hurt you."

Suzie's large, dark-rimmed eyes blinked. Her hands lowered a couple of inches and she looked at Jennifer. Marc took that as a sign of slight lessening in her fear and leaned closer to her. The child shut her eyes but didn't raise her hands again.

"It's okay. Your grandpa said I could borrow the purse. Nobody's going to give you the belt."

Marc's hand closed around the plastic strap of the purse. "I'm going to take it for a little while. See? I've got it and it's okay. I'm going now, and when I leave, you go to that door over there and knock and the priest will let you in."

But they didn't have to do that on their own. The receptionist was already bustling around her desk to guide the girls inside.

Marc drove to an automobile showroom gleaming with a Corvette, a Camaro, an S-10 pick-up and two large potted ferns. A salesman approached as soon as he was in the door.

"Good afternoon. You look like you're enjoying the summer. It's a pretty warm day out there, great for the crops. Can I help you with something? We've got a new vehicle for every budget."

Marc smiled and said, "Not my budget. Is Mr. Baker busy?"

"Can I say who's calling?" The young man washed his hands drily and grinned.

"Marc LePage."

"The newspaper, right? You guys are doing a great job over there. It's what this town needs, a real newspaper, not just Mrs. Spittoon had tea and cookies with Mrs. Jamjar."

"And then Mrs. Spittoon cut one that was heard across town. Thank you, but it's my last week at the paper."

"Moving on? Well, if your travels mean new transportation, I want you to remember me. Charles. Charles Adams. Charlie to my friends. Here's my card."

"Charlie, do you think I could see the boss? I'm losing my job— which doesn't make me much of a prospect— and I'm on a bit of a tight schedule."

Charlie escorted Marc up a set of carpeted stairs to a spacious office dominated by a desk and a tall thin man with white hair and a thin dark moustache. The brass plate on the desk said the man's name was Jonathan T. (Johnny) Baker. Two of the office's four walls bore certificates and plaques attesting to Jonathan Baker's volunteer efforts.

He shook hands with long, cool fingers. The back of one hand sported a brown liver spot.

"How you doing?" Marc asked.

"Fair to middlin'. At my age, you get out of bed in the morning and you're creaking, you're still alive. Every day above ground's a good one.

How are you? Looking a little like something the dog dragged home, I hope you don't mind me saying. Somebody hit you a couple of times? Sit down. Can I get you a coffee?"

"Thanks for the compliment and no thanks on the coffee. Can I smoke?"

"Only if you offer me a cigarette." Marc rolled him one. Baker used a desk lighter and inhaled and coughed and smiled along the creases of his face at Marc. "The doctors told me when I turned 69 that if I didn't change my ways, I'd never see 70. But we all know there's more old drunks than old doctors. So what I figure, it's like women— my age, you can still enjoy 'em once in a while, but you got to conserve your energy. I quit smoking and I scrounge three or four a day just so I know I still got a ticker." He laughed and coughed around a tongue startling in its redness.

When the coughing wound down, Marc said, "I'm out of a job."

"So we heard. That's not good news for this town. I always look at newspapers as if they were salespeople; if you gotta have one, you might as well have one with brass testicles. Are you here to pick up a new Corvette with your severance money?"

"I need a car, but I also need a favour. It's a little complicated, but that car of mine stands out like a sore thumb. And I've got a licence problem. Can you swing a rental for a couple of days?"

"Sure, no problem. I'll get Charlie to write it up."

"Okay." Marc hesitated and then plunged ahead. "I assume you're still interested in the mayor's job."

Johnny laughed at that and butted his cigarette, half smoked. "Let's say I'm part of the unofficial ABA movement."

"ABA?"

"Yeah. Anybody But Axel. Whether I win against the big guy this fall remains to be seen."

"I can't tell you much right now, but I'm looking into something he's mixed up in. I'm not exactly the richest man in town. I may need what I have to see me through this. So what about a discount on the rental? Even with my licence problem?"

"If somebody— anybody, my worst enemy, and believe me I got 'em—

told me they were investigating Klaus Axel, I'd give them the shirt off my back on the coldest day in January. You, sir, just got yourself a free rental. And gas. What the hell? Let's go all the way. If they ask about your licence, we'll plead senility, say we forgot to write it up."

Marc parked his new rental car two blocks from the *Sun* office and packed the pen set from the Rotary Club, the letter opener from the Optimist Club, a few ballpoint pens, some film and a couple of steno pads into his bags. It didn't take long to say the last of his good-byes. Everybody told him not to be a stranger— stop in from time to time— before they went back to putting out the next paper so they didn't have to think about him. Marc understood, but his throat caught when he said good-bye to the reporters. He covered his sentiments with a grin.

When he shook Barb's hand, he said, "No hard feelings, okay? Stay with it, don't let the bastards get to you, and you'll do fine."

"I appreciate what you did for me. Really." She gave him a little sideways hug.

Carmen was more generous. She offered him a full hug, a kiss on the cheek and a quick, "Call me some time."

Marc said, "Sure," and thought about, but didn't mention, his plan to leave town. So far, the decision to keep the women in his life at arm's length seemed to be working.

When Carmen let him go, he exhaled, ran his fingers through his hair and asked if she had anything for him.

"God, I almost forgot. It came by courier this morning. They like to cut things close."

"Nice," he said. "The personal touch. A little thank you for all my hard work."

"The pricks," she said and handed him a number 10 Brownrigg envelope.

With most of his worldly possessions in the trunk, Marc drifted through town in the rental. He enjoyed the air conditioning and the feeling of release now that little Suz was safe, he had Johnny's "emergency" keys, and he was driving a car that couldn't easily be identified. Friday afternoon traffic clogged 50th Street. Young people cruising, studying themselves and each other through mirrors and windshields and sunglasses. He drove sedately, idly observing their horseplay.

He parked in the wide Safeway parking lot and was surprised by how much he felt the tarmac heat through his running shoes when he was halfway to The Victoria. A quick one or two wouldn't hurt. He couldn't think of anything better on a day like this, hot and nothing to do for a few hours. Friday afternoon, everybody in a good mood, hoping to tie one on for the weekend.

A pick-up swept past him. A girl in a white lacy top and tight jeans was perched above the door frame, hanging onto the roof, the window open, her arms and legs inside, while the driver zigzagged crazily through the parking lot.

Memories of Teresa. Marc looked elsewhere. What he was about to do hit him, hard.

"Damn," he said.

To keep himself busy while he avoided any permanent decisions about anything, Marc drove all the way to Edmonton and wandered around the bookstores until 8:00. Time to head the rental to Rose Hill and see whether one of the keys in the plastic purse would work in a hotel room door.

When he allowed himself to think about it on the drive south to the village, going without a drink didn't seem all that tough. He had only walked by every small bar crammed with summer students on Whyte Avenue. He had only thought about stopping in a hundred times. Nothing a grown man with important things on his mind couldn't handle.

CHAPTER 22

Men and women in summer attire were lined up outside the showroom entrance for The Wild Rose. Marc drove past the hotel, parked on a street of poorly lighted bungalows five blocks away and walked back. He entered by a side door under a sign that said, "Lobby: Suites for rent." Inside were a leather couch, two leather chairs and a tired man watching television behind a counter.

"Can I help you?" Without switching off the set, the man moved to the counter, pen poised. His jacket was as dark as the furniture, his face as sallow as the wallpaper, bathed in yellow light from yellow lamps in the corners.

"Any vacancies? Yellow room, if you've got it."

The man grunted, ran a thumb down a desk calendar and said. "Just you?" as if he were suspicious of someone registering alone in this hotel. He emitted eau de stale old man and raised an eyebrow.

"Just me."

"I can put you up in 229. It's small, but clean. Most of our rooms are oversize and 229 has the movies and everything." The man shoved a yellow-looking card and a dark ballpoint pen across the desk at Marc.

"Can I have a look first?"

"Down the hall, take the stairs to the second floor." Raising a cigarette to lips that looked otherworldly in this light, the man rattled a key at Marc.

The hall outside the office was stuffy and dimly lit. A red sign at the end said "EXIT." Under the sign, a metal outside door had been propped open with a cement block in a futile attempt to circulate the hot hallway air. The bass line from a band at Alberta's longest bar throbbed in Marc's ears. He found room 4 easily and tried Johnny Basiuk's key.

The room was air conditioned and well-insulated. The bass beat stopped when the door had been eased shut, sealing Marc inside. There was only one sound, water swirling in an adjoining room. Different smells. Chlorine. Fresh smoke, both cigarette and cigar. The yeasty smell of beer.

A large room, it had blue lamps and an oak desk along the far wall.

An enormous chair loomed behind the desk. Above the chair hung a wide sign, its words inscribed in stylized western type: "The Four Horsemen. Meeting regularly for the good of ourselves."

A leather couch stretched along one wall under a bookcase lined with plastic video cases. Facing the couch were a television set, a VCR, easy chairs, a filing cabinet, and a refrigerator. In the centre of the room squatted a bed with a frilly bedspread not disturbed tonight, probably blue since it looked white in this light. Four stuffed horses' heads jutted out of one wall like safari trophies. The filing cabinet was under them.

Marc thought, "Stuffed heads? The way people feel about horses in this province?"

He brushed by the bed and lowered himself into the huge leather chair. On the desk were a telephone, three empty beer bottles, a pen set, a manual typewriter, and a television remote control. The centre drawer of the desk unlocked with a small key attached to Johnny's key ring. The other drawers slid open as effortlessly as if they rolled on ball bearings. Inside, he found file folders, stationery, a box of condoms, and a tube of waterproof personal lubricant. In the top right drawer, loose pens rolled over an invitation to a Rotary Club summer barbecue.

He relocked the middle drawer and tiptoed to a door between two of the chairs. Opening it a crack released the sharp smell of chlorine from a room with green lighting, a tiled floor and tiled walls. Water frothed and spun in a whirlpool bath with nobody in it. Towels on hooks lined part of one wall. Towels and clothing were tossed across two plastic chairs. Several pairs of boots were lined up against the far wall.

A sign on a door to the left said "SAUNA." Another door straight ahead of him had no sign. From behind it, noises of music and people emanated, none of it distinguishable. When he closed the door, all he could hear was whirling water.

The filing cabinet guarded by the horse heads unlocked with the same key that had opened the desk. The top file drawer screeched— to his ears, so loudly, the band could hear it— when he opened it. Marc quickly leafed through file folders labelled alphabetically: Agriplex, Axel Agencies, Bills,

Correspondence, Gasohol, Miscellaneous, Personal, Rent: Kuchik. The Bills file was the thickest.

Music rose and faded and rose again from the direction of the whirlpool room. Marc yanked out the Agriplex file and squealed the drawer shut. His fingers shook as he tried to relock the cabinet. No luck. He was sure someone was coming. He inhaled and exhaled four times, counting to 10 and back to one. He wiggled the drawer handle, tried the key, and it worked. Mouthing a "thank you" to God, he pushed the file folder into the front of his pants, tucked his shirt over it and left, making sure the door was locked behind him.

"Things check out?" the tired man behind the desk asked.

"No problem," Marc said, his voice shaking as he laid the key to room 229 on the counter. "Gotta sort out a couple of details first."

"You may be needing a double, then?"

"Maybe," Marc said. He winked in a way he thought the man with the yellow skin might appreciate. "Doesn't this affect the TV?" He waved his hand at the yellow lamps.

"A man gets used to almost anything."

Marc turned a knob in the dark interior of the rented car. A light shone under the glove compartment, and another glowed behind his head. He tried deep breathing again so he wouldn't spill the contents of the file folder all over the seat. Inside were blueprints and building sketches and copies of correspondence between Klaus Axel and various levels of government. The outgoing correspondence was typed on 4-H Enterprises stationery.

A series of letters from the previous year hinted at a connection between 4-H Enterprises and the sale of the land for the Agriplex. Since he wasn't able to cross-reference the numbered company involved in that sale, Marc couldn't tell for sure what was going on. Some of the land correspondence seemed to be dated after Klaus had become acting mayor. Hints of conflict of interest, but nothing solid.

Shoving the file folder under the seat, he closed his eyes, leaned on the steering wheel and said, "Man, oh, man." He wasn't trained for midnight sleuthing. He felt ordinary and so terrified of what might lie ahead that the only sensible thing to do was to start the car, tramp on the accelerator, and head for the nearest bus depot.

But he couldn't. There was a reason Johnny Basiuk had told him to come here, The Wild Rose Cafe, room 4, 11:00 p.m. So far, Marc had seen a whirlpool, four mounted horse heads, a dubious motto for the good life, and a file folder of correspondence that didn't add up to more than coincidence.

He had to go back. Slinging his camera bag over his shoulder, Marc locked the car and walked around the building so he wouldn't have to explain anything to the night man.

The metal door at the back was still propped open. The blue room was still blue. The horse heads guarded no more humans than they had a few minutes before. Marc listened at the door to the whirlpool room and heard no whirling water sounds and no voices.

He went in.

The steaming whirlpool was still. Behind him, the door shut and he panicked for an instant at the stealthy sound of its closing. But nobody yelled. No doors suddenly ripped open. The steady muffled beat of a country song from behind the door across the room drew him on.

Marc had changed to cowboy boots in the car after two hours of walking Edmonton's Whyte Avenue in running shoes. Boots were a disadvantage now. Removing them and his socks so he wouldn't slide on a wet patch of tile, he made his way barefoot to the clothes and towels piled along one wall, looking for identification.

There was more than identification.

There was a pistol sitting like a dangerous paperweight next to a black mask on a pile of clothing. Marc didn't know much about guns. It had been 20 years since he'd handled a rifle, when he and his buddies had gone groundhog hunting in the bean fields around Chatham, Ontario.

But that might not matter.

If he burst through the door, gun and camera in hand, would anybody in the room have any idea whether the safety was on or not? Picking up the pistol, heavy in his hand, he crossed the damp tiles and leaned his ear against the door. The music sounded like Dwight Yoakam.

Marc tried the knob. The door was unlocked.

He tried it again, opened the door a crack. Music filled his ears. Through the crack, he saw men, washed in red light on the far side of the room near a bed. Their arms were over their heads. They were naked except for cowboy hats and Zorro masks. A woman knelt in front of one of them.

As Marc watched, one of the men clicked the remote control in his hand and then dropped it behind him. On the television set, a naked child crawled across the floor and began doing something to an aroused man. Not a young woman, but a girl of six or seven. The child kept looking away from the man, as if somebody else were telling her what to do. The film was grainy, shot with a hand-held video camera, and the sound was bad and loud. The child resembled little Suz. He stared at her dark eyes, the ribbon in her long hair. It was little Suz. The realization staggered Marc, made him ill.

Easing the door shut, Marc went back for the black mask sitting on the clothes. He put the mask over his eyes, changed the filter on his flash and his camera settings, stuck the gun in his belt and came through the door flashing pictures and cranking the film as fast as he could. The first electronic strobe caught three men, naked, handcuffed to a horse stall affair set up along one wall. Two of them sported erections sheathed in condoms, and the third one might have had an erection. It was hard to tell, with the woman's head in front of his genitals.

The men quickly lost their interest in sex. The kneeling woman turned her head, her face hidden by a black leather hood with slits for her eyes and mouth. She screamed at him, "Hey, this is a private fucking party."

Marc had a sinking feeling in his stomach when he heard the voice. It sounded like Lise, and it didn't sound like Lise. The men very badly wanted to move their hands to cover their genitalia, but it was difficult with the handcuffs holding their arms fixed in the air. Their bodies writhed. One man was short, soft in the belly and slim in the limbs. Another was a little taller and tanned. The third, where the woman knelt, was tall and dark and heavily built. "What the fuck?" a man whimpered.

The woman brought herself up from her knees. She wore a black leather bustier and black high-heeled boots that came to her knees. She tottered toward Marc.

"Hold it," he shouted above the music. "Right there." He couldn't believe it. He sounded like a rookie cop on TV. Pulling the pistol out of his waist, he pointed it at the juncture where two orbs of flesh cleaved and protruded, defying gravity with the help of leather and wire.

That stopped her.

The Dwight Yoakam tape clicked off.

"Back off," she said in a voice that was a gravelly whisper in the sudden silence. That voice. Was it deliberately distorted? "You're trespassing. There's nothing illegal going on here."

"Oh, yeah?" Marc said, swinging the gun toward the television set where the grainy child pornography played on. A slim cattle whip lay curled on the bed among some ropes.

She had taken at least one more step toward Marc by the time he swung the gun back to stop her. The gun and his hand were shaking, but he didn't see how he could miss at this range.

"Shoot," she said in her husky voice, "and you'll go away for a long time. Maybe life."

All he could think of was what he'd seen in movies. "Down on your knees. By the bed. Head on the blankets."

She wouldn't listen to him, took another step.

"No," he said. "Down on the bed." He aimed the barrel at a spot near her high-heeled boots.

The roar was enormous in his ears. The bullet tore a hole in the carpet, ricocheted off the cement floor and buried itself in a wall somewhere. The woman dropped to her knees.

The soft man tugged frantically at his cuffs. Marc screamed at him, "Quit, asshole, or you're next." The man stopped.

Marc forced himself to move beside the woman. He had to admire her— not shaking or crying, just kneeling by the bed in her rather ridiculous S & M outfit, hands in front of her. He put the end of the barrel against her temple, ashamed because he was excited by the power the gun gave him.

"Off with the hood, please," he said in as measured a voice as he could manage.

"Okay," she whispered. "Just watch the gun. It's got a tricky trigger."

She peeled the hood off her head.

"Now," he told her. "Up, very slowly." He had to face what he had dreaded. That voice. And why she knew all about the gun. "Lise."

He let that sink in and confuse him.

His confusion cleared and it took all the rationality he could muster to not try the trigger again. His first instinct was to see how tricky it could be. "The masks," he said to her.

"No," the shortest man yelled.

"He's got a gun, asshole," Lise said. She removed cowboy hats and unmasked each man in turn— Robbie McLean, Klaus Axel, Nicky Kuchik.

"Well, well," Marc said, hoping that, with his mask, they couldn't positively identify him.

"Stay there," he said, trying to make his voice deeper than usual, going for a little Johnny Cash in it, indicating with his gun that he wanted Lise to line up with them.

"We'll sue your ass," Robbie McLean said, sounding frightened.

"All right," Marc said in his fake deeper voice. "It's a free country. Okay, police woman, get going. Join the line-up."

She did what he said. Before she could shield her eyes, he said "Smile," and took their picture, as if they were depraved relatives posing unhappily for a family photo. A second picture of the bed and the television. The whole time, he dangled the pistol under the camera, like an awkward light meter, balancing the camera on his wrist.

Popping out the video cassette, he said, "Come with me," to Lise.

"What about us?" Robbie McLean asked, sounding indignant at the idea of being left handcuffed and naked.

"I'll call your wife, see if she can get up here, give you a ride, cowboy. Looks like you might be impaired." Marc nodded at the bottle.

He shoved Lise ahead of him through the door into the whirlpool room. She slipped on a puddle of water and went down, face first. Her hands slapped the tiles, but not soon enough, and she banged one knee. Marc didn't move to help her.

"You got any clothes?"

"You bastard," she snarled at him from her hands and knees, her face contorted by rage and despair. "Fucking slime ball."

Marc lowered a knee into her leathered back. She reached around to claw at his genitals. He shoved the gun barrel into the base of her neck. She quit grabbing at him. The wind seemed to go out of her, and she sprawled on the wet floor.

Marc stood up. "You got any clothes?"

She nodded to the tiles.

"Then let's get them."

"Help me up."

"Sure," he said, but he stayed where he was and let her raise herself to her knees. A breast flopped out of the leather costume. She attempted no pretences of modesty. Leaving it out, she stared ahead. Marc didn't want to think about what she might be seeing.

After a while she tucked her breast back in and looked up at him like a pet that's been kicked. The anger seeped out of him, and he was suddenly tired to the bone. He waved the gun weakly in the direction of the towels and clothes.

Switching the gun to his left hand, he supported her while she got up. She didn't try anything on him. He removed his mask and found his socks and boots.

"I knew it was you," she said.

"Will they be able to identify me?" he asked in a depressed voice.

She shrugged. "Who knows?"

Lise disappeared into the sauna with some clothes and came out looking like a police officer who'd been gang raped. Her uniform was wrinkled, her hair a mess, her make-up blotchy.

But there were no tears. Very pale, she glared at him and smiled falsely. "What next, big boy?"

"Come with me. You walk ahead."

"You can't do this to the police."

"We'll see."

"That was the police commissioner in there. Our acting mayor. You, against those guys? Without me, you're toast."

"We'll see, I said. A few steps ahead of me. More than arm's length, but not too much more."

"Oh," she said. "You're in the wrong business. I like a man who takes charge."

"That's not what it looked like in there."

"You don't know anything and you understand less. Jerk," she said. Lise's eyes narrowed. He thought if she'd been any closer, she might have hit him, gun or no gun.

"Let's go," he said quietly.

They left the blue room to its blueness. In the hallway, she turned toward the lobby, but he said no, and waved his gun in the other direction. They left by the metal exit door and walked around the building like two Blackfoot in the old days, the woman walking ahead of the man. But not too far ahead.

Chapter 23

Marc had no experience with loading a prisoner into a car. Should he let Lise go around to the passenger door by herself? She might run away while he was getting in. Should he escort her to the passenger door, make sure she got in, and run the risk of an escape while he came back to the driver's side? Maybe it didn't matter. If she made a run for it, he wouldn't shoot her. He was calm, relieved at getting out of the room. Beginning to feel other things, too— jealousy, disgust, tinges of depression— after what he'd seen in the hotel.

A little ahead of him on the uneven sidewalk, Lise went over on one ankle. She limped a few steps, stopped and said something.

"What?" he said.

"Where's the bug?"

"What?" he said again.

She sounded exasperated. "The bug, the funny little car, *Das Bot* or whatever?"

"I got another one. Keep moving." Shoulders slumped, Lise trudged ahead of Marc, limping slightly on a sidewalk as fractured as Marc's hopes of putting his life back together.

They left the eerie glow of the street lamps for the dark shadows where the rental car was parked. He waited by the driver's door and lost her for a few seconds on the other side of the car. "It's locked," she said in a discouraged voice.

"Sorry," he said. God, he was stupid, apologizing to her when *he* had the gun.

Marc unlocked his door, snapped the power lock button and she slid into her side. Keeping the gun in his left hand, more or less pointed in her direction, he threw the camera bag and video in the back and dropped into the driver's seat, not feeling much of anything.

"What was that all about?" he asked, anger uncurling inside him like a snake in an enclosed place.

"I could have taken you, you know."

"*Tabernac.* Who gives a sweet fuck?"

"You don't know much, do you, babe?"

"Don't call me babe. Just don't do that."

"I can think of lots worse things." She yawned and the last word came out as "tha-a-angs."

"Yeah, so can I."

"I bet you can. I'll just bet you can, Mr. Clean. Like what?"

Marc looked at Lise and saw the back of a hooded head in the hotel room. He looked straight ahead, his eyes adjusting to the night. In front of him, in a kiddy park, he could see outlines of playground equipment— a swing and a slide and a twirly whirly at an odd angle. The skeletal equipment reminded him of little Suz, the abused. "There's such a selection, it's hard to know where to begin. Slut. S & M queen. Whore."

She backhanded him across the cheek, more swat than punch. His hands went up to protect his face from a second blow that never came and she grabbed the gun. Probing with his tongue, he tasted blood, salty along the soft tissue inside his cheek.

"Hey," he said, ready to throw himself across the seat at her. The gun stopped him.

"What about you?" she cried in anger and desperation. "We had an agreement, you bastard. An understanding. We weren't going to get involved with anybody else. Not seriously. We don't do involvement. And then, so typical... like any ordinary prick, you fell for that... that little slut. Couldn't you see..."

"What the hell is this?" Marc moaned. "You went with those guys because I pissed you off?"

Lise's wrist slackened and her hand dropped to her lap as if the gun were too heavy. Her other hand found her mouth. Clicking obsessively on her thumbnail with her top teeth, she half turned away from him. "No," she said.

"Then what?"

Silence, the clicking of her teeth against her thumbnail.

"I could take you."

She wiggled the gun at him, sarcastically, from her lap. When he didn't respond, she set it on the dash as if inviting him to grab it.

He left the gun there. "You want to tell me about it?"

Lise shook her head, her hair sluicing the dark interior of the car.

Up the street toward the lighted area near the hotel, a few couples were leaving, sated by revue dancers. "I know you like a good time. But that didn't look like anybody's idea of a good time."

"No," she said. "You don't get it."

"Don't get what? Maybe that's my problem. I have no idea what I'm *not* getting."

She tried to change the subject. "What are you going to do?"

He looked back at her and the thumb was still in her mouth, jiggling, but she had stopped testing the nail against her teeth. "I don't know," he said. "I thought I was leaving town. I've been a player in some game. But I have almost no idea what the rules are."

"Maybe we should get outta here," Lise said. "Those cuffs aren't the tightest, and the man with the little hands is going to wiggle free pretty soon. Sorry to think like a cop, but there's only two ways out of this burg: north and south on the Rose Hill Road. We might want to be off that road when they call the Mounties with some bullshit story."

He started the car and they drove back through the darkened village. In the middle of the night, everything except The Wild Rose was dead. At the highway, he turned left.

Lise started talking again, the car's motion acting on her as therapist and confessor. "You took pictures, right? I'm in some of them."

"One of the papers might buy them. Not the pictures, exactly, unless I wanted to sell them to the supermarket tabloids, which I don't. But the evidence, the story. Corruption in rural Alberta and all that. One of the dailies might eat it up, or maybe I'll go to the Mounties."

"I want out. I really, really want out. I've wanted out for a long time."

"So get out."

"It's not that simple. Let's stop for a drink. I could use a smash right about now."

"No," he said savagely, slamming the steering wheel with his open palm. "No drinks."

"Please."

Her pleading stirred up cravings in him, but he stuck to what he'd said. "No."

"Sorry I asked. Can we make a deal, babe?"

"Maybe. Stop calling me babe."

"Whatever happens, you keep me out of it. Will you do that? For me?"

"I'll try."

"Try's not enough. You gotta promise. God, I want out. Until you started hanging around, I never realized how much."

"You into porn?"

"Nobody's into it, if that's what you mean. It's around. Shit happens."

He heaved a sigh, weighed this in his mind. "Why didn't you do something when you saw the tape?"

"What tape? Their crappy amateur videos? I never watched. You're a film critic, too?" Lise said.

"The tape they had on tonight. The one featuring your friends and a six-year-old girl." Marc measured his words to get them through. Lise had been defending herself, not listening.

"No." Her shock was genuine, her voice rising.

"Suzie Basiuk." Marc was hitting her with the information now, spearing each syllable. "Naked with the Horsemen. Worse. Their usual."

In the dark, Lise's face, lit by the headlights of a passing car, was expressionless, deadly.

"I would have castrated them and then shot each one in the gut if I'd known. Are you sure?"

"I'm sure. And I took the tape."

They drove in silence. Three men in baseball caps urinated by the gloomy side of the road. Slapping each other's shoulders in drunken rowdiness near a half-ton, they reawakened Marc's need for answers. Answers and action.

"I don't get it. How could you be involved with anything like that? You were seeing me and them at the same time?"

"It started long before you."

He didn't respond to this.

"And we used condoms. Always."

"As if that helps."

"You think it doesn't?"

"It's rotten."

"It didn't start out rotten," she said. "Look, I'm not a bad person. And there's something you've got to understand. My job was everything to me."

He shook his head, believing Lise and not believing her.

"No, think about it. I can't start a serious relationship, because what's a guy going to do? Tie me down, right? I was going places."

"Going places?"

"I thought I was. Most guys you date wouldn't even let you wear the badge, right? And let's say I found one who would— say you— they're not going to move, are they? A man's not going to transfer with me. And I've

got to be able to transfer. I don't know how to explain this... I had a rough start. I wanted to be a cop all my life, my ticket out. It was my answer to everything. But once I joined the force, it wasn't enough. I knew right after I graduated. It's so easy for women to get in. Especially these days. It doesn't prove anything. So I set a new goal. First woman chief in the province."

It was such a ferociously held, private admission that Lise seemed embarrassed by it. She had trouble getting it out. Having said it, she waited to see whether Marc would say something in reply. He couldn't stop himself from playing the newspaper reporter, saying "Uh-huh" to keep her talking. But he wasn't sure he wanted to hear what was coming.

Lise stared out her window before she picked up the thread of her monologue and chewed on it, leaving her thumbnail alone. "I met Klaus a couple of years ago, when I came to town. I knew he was married, but that's not a problem. Married guys don't tie you down. He was sexy when he wanted to be. We had fun."

"Fun?"

"Yeah," she said. "It used to be, before all the weird shit started. You can't predict who you're going to find attractive— least I can't. With me, they're often older and married. I never had a problem with that until lately. I figured it wasn't going to hurt to go with the police commissioner. That had to give me an edge somewhere. But then it changed. He gets carried away, and pretty soon he's got me playing Madame Dominatrix one week, sex slave the next. That was his way of controlling me, tying me down."

"And you couldn't get out."

"You got a cigarette?"

He gave her tobacco and papers. Lise rolled them each one. Marc opened the power windows a crack. They polluted the night air with streams of smoke. "It didn't happen all at once. I got in some trouble a few months ago. He helped me out. So one night, he adds a little coke and we get a little wired. No big deal. But then it's more than a little. He introduces me to this number with his friends."

"And you thought you could handle it? Or control them? Or what?"

"Sometimes when I got wasted and didn't have to look at them or think about it, it was like thumbing my nose at the whole uptight town...

"Lately, it's been bothering me," she continued. "Where's the payback? I don't see it coming. I've been in the force for damned near ten years, counting my training, and I'm still basically a beat constable. All I'm doing is getting in deeper with them.

"Then you came along." Reaching over, she stroked the hair at the back of his neck with her fingers.

Marc jerked his head away, but her fingers wouldn't leave him alone. "So what am I? One more notch in your garter belt?"

"Give me a little credit, will you? I like you. You never seemed to have an angle, no ties to the place. The first guy in a long time— maybe ever— who didn't see me as anything but me."

"No, erase. Back up, damn it. If that's right, why couldn't we do it straight? Why'd we get so goddamn drunk all the time? And something else. If you liked me— as me— why were you always playing the control freak?"

"Or a better question, why'd you let me? I don't know. Maybe it's stages. So what if we got bombed once in a while? Maybe it was something we had to do at the time. And then we hit other stages, such as lately I've had trouble living with myself. Hanging around with you and those guys... giving out parking tickets while nobody's touching the big stuff."

"Big stuff?"

"Yeah. Putting the wrong man in jail, that seems big to me."

"You know that? And the right guy is?"

"You've been close, I'll give you that, closer than a lot of people on the force who should've been looking."

He wasn't following her again. "Close to what?"

"What's going on. It was a good question about the night Stephanie was killed: why the crack started on the passenger side."

"In a car without any insurance."

"Yeah, how'd you know? Did my letters help?"

"You wrote me letters?"

"Dear editor... Like I said, I wanted to get out. And I was trying to tell you a few things— hoping you'd get out. I hung around with them, but I never trusted the Horsemen. They'd do almost anything under certain circumstances."

"For example, if somebody started threatening their power base in town. And when I didn't quit, you sent me more letters."

"Yeah. You and Miss Tight Ass kept going, so I thought, what the hell? Couldn't hurt to keep warning you. I'd have told you more if I'd known more sooner. I didn't get the whole story until earlier tonight— Klaus is getting wilder and more desperate. They did Teresa. He told me a few things."

"They did Teresa?" Marc felt a chill run through him. He thought about her desperate phone calls, the man's voice in the background, water. Had Teresa phoned from the room he and Lise had just left?

"They didn't like the questions you and Teresa were asking. Got her so stoned she didn't know what she was doing, and made her eat ice cream laced with sleeping pills. They thought they'd finish her off, but she's tougher than they counted on."

"They thought she was a threat, but to what?"

Lise's laugh was harsh in the car. "Klaus couldn't stand it when things started to go sour. When you're the biggest guy in town, you hate to lose your status. He got in way over his head on this gasohol plant. Trying to be some environmental hero and make a million dollars while he was at it. The man had the money all lined up until the oil lobby boys got to the government and put the squeeze on. Klaus is cash starved; he went ahead with the plant before he got the grants. He needed the sale of the Agriplex land to bail him out. Meanwhile, the banks were crying."

"The man was short of cash. That much, I already heard, though I wasn't sure why."

"It's hard to give up the lifestyle."

"By lifestyle, you mean some of what we saw tonight."

"Shut up," she said, sounding dispirited. "Klaus starts depositing insurance premiums to his own account. And he keeps issuing pink slips so the clients don't know the difference. He just forgets to send the money to the parent company. People write cheques all the time, leave it to him to fill in 'Pay to the order of...' Minor technicality. A policy here and there hardly gets noticed. But it adds up to thousands. Enough to pay the interest, keep the wheels spinning."

"And you got all this from the files?"

"Part of it's in the files, if you know what you're looking for. He's careful what he puts in writing. Mostly, the man's got such an ego, he can't help boasting. He figures he's got me six ways from Sunday, so he gets things off his chest with me that he can't tell anybody else."

"Including the other Horsemen?"

"The 4-H Club that never grew up. Yeah, they were in things up to their assholes, but he didn't tell them half. Johnny Basiuk was a handy guy to toss to the local constabulary. Klaus figured us small-town cops'd eat it up. Did we prove him wrong?"

"I understand that," Marc said. "Johnny's odd man out. If there ever was a natural fall guy, it's him. But maybe he did kill his wife. He was so plastered, he's not sure himself."

"Who was his wife talking to the day she died?"

"You're talking to him."

"See?"

Marc knew that he wasn't directly responsible for the death of Shirley Basiuk. But he'd been at her house. And he'd chosen not to report a violent domestic dispute. "Nobody who talked to me was safe. You said so at the slowpitch dance. Why didn't they just kill me?"

Lise thought about that for a few minutes. Marc had the car on cruise control, 18 kilometres over the speed limit. Fast enough to get them to Crooked Elbow in a hurry, but not fast enough to draw police attention, he hoped.

The pause was long enough that Marc wondered whether she'd forgotten the question when Lise said, "I think it was something like this. Brownrigg is a lot bigger than the companies Axel and McLean run. People like the Basiuks get killed, it's news and it's over, but I think they were scared to seriously harm you while you were on payroll. They leveraged what they could from Brownrigg, using their advertising commitments to the paper as a weapon. But they weren't in bed with Jeremy Brown. Klaus and Robbie were worried about messing with a large media organization."

"How do you know that?"

"I don't. But I'm pretty sure. I was with them for a while the night of the accident. They were scared. And they've been scared ever since. Scared of the paper, of the cops— no matter what face they've been putting on things. Intimidation, beatings, theft— Klaus had come to that. But they'd never murdered anyone before."

"You were with them the night Stephanie Basiuk died? You've got to be joking."

"Klaus invited some of us to the world-famous revue, planning to take us to the room later. The place was jumping, everybody getting pretty polluted. The Basiuk girl came in with Bobby."

"The grocer's son?"

"Mr. Axel's protegé. Steph leaves Bobby, starts dancing with Joe. Bobby gets huffy, they take it out to the parking lot. Bobby's drunk, goes after Joe with a tire iron— mostly flails around— ends up punching out Joe's headlight with the iron. I went over and tuned them down, but I guess Bobby had already challenged Joe to a little showdown on the sideroad."

"And Stephanie went along."

"She must have."

Lise asked Marc for another cigarette. He tossed her the makings. The end of her smoke bobbed and quivered when she finally lit it. The car's headlights flashed on a checkerboard dead end sign. Marc signalled left for Crooked Elbow.

"Thanks," she said.

"You're such a good cop, why didn't you call it in?"

"The fight wasn't serious— nothing you couldn't see a hundred times at other bars on a Friday night. I didn't know Steph wasn't driving until a few hours ago."

"Didn't that hit you like a ton of bricks?"

"Yeah, especially when Klaus had this crazy idea that I should go into the computer and modify the car's registration. As if... I didn't tell him I wouldn't. Just played along to see if there was a way I could blow his cover."

"Or blow him."

"Fuck you and your sweet ass and your goddamn girlfriend, too. You think I cared about those low-life scumbags?"

Marc didn't say anything for a while. The lights of Crooked Elbow glowed in the west. At night, the petrochemical plants were transformed into futuristic space modules.

"Sorry," he said. "So you heard some things at The Wild Rose that night. And Klaus told you the rest."

Lise was still angry. "I don't know why I'm telling you anything."

"Don't be like that."

"Sometimes I hate myself," she said. "I can hardly look in the mirror."

"You don't suppose that, strange as it sounds, the fates were conspiring to put me in that room tonight so we could both get out of Sin City?"

"Maybe," But Lise wasn't paying attention to him. "Did you know Bobby was thrown clear? Born with a horseshoe up his ass— a one-in-a-thousand accident where you're better off without a seat belt. Bobby was all boozed up; he freaked when he saw Joe was still alive. He finished Joe off with that tire iron he keeps in the car.

"Bobby comes walking back to the village, practically wetting his pants when he thinks about what he's done. He gets Klaus and Robbie paged to the lobby. They meet in their little office with the horses' heads. When Bobby tells them about the accident, Klaus nearly has a coronary.

"If Steph was hurt or paralyzed— and still alive— this thing could run into big bucks. What was Klaus going to do? He had nothing backing up the pink slips. Klaus was carrying the Trans Am, and the pick-up. Hadn't sent in the premiums on either.

"He practically collapsed in a chair. He'd been covering the fender-benders as they came up, but he'd never be able to cover a major liability suit."

Marc said, "Dead people don't talk."

"Klaus and Robbie roar out there. Klaus checks Joe, and he can tell Bobby killed him. He checks Stephanie, and they snuff her with a sweater to be sure there's no personal liability claim and to keep Bobby out of it. They manhandle her over the console to the driver's side, make it look like she was driving.

"Klaus tossed the sweater in the back seat and they drove back to Rose Hill. He had a shower and threw his clothes in a dumpster."

"I saw it from there, more or less."

"Looked like Klaus was safe. The parent company never heard about the accident. Klaus can cover 50 or 60 grand for a couple of vehicles, one of them owned by his buddy McLean. Even if he has to borrow the money, he can still raise that kind of cash. Maybe he paid off the parents, too, I don't know. Johnny Basiuk never found out what happened to Steph, and he might have gotten some cash after the accident. I heard he signed something for Klaus when he was drunk."

Marc thought about that. "So Klaus was worried about a lot more than Crooked Elbow's image when he sent Robbie to keep the names out of the paper."

"Then you run the story, and you start sniffing around. You and Teresa, not sure what you're looking for, but looking. Once you started checking out the car, Klaus figures that's a little too close, so he puts Teresa out of the picture with a drug overdose."

Lise pulled hard on her cigarette, exhaled a lot of white smoke and a cough. "And Johnny Basiuk beats his wife and she dies. Sure. Tell it to the Mounties. The man's so drunk, he doesn't remember a thing. He could have done it, but my instincts tell me it was Klaus or Robbie, or somebody who works for them. I'd be interested in an honest autopsy on that death."

Marc thought about the bottle of Scotch on Shirley's kitchen table.

They passed a huge beaver statue guarding the entrance to Beaver Park. Off to the right, in the darkness, a few sparks filtered into the air from late night campfires. A "Welcome to Crooked Elbow" sign flashed by, with an admonition about protecting children. Vehicles rushed down the main highway. A police car at the 7-Eleven gave Marc pause, but the driver was apparently on radar check, or looking for a Volkswagen, or snoozing. The rental car didn't interest the cop in the least.

"What are we going to do?"

"I could use a drink," she said. "I could use a long drink and a longer bath. Do you know how long it takes to wash those guys out of my hair? Or we could get out of here, right now. Before they have time to find us."

"What about your clothes? Money? Your job? Little details like that?"

"My job— yeah, right. As far as money goes, isn't that why they make bank machines? I've got credit cards. We could keep on truckin', west into the interior of B.C., get lost among the cowboys."

"I'm not sure I can go with you." He felt stiff saying it. But it was the truth.

"After tonight, you mean? Men and their egos." She ruffled his hair.

He wheeled the car into a dark visitors parking spot outside her apartment building. Lights shone from several sliding windows onto the balconies of night revellers. "Yeah," Marc said. "After tonight, I've got to think."

"And what about me?"

"You can't blame me."

"I guess not... But I'm the same person I was before. I never did a thing in my life I didn't have to do. And I take precautions. I'm not carrying anything, if that's what you think."

He was suddenly sad and tired beyond belief. "That's beside the point. What about Teresa?"

"What about her? She was an adult, no blood relative, at least that's what they kept saying."

"I mean at the hotel, in the party days. I'd have to check a video I've got. She just turned 18. If there was anal sex involved and it was filmed when she was 17, that's a crime. For sure, the bit with little Suz is."

"I was never there when Teresa was there."

"So your conscience is clear? What about Stephanie?"

Lise didn't say anything. She chewed at her thumb for a few minutes. "You and I are in deep. We can't stay here," she said at last.

"I've got to do something for Suzie," he said, thinking about Vancouver.

"What do you mean?"

"I know where she is."

"Can we get her out of town?"

"Maybe."

"Her life's pretty much fucked, but I think we've got to try," Lise said. "The poor kid."

Lise looked out the window and tears were sliding down her cheek. Her thumb was back in her mouth, the nail clicking, clicking against her front teeth.

CHAPTER 24

Marc didn't think he would ever know exactly what it was that made him decide that he and Lise could escape Crooked Elbow in the rented car.

It could have been a capacity for letting go, the seeds of which had been planted by Father Larry months before.

It might have been basic weakness— Lord knows, he had enough of that.

Maybe asking Lise along was simple expediency. It occurred to Marc that Lise was far better off with him— for his safety and for hers— than if he abandoned her to the nonexistent mercies of Klaus Axel. She had been powerfully swayed by Klaus more than once already in her life. Marc wasn't sure he could trust her in Klaus' clutches again.

Then again, perhaps it was her knack for knowing when to shut up. When they went up to her apartment, she made no attempt to continue her monologue. Nor did she try to justify anything she had done or failed to do. When he said, "Lise, I'm really, really sorry that I didn't..." she wouldn't let him finish telling her how much he regretted not doing more to help her or Teresa, sooner. She put her fingers to his lips and said, "S-s-s-h."

Or it could have been the eggs.

Inside her apartment, she showed him where the coffee grounds and filters were, where the machine was stored under the sink. "I need a shower," she said and left him in her rigorously clean kitchen where the only personal item he could find was a men's swimsuit calendar. She seemed to prefer balding men with the physiques of weight lifters— the calendar had yet to be changed from Mr. April.

Marc sat at one of four brass chairs with netted seats around a circular glass kitchen table and waited for the coffee to drip. He was on his second cup when Lise emerged from the bathroom with red feet, a white bathrobe and a white towel swirled around her head, looking more like a full-grown child than a cop capable of blowing the police commissioner as part of her career plan.

"You like eggs?" she asked, resting a hand on his shoulder as she squeezed by Marc.

"Sure," he said.

The media hype about bad cholesterol must never have reached Lise. She cracked six eggs into a bowl, whipping them with a fork, yolks and all. She added milk, diced onions, green peppers and celery. At this juncture, she pulled a black frying pan from under the oven and turned a stove burner to a setting just above medium. She put thick slices of bread in a toaster oven. Adding butter to the frying pan, she let it melt, shared some with the egg mix and poured the raw omelet into the sizzling pan, all with such silent concentration that Marc began to wonder if she had forgotten about him. At a time that satisfied her, she flipped the omelet and added chili powder and thin slices of sweet red pepper.

When she served it, with thick slices of toast slathered in real butter, Marc forgot his enemies, his anger and the fact that there was a world outside the apartment that mattered in the least.

"You do like me," he said.

"Maybe. Or maybe I was starving," Lise said. "What are we going to do about the little girl?"

"I don't know," Marc said. He'd been tossing around some options while Lise was in the shower, contemplating another night visit to Father Larry.

"Before we get into that," Marc continued, "I've been thinking that you were right. We have to get out of town— at least for a while. And maybe we should do it together." Putting it that way, Marc avoided the touchy topic of whether or not he truly wanted her to go with him.

"I'll pack some things while you go check on Suzie," Lise said.

Marc wondered how she could read his mind.

"You won't be satisfied until you risk your neck at least once more to save a Basiuk."

Driving to the church rectory with take-out coffees from Tim Hortons, Marc mulled over the possibility that Lise might be gone when he returned to her apartment. Would he care if she was? Probably.

Parking on the street, Marc threw gravel at Father Larry's window until a light came on, the window was raised, and Father Larry's head poked out.

"Have you lost your ever-loving mind?" the priest asked sleepily.

"Yes," Marc said.

"Full marks for honesty. Come to the office door, and I'll let you in. When they take me away, I shall plead Christian charity as well as insanity."

Father Larry, in jogging clothes, shuffled ahead of Marc to the priest's study.

"Thanks," Larry said when Marc offered him one of the coffees, and declined the offer of a hand-rolled smoke. Instead, he took a long, extra-mild cigarette from a package on the desk.

"I don't want to know why you are here, Marc. If I had a modicum of common sense, I'd call the police. Any further involvement with you, and I think the bishop will be warming up a nice chair in Inuvik for my next posting."

"I'm here about the girls," Marc said innocently. "Like I said I'd be."

The priest took a long sip of his coffee. "It's interesting what you leave out of what you tell me, Marc. I did not expect an APB on those girls."

"The police have already been here?" Marc asked, trying to act surprised that such a thing could have happened.

"No, I went to them. And don't look like I'm betraying you. My secretary heard a missing kid report on mighty CFCW Radio. They were looking for Jennifer Black."

"Nothing about Suzie?"

"See, I noticed that. I'm not a Jesuit, but I've always admired their discipline, their love of learning and their rationality. Sometimes, I can almost hear Ignatius Loyola and Francis Xavier coming at us, down through the centuries, 'To be Christian doesn't mean to be dim-witted. Think, dammit.' So I thought about that radio report. And I asked the girls their full names."

"And they told you."

"Of course. I'm a pastor in the Catholic school system. I know how children respond to displays of genuine interest in them. Just as I know the price we pay for their systematic neglect. Jennifer warmed right up to me, said she was Jennifer Black. I knew she was fine. Suzie was reluctant. She gave me her first name easily, but it took some work to get the last name. Once I had it, I thought about the news stories I'd seen and the tragedies in that family. And I couldn't believe you had dropped them off without a powerful reason. So I left Suzie playing a video game on my computer with my secretary and took Jennifer to the police."

Marc was wide awake, alert to tiny sounds the room made when there was no traffic outside. A humming noise. The scratching of an insect or small animal in the wall. "And told them what?" he asked.

"The truth. But like you, I was selective." Father Larry butted one extra-mild cigarette and chose another from his pack. "I said some man had dropped her off, that she didn't seem to be harmed.

"They wanted to pursue the angle of how she got here, but I simply told them that he'd found Jennifer by the road, that he'd brought the child to me instead of the police because in the modern climate of child abuse accusations, he was afraid they'd give him the third degree."

"And that satisfied them?"

"I think so. But if I were a gambling man, I'd be wagering that you're not here for Jennifer."

"You'd win," Marc said. "I want to take Suzie with me."

"I can't let you do that. There's more than my respect for the bishop and my dislike of places colder than this at stake. Child custody is a legal issue."

Marc hesitated only a few seconds before he relayed the story, as briefly as he could, of how he had come to snatch Suzie and her friend Jennifer off the lawn in front of Klaus Axel's mansion. He left out most of Lise's involvement with the Four Horsemen. But he included the fact that a bewildered little Suz was the child in the tape he'd stolen from the hotel room in Rose Hill. And he passed along Johnny Basiuk's certainty that Klaus Axel was taking steps to gain custody of the youngest Basiuk.

"You're sure of all this?" the priest asked, slurping the last of the cold coffee from his cardboard cup.

"Father, if I still had a newspaper to write for, I'd be putting it on the front page, at least the stuff that isn't too lurid for community standards."

"I'll wake the child."

Marc drove the car west, then south, then west again, staying off Highway 2 or any other main highway. Most of the roads he chose were paved, some were gravel.

Lise and he didn't talk very much. She dropped off to sleep about 2:30 a.m., releasing him to the solitary reflections inspired by night driving without human interruption. The miles softened the edges of his mind, took the roughness off the anger that had come and gone since he'd left the hotel.

He wasn't sleepy.

Neither was Suzie.

Eyes round with the shock of being awakened in the night, hustled into an unknown car, brought to an apartment, reloaded in the back seat and driven for miles down unfamiliar roads, she rode, wordlessly alert, in the back seat.

Glimmers of first dawn emerged in his rear-view mirror at 3:00 a.m. Suzie must have found the promise of light comforting, like a child who can only get to sleep with a night light. Some time between 3:00 and 4:10 when the enormous red-tinged sun rose behind them, she laid her head on one of his pack sacks and slept. Lise's bags filled the trunk.

The land elevation was rising with the sun, although the rise was not always perceptible. The countryside was changing and the farming with it. More huge round bales, cattle, more roll to the fields. Still some grain.

When the car approached Rocky Mountain House at 7:00 a.m., Marc experienced one of the illusions that light and space create in Alberta. They were still about 60 miles from the mountains, but the Rockies seemed to be almost on top of them.

Liz and Suz woke groggily.

Marc gassed up the car and signed them into a cheap motel, paying cash from the $400 he'd taken from the bank machine in Crooked Elbow in the middle of the night after depositing his final Brownrigg cheque. The licence plate on the rental was obscured by dust from some of the gravel roads he'd taken. Signing in as Mr. and Mrs. I.M. Kant, he gave a fake Edmonton address, put Chevrolet down as the make of car and left the licence part blank. The snappily dressed senior at the counter didn't seem to care as long as Marc paid cash.

They went for breakfast at a Husky gas station and restaurant. To fit in, Marc should have been driving a cube van, an 18-wheeler, or an F-150 pick-up that hadn't been washed since it came off the assembly line. George Jones and Patsy Cline tapes were $5.99 in the display case by the cash register. "No provincial sales tax in Alberta," a sign reminded out-of-province truckers.

Breakfast consisted of coffee, toast, and eggs that couldn't hold a match to Lise's. Never mind a candle. Sugared cereal for little Suz.

"How're you feeling?" Marc asked Lise.

"Like something the dog dragged in and the cat forgot to take back out. Will you excuse me?"

She left and Marc ordered more sugared cereal for Suz. Silverware clashed. Cups banged saucers. Orders were shouted into the kitchen.

When she came back, Lise had applied new make-up. Her hair was slick with water, but it looked more presentable than the tangles she'd picked up sleeping in the car. After more coffee and a smoke, she started to wake up.

"You'll like Vancouver," Marc said.

"Yeah," Lise said. "You know, I've been thinking."

"Uh-oh," Marc said. The way she said it made him tired for the first time in the last 24 hours. For the second time in the last nine, he had a terrible, sinking feeling.

"We're not going to make it," Lise said.

"Yes, we will," Marc argued. Even to himself, he sounded like a motivational speaker who had lost faith in his message. But he gave it another shot, "People do it all the time. They disappear, with a kid. Get new identities. Why do you think child support orders are so hard to enforce in this country?"

"I know," Lise said. "But this is a little more complicated. There are powerful people who have a very strong interest in finding us. They will allege kidnapping, and they will have a point. They have connections with police forces across the country, and will not be afraid to exploit those connections. It's a little different from a single mom on welfare trying to locate a deadbeat dad."

Suzie had finished her second bowl of cereal and was leaning against the side of their booth. Her eyes were beginning to close, the lids drooping, as she fought sleep.

Marc watched her set down her spoon. "I still think we can do it."

"How much money do you have?" Lise asked.

"On me? About $300, after the gas, the motel, and breakfast."

Traces of Lise's impatience returned. "No, dingle-arse. In the bank?"

Marc found the bank machine slip in his wallet from the night before. "$12,124.84. I saved money living at my aunt's, plus I got the severance. I can take out $400 a day from the bank machine."

"And I've got nearly 20 thousand."

"We have the money to get away. What are you thinking, that we should leave the country? Get to Mexico or somewhere? Sorry, but could we discuss that later? I'm beat."

"Just a minute. Let me finish. No, let me get some more coffee while you make a phone call."

"Who am I calling?"

"St. Jude's Hospital. You might as well get it over with."

He used his "Uncle Marc on the road" routine. The hospital staff acted as if they'd been expecting him to check in. And there was good news. "Teresa regained consciousness last night," a nurse told him.

"Does she seem all right?"

"We think so."

Relief washed through Marc, and recklessness. He sifted through the change in his pockets, shoved coins into the slot, and dialed a number he'd tried very hard to forget. The right voice answered, not Cindy's. Sky didn't hate him. She missed him. He heard a hundred perfect echoes in her sleepy voice when she said, "Daddy?"

The lifting of darkness must have shown on his face. As he approached the table, Lise said, "Teresa woke up."

Marc didn't say why he'd been five minutes on the phone. "It's some kind of miracle."

Once again, Lise proved that she knew the value of silence. She let the miracle and some of its implications sink in. Little Suz slept beside her, exhaling breath in a child's version of snoring.

Marc said, "You were talking about trying to get away. You were talking about money. Does this add up to something?"

Lise smiled. It was the first smile he'd seen from her in a long time. He liked the way she smiled, with her small mouth and her full lips. She said, "Sure it does. We might get away— we might not. We have enough money to last for a while, a few months, maybe, if we don't get caught in the next week. But we also have enough money, I'd guess, to put out a paper in Crooked Elbow."

"Excuse me. Rewind. Erase. What did you just say?"

"Put out a paper in Crooked Elbow. I thought Teresa would recover. If you live the first day after a drug overdose, you usually stand a chance. So what we need to do to redeem you and me— and save her and her sister's ghost from the wolves— is blow the cover on these guys."

Marc thought about the work involved in putting out a newspaper by himself. The work and the money and the hassle. But he also thought about the sycophantic newspaper coming to Crooked Elbow now that Barb was the publisher.

"So what are you saying? We put out an edition that chronicles the dirty deeds of the Four Horsemen?"

"Yeah. We use the videos and your camera shots as evidence. You interview me and I tell as much as I can on the record. Teresa will talk, I'm sure of it. We publish the whole, sordid tale in one edition. After that hits the streets, Klaus will be replacing the "No Trespassing" signs on his estate with "For Sale" signs. And somebody else will be taking over the bulk of the insurance business in town."

Marc looked at her, at the street, at the mountains. "I need some more coffee."

Lise laughed. "I could apply for the job as head of the police commission."

"And I'll run for mayor. There's irony for you. If we do this right, I could also be the new grocer in town. Depends whether we can prove anything illegal about Robbie's activities. But we know Klaus Axel and Bobby are dirty as sin."

"You see where I'm going with this."

"I don't trust the printers in Edmonton. They might call Brownrigg if they saw a competing paper for Crooked Elbow going on their presses. But I know a guy up north who escaped from eastern Europe in the '50s. He's getting old now, but nobody believes in the freedom of the press the way he does. He's got typesetting equipment we can use, and he'll print it for us, no reprisals, long as we've got the cash."

"What would I do, sell ads for this edition?"

"Nobody's going to buy advertising until they see the product. We'll get this one composed and printed and we'll distribute it to every household in Crooked Elbow by Canada Post's Admail." Marc could see the front page, the photographs of Klaus Axel and Bobby McLean, the headlines.

"Why don't we do more than one edition?" Lise asked. "Start a competing paper in town? Most start-ups fail, but with personal computers, isn't there room for somebody like you? We don't try to become the *Crooked Elbow Sun*. Just sell a few thousand papers and enough ads to keep the doors open."

"And what? Join the establishment we aging hippies always said we loved to hate?"

"Maybe," Lise said.

"Let's get one edition out. We'll see who goes to jail and who wants to sue us when that hits the streets. You're right about one thing. It's our best shot at clearing ourselves. And we might get Teresa and Suzie out of this mess. But we have to move fast, if we're going to get one out before they hamstring us with a kidnapping charge."

"Right." Lise drained the last of her coffee. She looked tired. With her blunt, strong hands, she picked up the sleeping girl. Lise rested Suzie against her shoulder so gently that the little girl didn't wake up until mid-afternoon.

By then, Lise was driving, and they were north of Edmonton.

A nightmare woke Suzie. She screamed in her sleep, and when Lise pulled over to comfort her, that woke Marc. His eyes felt as if they'd been subjected to summer fallow dust forced directly into them by a west wind. Blinking and rubbing made them worse.

Coffee at the next restaurant helped.

Lise said she wanted to call the first edition of the paper *The Crooked Elbow Independent.*

"The first *and only* edition," Marc said. "I don't need the hassle of trying to transform myself into some fucking capitalist."

"We'll see," Lise said. "You'd look cute in a blue three-piece."

"Can I call the editorial slamming these guys 'The Critique of Pure Evil?'"

"Sure," Lise said, signalling for more coffee. "You can say whatever you want. It's our paper."